Finders Keepers Detective Agency

A Novel by

Philippe Dubé

JULY 6, 2011

TO KATHERINE

NEVER LOSE

YOUR LOVE OF READING

Philippe Dubé

Order this book online at www.trafford.com
or email orders@trafford.com

Most Trafford titles are also available at major online book retailers.

Note for Librarians: A cataloguing record for this book is available from Library
and Archives Canada at www.collectionscanada.ca/amicus/index-e.html

Printed in Victoria, BC, Canada.

ISBN: 978-1-4251-8888-7

*Our mission is to efficiently provide the world's finest, most comprehensive
book publishing service, enabling every author to experience success.
To find out how to publish your book, your way, and have it available
worldwide, visit us online at www.trafford.com/*

www.trafford.com

North America & international
toll-free: 1 888 232 4444 (USA & Canada)
phone: 250 383 6864 ♦ fax: 812 355 4082

Dedication

I owe a debt of gratitude to my parents, Paul and Bernadette, for all their help and moral support in the writing of this novel. To my wife, Pat, for her love and editing, and my father-in-law, Jim Dooley, for his financial support in getting this book finalized and published. And to my ever-faithful writing group members: Adrian Zorzut, Cathy MacKinnon, Lorna Loewen, and Monica Rosborough, I owe immeasurable gratitude for their years of invaluable critiques.

Prologue

This novel is written in a 4-book format.

Book One is the story of Jack Valencz, a private investigator.

Book Two is the story of Kathee Marani, a stage performer and mentalist.

Book Three is the story of Cliff Bowen, a pick-pocket.

All three of these characters have many things in common, but their main dislike is organized crime, and they'll do whatever it takes to put a crimp in the criminal activities around them.

Book Four is how all three of them find each other and face a major criminal organization.

The first three books all begin around the same time and flow into a common time in Book Four.

The author hopes you enjoy the story and reminds you that any similarities to actual people, places, or events are purely coincidental. This is a work of fiction.

BOOK One—Jack's Story

CHAPTER 1

312 OD—September 3—10:15pm

In my line of work you get to meet all types of people. Unfortunately, most of them are trying not to be found, and they tend to hide in the seediest and most dangerous of neighbourhoods.

My name is Jack Valencz, and I'm a private investigator. The big flashy cases that fall across the desks of well-known PI's or the big professional companies don't normally come my way.

That's okay with me. I prefer the anonymity that my Finders Keepers Detective Agency gives me. Also being a psychic helps, since my particular talent is very useful in my chosen occupation. No one knows about my psychic abilities. If they did, I'd be dead.

There was a lot of paranoia, dating from the twentieth century, concerning Freedom of Information and Privacy. People were so fearful of someone getting sensitive information about them, that the psychics of that day were looked upon as invasive pariahs. Anyone who showed the least psychic talent had been sequestered away from the rest of society. They weren't jailed, just hidden away for their own protection. Psychics died out in the late twenty-second century. If there are any around today, they keep a very low profile and don't advertise themselves or their gifts.

I'd always wanted to be a cop, but couldn't make it through the academy. Being as introverted as I am, I can't seem to be a team player like cops have to be. Even when I tried to become a lawyer, I couldn't. Oh, I passed the bar, no problem, but I couldn't make it as a junior partner in the three law firms I tried to work for. That's when I sort of fell into the PI business. Its solitary nature appealed to me, and my talent has proven to be extremely valuable.

Take for example the bail jumping case that I'm currently working on. I'm looking for a Mr. Paul Dunne, a small time numbers runner who works for Kevin Pharen. My files on Kevin are sketchy, and I would dearly love to put him away. But, I don't have the ammunition necessary to keep him put away. Paul, on the other hand, tends to take the fall for his boss, and that's why I'm chasing him now.

According to his file, Paul seems to be a well-to-do executive. But, when you look at him closer, you can see that his expensive tailor-made Italian suit is actually a few years out-of-date and getting to be quite shiny in the seat and elbows. His silk ties are very fashionable and the best that money—usually someone else's—can buy.

My talent gives me hunches and fuzzy visions that prove to be remarkably accurate. Once, when I concentrated on Paul, I got a blurry image showing a painting of a smoke-filled, crowded room. When I squinted, I could see a hazy squat building with a red rose wearing a sombrero. It was just a matter of looking through a directory of ethnic restaurants. Soon, I'm standing in front of Mexicali Rosa's and looking at the sombrero-wearing rose sign perched atop the low building. A neon sign is glaringly bright in the early hours of the evening. When I wrinkle my nose, I can almost sniff the unmistakable aroma of the acerbity of beer and Tequila.

Mexicali Rosa's Cantina started out as a Latino hang-out, but now it's a mutants' bar. Even through the closed doors I can hear the subdued murmuring of the occupants who have finished their strenuous daily work and been relaxing with their friends before going home to their families. In fact, the muties have probably been sitting here since the bar opened, knocking back one beer after the other.

Look, I've got nothing against mutants. In fact, I think they're getting a raw deal from society. They're treated like garbage and have no civil rights. As far as I'm concerned, they're just as normal as me, at least on the inside, and should get better handling from the government.

Both experience and common sense tell me that walking in at this precise moment can certainly be damaging to my well-being, if not downright hazardous to my health. Unfortunately, Paul Dunne is not going to simply walk out and surrender to me. That would be far too easy.

Instead I take a deep breath as I mentally prepare myself for the ordeal about to occur. I'm going to have to go in and bring Paul out—peacefully if possible—and that's going to take some doing.

My psychic sense gives me a picture of a blurry figure sitting in a chair in the middle of a desert. Paul has to be alone someplace, but this doesn't jive with the vision of him being in this place, or does it?

My father was Latino, and therefore I have a Spanish surname. But I inherited my looks from my Irish mother. My short black hair, dark brown eyes, Roman nose, and light-coloured skin all mark me as a "normal". The fact that I also stand almost one quarter of a meter taller than the average person usually gives me the advantage in a fight.

Paul, on the other hand, doesn't have these problems. He has a more rounded face with dark brooding eyes. His features and coloration allow him to easily blend into numerous ethnic backgrounds. He'll still stick out in a mutie bar, just like I would, but he can pass as a local much more easily than I ever could.

Before going in, I reassuringly pat my 9MM railer that I carry in a shoulder holster. The weight of my concealed second weapon, a snub-nosed .38 police foamer, is comforting in its ankle holster. There are two stilettos in sheathes attached to the inside of my sports jacket at collar level. They are easy to reach if, by some unfortunate circumstance, I am told to clasp my hands behind my head.

Taking another deep breath of the stale night air, I push open the heavy, badly-dented brass doors to the cantina.

The noise level decreases perceptibly as all eyes automatically focus on me. The streetlight from outside frames my body, making it difficult for anyone staring at me to determine who I am. The door closes behind me. The eyes that were, a moment ago, squinting in the light now re-adjust to the dimly-lit interior. A dark muttering replaces the silence among the cantina patrons.

It's clear to see that they recognise me for an outsider, and it's obvious that there is little love lost in their feelings towards me. A normal in a mutie bar is like a red flag to a bull.

Like a practised thespian, I slip into my bumbling persona and walk hesitantly, as if I'm lost, towards the long bar set up at the far side of the room. I'm very careful as I thread my way through the maze of tables and outstretched legs, making sure that I bump against certain tables. My clumsiness creates a slightly wider aisle for a potential easier escape. Secretly, I study each face in my search for Dunne, without success.

Once I reach the bar, I stop and pause for a second in silent deliberation. Though fluent in Spanish, I choose not to reveal that fact to this crowd. Using broken Spanish, much as an anglo would, I ask, "Uno beer-o, pour favour, Si-nor?" while pasting an innocent smile on my face. The odds are that the muties are not yet dangerously drunk, and they will only try to tease and humiliate the crazy anglo.

The heavy-set bartender snorts in derision and continues to clean the glass in his hand with a grey cloth obviously stained with countless soakings from numerous alcohols. Again acting as the rich-but-stupid anglo, I reach into my inside coat pocket and pull out a single hundred-dollar bill. Dramatically, I place it on the table.

The bartender's dark brooding eyes widen. He licks his fat lips in eager anticipation. Keeping one hand on the bill, I nod towards the far end of the bar where the tapped beer dispenser stands. The bartender looks at me, at the hundred-dollar bill, then back at me before finally shrugging his shoulders, picking up a "clean" glass and walking slowly to the dispenser to draw my brew.

Even though he moves at a leisurely pace, I can tell he is anxious to get the drink to me and grab the bill before any of the patrons decide to take offence at my presence and start the inevitable fight.

Turning my back to the bar, I nonchalantly lean my elbows against it. Scanning the sea of faces before me, I hope to find Dunne and determine the best way to get him out of there—hopefully with the least amount of damage to either of us.

My private investigator training taught me to look for a solitary figure hiding someplace. Sure enough, there he is in the back. His gaze is averted while everyone else is staring at me. Obviously he doesn't want to make eye contact. He can't know that I don't need to see his eyes to recognise him.

Another aspect to my talent is that when I get close to what I'm looking for it acts like a Geiger counter. An inaudible clicking, that gets louder when I focus in on my target, helps me zero in on what I'm seeking.

Looking at the figure in the shadows, I hear the clicking loud and clear in my head. When I glance away, it fades. That's definitely Paul.

The bartender's plodding footsteps and laboured breathing get louder as he nears. I see him deliver my $2 beer from the corner of my left eye. Some of it spills out onto my money before it vanishes into his greedy pocket. Without removing my gaze from my quarry, I fumble slightly until I manage to grab the mug and begin walking towards Paul. The rest of the patrons start to stir restlessly, and they goad themselves with hushed whispers to action.

There's very little time left to carry out my plan and leave with my skin still intact.

"Hello Paul." Pulling a chair from the neighbouring table, I strategically place it between him and the door, blocking any escape route. Purposefully, I break the first commandment in the Jack Valencz Private Detective Handbook—*never sit with your back to a door or window.*

"No habla Inglis." This, along with a blank stare, is the only reply I receive to my greeting.

You have to give Paul credit in his attempt to maintain the almost flawless disguise. He has darkened his greying hair to match his jet-black eyebrows, and he has adopted a false moustache that rivals the real ones sported by many of the cantina patrons. His clothing is no better or worse than that worn by the locals. Any other bounty hunter would have been taken in by his camouflage.

Even if he had the neighbourhood priest vouching that he isn't the one I am searching for, my ability makes it impossible for him to fool me.

"Paul Dunne!" My voice is much harsher now. "I am an officer of the court, and you are under arrest for failure to appear before the magistrate for sentencing on August 30th of this year."

Paul's hazel eyes dart from side to side in a frantic search for an escape. His hands tightly grip his beer mug. He looks at me to protest his innocence.

Almost every bail jumper tends to behave in much the same manner, so it's easy to surmise every one of his actions.

Shaking my head, I admonish him, "Don't bother trying to tell me that you aren't Paul Dunne. I know better."

His mouth closes, and a puzzled look fills his eyes. "How did you find me?"

I'm not about to tell him the truth.

"Diligence, hard work, and a host of your fellow street snitches. Did you know that they don't like you very much? They fell over themselves in their haste to help me. Guess there really is no honour among thieves."

Normally, at this point, the bail jumper would hang his head in resignation and allow me to lead him away, but Paul doesn't do this. Instead, he seems to smile pleasantly at me. Then I see that his eyes are focused over my shoulder.

The hair on the nape of my neck rises and an image of a wagon train being surrounded by a band of Indians flashes into my mind. Not a lot of time is wasted in interpreting this image. Slowly, I stand, making sure that I move with great care and deliberation. Tossing aside my bumbling persona as I turn around, I face the reason for Paul's happiness.

Almost to a man, the rest of the bar has risen and formed a rough semi-circle behind me, effectively blocking the exit. I've made a dumb mistake and neglected the tenth command-ment in the handbook—*locate a secondary exit or defensible position before proceeding into a room.*

My gaze scans the throng as I try to determine who the ringleaders are.

In the three hundred and twelve years since ozone depletion (312 OD), there have been numerous mutations, most dealing with skin texture and colour. The majority of these muties have dark skin tones, but there are some blue and green mutations among them. As well, it seems that Earth's diminished ozone layer and increased cosmic radiation has also conspired to make this group's secondary mutation a set of antennae—almost everyone sports them. The majority are ant-like, but there are a few sweeping and graceful butterfly-like ones present. One or two even have large and furry moth-like antennae, and now they all seem to be quivering in anticipation of my next move.

Looking at the three larger specimens in the centre of the advancing throng, I decide that they are probably the ringleaders. The middle one has a scar running from his right temple near the base of the furry antenna to the bottom of his cheek, and I dub him "Scarface". The one on his right is a brilliant shade of cobalt blue, so I name him "Blue Boy", while the one on the left has a gold tooth to differentiate him from his compatriots, and I christen him "Goldy".

It's towards them that I walk. I want to put as much space as possible between my prisoner and his allies as I can. This isn't much considering the size of the room.

Moving forward, I purposefully bump into a table with enough force to slide it into the path of the oncoming group.

"Is there anything I can do for you gentlemen?" My winning smile and charming personality will get me out of this situation before it gets much worse. I hope.

Something tells me that the patrons don't think too highly of my question. Their faces darken in anger, and many reach into pockets to place their hands within easy reach of their make-shift weapons. Others merely change their grips on the bottles they are holding, getting ready to use them as clubs.

It looks as if my smile and personality aren't going to be of much help.

I reach for my pistol.

The advancing line halts like automatons programmed to stop on cue.

Unfortunately, they don't stop for too long. The three leaders obviously recognise the make of my railer and correctly presume that it only holds nine projectiles. There's a lot of damage I can do, but in the end, even if all my ball bearings find their marks, I will still have to face the other ten. They would overrun me long before I have the opportunity to pop in another clip.

Silently, I vow that my first shots will find themselves in the three ringleaders. Sighting on Scarface, I begin gently squeezing the trigger when, without warning, a bottle comes flying from the direction of the bar and knocks the railer out of my hand.

Where the hell did that come from? A wave of tiredness washes over me. My psychic sense got so overloaded with the imminent danger, that it failed to register the bottle thrown by the bartender.

When the railer goes flying it's a signal for the mutie mob to attack.

Luckily, I've studied various unarmed fighting techniques. I make judicious use of my skills in countering my opponents.

The three leaders are the focus of my attention. I disable "Scarface" with a flying kick to his chest as I leap over the table. I'm still in the air when I swing my right foot out and connect with "Goldy's" temple. Spinning in mid-air, I grab "Blue Boy's" shoulder to regain my balance. As my feet hit the ground, I deliver a right-cross to his chin. He joins "Scarface" and "Goldy" in the pile forming at my feet.

I shift my weight and brace myself for another attack. I'm panting slightly. My leg muscles are tensed to allow me to move quickly in any direction. My swift and decisive moves have startled the rest of the mob. They pause for a couple of seconds in their forward movement.

One of the men on my right screams, "He's only one man! We can crush him easy! Ghost the bastard!"

The rest of the sheep rally around their new leader and begin to press forward once again. But their hesitation provides me with a plan.

Their line is ragged and open to a counter-attack. Fortunately the momentary weakness has abated. Charging the nearest men, I surprise them by jumping over their heads. As I reach the peak of my leap, I straighten my body and pump my legs onto the tops of their heads, just missing their sensitive antennae. Continuing into a somersault, I hit the floor with knees flexed. Without pausing, I push myself into a backward flip and land on my hands in the perfect position to deliver a roundhouse kick to the temple of one unfortunate foe.

I continue the handspring and find myself beside two more men who are gaping at my gymnastics. It's almost too easy. I punch the shortest one with a single right-cross, and down he goes. Spinning around, I get the larger one with a straight-arm closed fist to the sternum. He grunts once. His eyes glaze as he sinks to his knees and collapses in a heap.

My gaze hypnotically follows his motion, so I don't see the two creeps coming up behind me. Fortunately, my talent saves me, but in a way I've never had happen before. A crystal-clear flash image of them sneaking up on me causes me to hesitate. I suddenly feel like a superman. Without looking, I take one step back with my right foot. Now, I'm directly between them. Both fists come up to strike the point directly between their eyes. Their forward momentum combined with my blows causes their legs to fly out as if their upper bodies have been forced into a sudden stop.

All motion in the cantina ceases. With feet braced, my head swivels, searching. My sense warns me with a clear vision of somebody getting ready to attack me with a bottle from behind. Spinning, I take a rapid step in his direction. The attacker isn't even looking at me. He's staring stupidly at his empty hands. Butter-fingers has obviously dropped the bottle. He looks at me, blank expression on his face, then turns and bolts out the door.

The mob stops. A clear image forms in my mind of a tidal wave crashing ashore and burying a village of straw huts. The image fades quickly and I get tired again. There's a sick feeling building in the pit of my stomach—I try to ignore it and shake off the tiredness. It doesn't take a genius to know what's coming next. The horde surges forward. I'm buried by the rabble. As good as I am, I can't beat off the hail of blows.

I unexpectedly find myself being carried by my attackers, then feel a cold breeze as I'm flying into the back alley. The door slams shut as I hit the slick pavement and skid into the dumpster on the other side of the lane.

I'll admit that there's one thing in this world that scares me to death. Spiders! I have arachnophobia, and I have it bad!

When I hit the wall, the first thing I see is the remnants of a spider web; the one I'd just crashed through! A cold feeling of dread fills me. I feel the tickle of tiny feet on my cheek. I panic.

I take two quick strides backwards as I'm swiping at my face with the sticky silk surrounding it like a harem girl's veil. Unfortunately, I'm heading straight towards the door I'd just been hurled through.

The door opens again.

"...and you, too!"

Paul's body crashes into me and knocks me down.

The door slams shut again cutting off the raucous laughter of the muties.

Paul and I hit the lane in a tangle of arms and legs. Not wanting to be at the same level of any potential bugs, I struggle to disentangle myself and stand up. Paul's still in a daze. Wasting no time, I roughly cuff his hands behind his back. Someone has to pay for my defeat—it might as well be Paul.

"Well Paul, it looks like Pharen is going to have to look for another runner. You have a date with the judge. And I'm going to make sure you keep it."

Paul shakes his head to end his stupor. In a sheepish voice he looks up at me as he inquires, "You were doing damn good in there until they ganged up on you. How were you able to do what you did?"

"Practice, practice and even more practice."

"No." He shakes his head once again. "When you struck those two who were coming up from behind you... I saw that move... in the last movie I went to! How'd you know that one guy was closer than the other?"

I'm also amazed at the clarity and accuracy of that particular vision. But, I want to get Paul to the police station as quickly as possible. Grabbing his arm, I begin to move towards the mouth of the alley.

"Paul, Paul, Paul. You watch too many movies instead of learning how to fight."

Unfortunately, Paul is a good observer. I know I haven't deflected his curiosity. Suddenly, my ability gives me a blurry image of a group of men charging out of a building. Interpreting this as meaning that the muties are getting ready to come out and finish us, I hustle Paul along.

I don't have to worry about Commandment Six in the handbook which states—*never go out the front door when the back door is available*. The cantina occupants have provided us with the back door. Now, I have to provide us with the rest of our escape.

CHAPTER 2

312 OD—September 3—4:10 pm

"I don't care how you get it done, just get it done!" Jonny Paggett yelled at his three underlings.

Lori was hiding behind the barely-opened door of the bedroom suite, which Paggett maintained beside his home office. She warily watched her older brother pace across the office like a tiger in a cage.

"Boss," interjected Slim Jim. At almost two meters he was the tallest of the three men as well as their obvious spokesman. He bravely straightened his shoulders and said, "We don't have the expertise to hit deSalle."

"Don't tell me about expertise!" Paggett grabbed the cigar from his mouth and clenched it tightly in his right hand. "I've got well over three hundred men and women working for me. Out of all of these you're telling me no one can go out and ghost Sharah deSalle?"

The three nodded in unison. Jim, with a tangible amount of pride and defensiveness, straightened his shoulders and boldly stated, "We don't lack the resources to have him ghosted outright. But, if we do, the cops will be all over us. That's one thing we can't afford to have happen."

Lori shuddered slightly. Jonny had stopped pacing and stood in front of the three men, his forgotten cigar still clasped in his hand. She had grown up in fear of her older brother's sudden fits of anger. Lori knew Jim's voice of reason and simple comment could easily trigger his violent temper.

Paggett had to look up to all three of them due to his short stature. Having endured his glare before, Lori could imagine the intensity of Paggett's look as he glared hotly at Slim Jim, Brik and Terry for a few moments before he put the cigar back in his mouth and continued his restless pacing.

Paggett had learned to lessen his violent anger attacks by walking off the angry impulse and not blurting out the first epithet that came to mind. He paced a lot.

He stopped his pacing and walked directly to the bedroom door behind which Lori hid. She gasped as his hand reached for the door handle, and she tried to make herself as small as possible in case he swung the door open.

Paggett paused. He slowly released the handle and turned to look back at his men. "There must be some way we can hit deSalle?"

Terry—who was barely taller than Paggett and whose face was textured in a terry-cloth pattern similar to a hand towel—suggested, "What about Simmonds and his people?"

Paggett violently shook his head. The cigar tip flared and burning ash fell unheeded to join similar burn marks on the carpet. Paggett snapped, "Absolutely not!"

"Why not, boss? His boys are good at staging accidents. Then we won't be involved."

Paggett vibrated in anger. He looked at Terry, opened his mouth to speak but closed it without saying a word. He shook his head then took in a deep breath. "I KNOW, Terry," he countered in exasperation as he moved a few steps closer to his men, "I know."

Lori released her pent-up breath and took this opportunity to move further into the bedroom, closer to the other door leading into the hallway. She moved only as far as she could to be safe from discovery. She desperately wanted to hear the conversation going on in the other room.

Paggett continued, "We already owe Bill Simmonds too many favours for the last hits he did! Any more, and he could wind up owning my operation—lock, stock and barrel!"

"B-b-b-boss," Brik stammered. That one damnable letter always had Brik shaking his head in frustration.

Lori could just see Jonny's back through the slightly opened door. She moved slightly closer in order to see the stocky individual he was talking to. Brik was the gentlest of Jonny's henchmen, most of the time. When angered, Brik became victim of a "berserker rage". Most berserkers tended to die a young death, fighting wildly in the middle of battles.

Brik was the exception. His mutation gave him a bumpy grey skin as tough and impervious as a paving stone. His invulnerability made him a perfect fighting machine and a valuable addition to Paggett's bodyguard staff.

"Yes, Brik?"

"I—can—do—it," he stated slowly and with great deliberation.

Paggett shook his head in denial. "I know you could easily take him, my friend. But you know as well as I, that you could never force yourself to ghost anyone while you were in your right mind." Paggett patted Brik's broad shoulder. "Thanks for the offer, but we'll find some other way."

Lori saw Jonny begin to turn, so she rushed to the other door. She jerked it open then closed it noisily.

———•◆•———

Paggett's head came up at the sudden noise. He saw his sister walking towards him and a fleeting thought crossed his mind. *Did she hear anything?* He shrugged and smiled warmly.

"Sis. What are you doing here?"

"I just came in to tell you that I was home and ask if you wanted me to tell the maid to set out dinner now or wait a little longer?"

He looked up at her and remembered his promise to their dead father. *Don't let her get involved in the family business.*

"No, I was just finishing up some minor details with the guys. We'll eat in an hour or so. Did you have a good shopping trip?"

Lori's amber eyes glinted with the excitement her voice showed. "The mall was packed! It was crazy! I must have spent most of the day walking through a thousand shops."

"That many stores? Then, you must have gone to MallWorld," a gruff tone suddenly tinged his voice, "instead of City Centre Mall."

Paggett knew that MallWorld was the biggest in the world. It not only had retail shops but theatres, a hospital, high-rise apartments, churches, schools, a water park, rodeo grounds, a botanical garden, two immense Atriums, as well as food courts that catered to every known taste. It was held that you could spend your lifetime in MallWorld and never be bored. He also knew that his sister wasn't supposed to go there alone.

"Uh... yes," she hesitated and took a step backwards. "Is there a problem?"

"You know I don't like you going to MallWorld without an escort."

"I know. But last night at supper you said you were going to be busy all day today. I didn't want to be a bother."

"You could never bother me, you know that, Sis. And when I'm at home, I don't need the guards with me." Paggett gestured to the three men standing behind him with his ever-present cigar.

"I know, but Jo was with me and he..."

"But, nothing." He wagged the cigar at her. "Jo is nothing but a glorified taxi driver. He can't protect you. The guys are here to be used, so use them!"

"Oh... okay," she mumbled, then brightened. "I have to go back tonight, anyway. I've got to pick up some things that I couldn't bring with me. How about Brik comes along?"

"How about Brik and Terry?" he countered.

"Then I'll look like I'm leading a parade," she complained. "I don't have that many packages. Brik will be able to handle it. Please?"

Paggett sighed in defeat. "All right."

312 OD—September 3—9:35 pm

The entire first floor of the deSalle mansion sparkled with light. One limousine after another cruised slowly up the circular driveway and dropped elegantly-clad couples at the front door.

Lori pulled her shawl around her shoulders as her Black Forest Motors Special Issue drew up to the front door behind another BFM S-I. She looked over at Brik while Jo walked around the car to open her door.

"Brik, I want you to stay here with Jo, and be ready when I come out." Lori pulled on her short, black evening gloves, and then reached for the door handle.

"I can't let you go, Miss." His arm blocked her exit. "Your b-b-brother would ghost me if anything happened to you."

"Nothing's going to happen to me."

"B-b-b-but..."

"But nothing. I'm a big girl. I know what I'm doing." She tried to open the door.

"B-b-but your b-b-brother..." Brik kept pushing the handle down so she couldn't get out.

"My brother is a worry wart," Lori snapped irritably, then noted the pained look that crossed Brik's face at her comment. "It's okay Brik. It really is. My brother doesn't need to know what I'm doing. He's fussed over me ever since mom and dad died. He doesn't think I know about the family's business. I'm not stupid."

"I never said you were stupid."

"I know, Brik." Lori reached out and gently put her hand on his arm. "I think that it's cute when Jonny calls you guys guards. I know what you really are."

"B-b-but we are guards, Miss," Brik protested.

"Okay guards it is. But you're guards with attitude. I know you guys are muscle. You do whatever Jonny needs done… without question. If that means escorting a drug shipment across the border or beating one of Jonny's pimps into line or even escorting some of the girls on their dates, then that's what you do."

Poor Brik. I shouldn't have been so blunt. But that shocked look on his face is priceless.

"I want you and Jo to wait in the car for me

to give you the signal. Is that understood?"

Brik looked down at his grey stone-like hands. "B-b-but Miss..." he murmured.

"But nothing Brik. I know what I need to do. Everything will work out okay if..." she paused for a second, "...if you and Jo do exactly what I want."

She patted his hand and added, "I promise."

"The b-b-boss will ghost us if anything happens to you."

The door opened, and she moved forward slightly and put one foot out then looked back at him. "Just park the limo, then make sure that you're under the third window on the north side of the house away from all the guests and cars. Okay?"

Lori barely heard his muttered "Yes ma'am," as she took Jo's hand and stepped out of the car. She leaned towards Jo and whispered, "The third window."

Jo nodded once.

——— •◆• ———

The party was in full swing as Lori walked through the front door. A steward waited nearby with a tray of fluted glasses filled with sparkling champagne. Lori took one and circumnavigated the dance floor stopping here and there to say a few words to people she knew.

"Good evening, Lori. Where's your brother?"

"Oh... Hello, Sharrah. I didn't see you there." She turned away from a couple she was talking to and smiled politely up at her host, Sharrah deSalle.

At first glance, the tall, athletic, and very handsome black man looked more like a football linebacker than the Haitian drug and prostitution gang lord that he was. His beaming smile and sparkling eyes hid a dark and sinister side that Lori was well aware of.

"Jonny couldn't make it tonight." She held out one of her hands, and Sharrah bent down and gently kissed it. "He had some last-minute business to attend to. He sends his apologies."

Actually, Paggett had sneered at the thought of attending this party. He would be livid if he knew that she had come here unescorted.

"That's too bad." Sharrah's smile couldn't hide the sarcasm in his voice. "I really would have liked to talk to him about a business deal."

Right, like that would ever happen. Lori was familiar with the only deals that Sharrah was interested in. Preferably one in which Paggett either wound up dead or in jail. Either way Paggett would be out of the way of Sharrah's expansion plans.

"Maybe you could call him tomorrow and talk about it?"

Sharrah's grin widened. But before he could respond, his attention was drawn to someone standing behind Lori. A dark look crossed his face and was quickly replaced by his mask of respectability. "You'll have to excuse me."

"No problem. We'll meet up later." Lori shivered slightly as Sharrah bowed and turned away. She stopped a passing waiter and gave him her empty champagne glass, then continued on towards the stairway leading up to the guest washrooms.

Lori smiled at the two ladies walking past as she entered the powder room. She locked the door and moved to the toilet before unrolling most of the toilet paper and wadding it into a large mass and placing it on the counter. Slipping off the skirt part of her floor-length black gown, she took a pair of soft gloves out of her handbag. Now she was dressed for action in tight-fitting black slacks. She kicked off her high-heels, grabbed the bundle of paper and opened the door leading to the small, meter-wide, balcony.

It was dark on this side of the mansion. Guests were not supposed to be wandering around the estate.

Her driver, Jo, was waiting. Lori dropped the bundle of toilet paper to him. In return, he threw her a pair of black runners and a compact black case containing a small railer, a throw-away up-link, and burglary tools.

Lori put the railer and up-link in her pockets and tucked the tiny lock-pick kit in her waist band. Making sure that nobody was wandering by, she climbed out on the balcony rail and jumped the meter-wide gap over to an adjoining balcony. The lock-pick made short work of the French doors. She slipped quietly into Sharrah's office. Positioning herself beside the door, she pulled out the up-link and dialed.

Lori made her voice huskier than it normally

was. "Hello. Is Mr. deSalle there?"

She waited for a second.

"I don't give a damn if he is hosting a party. I need to talk to him. NOW! Tell him Paggett's on the move. I'll call him back in five minutes. Tell him to be ready."

Lori put the up-link in her pocket and grabbed the pistol. She only had a few minutes to wait before the ornate doorknob of Sharrah's office rattled and masked the almost inaudible click of the safety being flipped off.

Sharrah entered the room and called over his shoulder, "I'll be right back. Have Tony get the car ready."

The door closed with a soft click. He took two steps into the room before he stopped and looked at the open balcony doors. He spun around. By then, Lori had the railer aimed at him.

"I'm sorry," she whispered as she looked into his handsome face and watched it transform into a snarling mask of fury.

It never got easier. Taking someone's life no longer filled her with the mind-numbing panic that her first ghosting had. Paggett never imagined that two of the ghostings that Bill Simmonds was taking credit for were actually hers.

Three soft pfft sounds preceded the harsher thud of his body slumping to the carpet.

Lori put the safety back on and placed the railer in her pocket. She raced back to the balcony and didn't bother to close the French doors before leaping back to the powder room balcony.

Moments later, she had put everything back into the case and dropped it and her runners down to Jo, then put on her high-heels and the lower portion of her gown. She pulled up the hem of the dress and used it to cover her hands as she closed the balcony door.

Stepping out of the room, she looked to her left and saw two of Sharrah's guards standing by the door. Now it was time to set up her alibi. She needed for them to remember and vouch to the police that they saw her using the facilities at the time of deSalle's death.

"Excuse me," she smiled her sweetest smile, "but you're almost out of toilet paper in there. Could you have someone replace the roll?"

The taller of the guards nodded. "We'll have someone look into it right away, ma'am."

Lori managed to get down to the dance floor before the guards opened the door and discovered the body. Sharrah's men were all wearing ear receivers and belt up-links so they were able to quickly block off the doors to keep anyone from leaving.

The police were prompt. A trio of squad cars arrived within two minutes and the detectives five minutes later. Everyone was questioned. Some more so than others. Lori was in this unlucky group due to her last name and having been noticed in the vicinity of the crime scene.

She wasn't surprised that the detective's

eyebrows shot up when she identified herself. It was a well-known fact that her brother and Sharrah were business rivals—both in legitimate and illicit business aspects.

The police had more questions and decided to ask them in police headquarters. Even though the trip to the station was fast her lawyer was faster. And though she hadn't been charged with anything, he was waiting for her—writ of *habeas corpus* in hand.

312 OD—September 4—5:12 pm

"Why didn't you stop her?" Paggett tried to keep the anger out of his voice. He failed miserably.

"Brik. You were supposed to go to the mall, not deSalle's. Why didn't you call me and tell me what was going on?"

"I'm sorry b-b-boss." Brik stared down at his feet and shuffled in anxiety. "B-b-by the time I thought to call you, the cops were already there. I didn't know she was planning on killing him."

"Jo." Paggett spun around and glared at his driver. He almost bit through his cigar in suppressed rage as he asked, "You drive her everywhere. Did you know what she was planning to do?"

"No sir. I tossed her the case of tools..."

"She has a case? How many times has she done this that she needs a case?"

"Only when I have to break in somewhere,"

Lori answered him from the doorway, "and this is the third time I've ever used the railer."

Paggett spun around and looked fiercely at his younger sister. "Three times? Three…" Paggett gasped. "Are you out of your damn mind?"

Lori took this moment to stand up to her brother. "No. Just helping YOU out in the family business. You wanted Sharrah disposed of. You didn't want Simmonds' men doing it. So I did it."

"You're not supposed to …" he shook his head in disbelief and sat down heavily in his chair.

"I know, I know. And I'm also not supposed to know you're a gangster dealing in drugs and prostitution." She glared back at him then sat in the chair facing his desk. "I'm supposed to be a good little girl, shop all day, party all night, and never, ever wonder where our family's money comes from."

"But...?"

"I don't want to be sheltered! I'm NOT a brainless airhead! I've shown you what I can do! I want to help you!"

Paggett's jaw dropped, and he stared at her for a few seconds before he threw up his hands in defeat.

"Besides, the police don't have anything on me. I've covered my tracks completely. The up-link I used was stolen and un-traceable. I even tossed Jo a large wad of toilet paper to make it seem as if I used the washroom. Then I told the guards that they were running low on paper."

Paggett's gaze narrowed as he pondered her procedures. He crushed the butt of his cigar in the nearly-full ashtray and pulled a new one from the humidor. He took another moment to prepare and light it. All the while, thinking.

"Did you use the taps and flush the toilet?"

"Uh... No, I didn't. Why?"

"They're going to dust the place for prints. The guards will tell the cops you were in the washroom next door. They'll check for finger-prints and discover you didn't use the facili-ties. Even the dumbest detective on the force will be able to put two and two together and come up with you as a suspect. Then they'll come here to arrest you."

Lori's eyes widened, and the blood drained out of her face.

"You're going to have to hide out for a while until I can arrange for you to get out of the country. I want you to go to the warehouse and wait there. Brik, you, Slim Jim, and Terry go with her. And this time, make damn sure that she goes there and nowhere else. And stay with her at all times. Understood?"

CHAPTER 3

312 OD—September 4—3:18 pm

Well it may not be much, but people can
look at it and say that Jack Valencz owns the
entire thing. My offices are on the top floor of
the 4-storey office building. The bottom three
storeys are leased to a variety of businesses
including a dentist, a doctor, and a radiology
laboratory.

Finders Keepers is not a big company, so I
only use two of the offices on the top floor.
The others are kept for storage and to ensure
my privacy. The front office is a waiting room
with a couple of couches and some comfortable chairs. The magazines are the latest
issues, because I hate reading old and dated
material.

Directly across from the door is the space
where my CompSec, a Rosie 4000, is located.
She's beautiful from the waist up, but below
the desk she's just a metal pole stuck in the

side of the desk where her main processor is located. Because of my talent, I opted for an electronic secretary. It answers my up-link, takes messages, and doesn't ask nosey questions.

My psychic talent helped me to build up *Finders Keepers* and to purchase this building. The most lucrative aspect of my power is the ability to find things—ergo the name *Finders Keepers*. The building was purchased with the money I made when I recovered 12.5 million dollars worth of jewellery stolen from a downtown store.

———·◆·———

In that case, the news reporters surmised that the thieves had known the gems were brought in as part of a trade show exhibit.

The police had no clues on the case, be-cause the crooks were good—very good. They had masked themselves completely. Once outside, they vanished without a trace. People who had seen the trio described them as average with no accents—not much to go on.

When I first heard about the diamond heist on the evening news, I got an image similar to a choppy old movie. It was a game board with a huge arbour over two large homes and a smaller ranch-style house. That was enough for me. Checking with the Park County offices, I found that a multi-parcel sub-division titled "Arbor Estates" was a few kilometres southeast of the city.

It didn't take me long to get to the jeweller and give him my pitch.

He was, needless to say, a little hesitant when I had offered, "Finders Keepers specializes in cases like yours. I can guarantee you that I will locate the stolen gems within 24 hours."

His eyes narrowed, and a frown appeared on his face. "And how much will it cost me?"

I knew he figured me to be one of the crooks trying to sell him back the gems. "Look, the police know me and my reputation. Sometimes, when they're stumped, they've come to me for help."

"Again, how much is this going to cost me?" the jeweller inquired suspiciously.

"I normally collect 10 percent and charge a per diem of two hundred dollars with a minimum rate of 10 days."

One of his eyebrows twitched.

"But," I continued, "that's only when I don't have a limited time frame to work with. My rates are triple if I have to find things fast. If the jewellery isn't located within 24 hours, the stones will be pried out of the settings and it will be impossible to track them."

He nodded, knowing full well that this was the truth.

Taking a gamble that I wasn't pricing myself out of a job, I told him, "For this case, I'll only charge… say a 20 percent flat rate, payable when the police notify you that I've found the jewels. If I don't locate them in a day," I shrugged, "then I'll find them for free."

He knew the police would never find the crooks without clues. The gems would then be lost to him, and his insurance deductible would be far more than what I was asking. He agreed to my terms.

I put on a show. Talking to a few of the staff and filling up a couple of pages in my note-book. Making a big production about going out-side and questioning some of the local street vendors was my first step. Then I left in the same direction the thieves had. Within an hour I was pulling up to the Arbor Estates drive. After I parked, I walked the short distance to the ranch-style house. Sure enough, the closer I got to the building the louder my psychic Geiger counter got.

The element of surprise was on my side. The crooks didn't have a chance. While waiting at the door I had a flash—a fox charging into a henhouse. A couple of glances around the side of the building told me they were all inside. Then I kicked in the front door. I literally caught them with their pants down. They had just finished divvying up the jewels and were changing into different clothing.

My 9MM railer and I convinced them of their limited options. Unless you have a death wish, a stainless steel ball to the head is never preferable to jail time.

Needless to say, the police were totally flab-bergasted when I brought in the trio. The jew-eller was just as stunned when I told him the gems were in police hands and locked up for evidence. Once he verified this, he wasted no time in writing me a cheque. He was conflicted—happy to have his jewels back, unhappy about having to pay me.

The building I wanted to purchase was in an ideal location, and now was my chance. After cashing the jeweller's cheque and buying the building, there was enough money left over after the purchase to renovate the top floor into my office. Renters for the other floors were not an issue. Purposefully setting the rental fees low, just enough to cover the yearly taxes, utilities, and contingency repairs was my first priority. The tenants were cheerful to sign long-term leases.

—— •◆• ——

I have lots of work to do before I can transcribe my notes on the Paul Dunne case. More specifically, the Kevin Pharen file needs to be finished. Pharen heads a big time numbers operation working out of the west-end. I'd located three of his betting parlours and passed on their locations to my police contact.

As I upload and save the file, I hear someone coming into the front office. Getting up, I walk to the door.

Rosie is playing her pre-recorded message. "Please be seated. Mr. Valencz will be with you shortly."

A grey-haired gentleman, with a neatly trimmed moustache hiding his upper lip, is standing just inside the doorway looking at Rosie. He is about half a meter shorter than I am and dressed in a very expensive suit. I know this because I wear the cheaper version. Oh, don't get me wrong. I like the good stuff. It's just that anonymity is preferable to flashiness. And thousand-dollar suits scream `Hey, look at me' very loudly.

A greyish haze, visible only to me, surrounds him. This phenomenon is not rare—usually it appears when I listen to politicians or corporate mavens. They also tend to have the same cloudy aura. I presume it's due to the nature of their occupations. Businessmen lie. Politicians—well everyone knows the relationship between politicians and the truth. This fellow may very well try to lie to me.

"Good afternoon. Can I help you?" I call out from the doorway to my office.

He's startled, and his eyes squint behind his gold wire-rimmed glasses, as he looks me up and down. "Are you Jack Valencz?"

A quick nod is my answer.

"Name's Simon Johnson, and I need you to steal something for me."

"I think you have the wrong place. I'm not a thief. I catch them."

He shakes his head. "Sorry that came out wrong. I need you to steal back something of mine that was stolen from me."

I'm intrigued. "Okay, Mr. Johnson, right this way."

He finds his way to the chair in front of my desk.

"Tell me more about what you want me to recover for you?"

"Well it's like this," he squirms, and I can tell he's more than a little uncomfortable—this is where the lies will start flowing. "I own a small import and export company. My primary competitor, Jonny Paggett, got his hands on my list of suppliers and clients. I need it back before the jackass takes over my business. Once he knows where I get my goods, he can price me out of the market."

Okay, this all seems to be the truth—at least my psychic alarms aren't going off. "Let's go back a step. Exactly what is it that you import and export, Mr. Johnson?"

Without missing a beat he rattles off a list. "Spices, toys, knick-knacks, all sorts of things normally found in dollar stores."

Ding—Ding—Ding. There goes the alarm in my head. This is a well-practiced list that he recites a little too readily, almost as if he's had to tell it to the police a couple of times before. Something's missing. Maybe I'll have to steal his client list back in order to find out exactly what it is that he's hiding.

"You said that Paggett stole this list. How?"

"Gangsters like him don't like competition, Mr. Valencz, legitimate or otherwise. He's muscled in on all the businesses in our district. The banks are only too happy to have his loan company take over the notes on our companies. They get their money back and don't have the worry of our going tits up."

While he's talking, I quickly access the police files on Paggett. I realize I'm not supposed to be hacking into the police computers, but as long as I don't muck about with their data, no one will ever know. One of my better illicit purchases was "back door" codes.

I know Paggett from a previous case, but I hadn't realized that he'd moved up in the ranks since I first met up with him. His file now reads like a crime directory. He has been arrested for everything from arson and loan-sharking to drugs and prostitution. From what I can see, there is no crime that Paggett hasn't committed or at least been accused of in the past five years. And sure enough, the latest data indicates that he's indeed trying to weasel his way into various legitimate businesses.

"Paggett sent his thugs to try to force me to sign my business over to him." Mr. Johnson pauses for a second. "I refused. That's when they broke up my office and took the list."

Not detecting any new lies, I nod and continue to listen while looking up Mr. Johnson in the police files. I'm not surprised to find the complaints he has filed against Paggett. His mother had come from "old money". Her parents had disowned her when she married Johnson Senior. He had a rap sheet almost as long as Paggett's. A thought came into my mind. *Did Junior inherit daddy's business as well?* A few keystrokes later gave me my answer. Simon was clean.

"I need my client list back from Paggett ASAP! The longer he has it, the more shit he can do to me." Simon wrings his hands in obvious frustration.

"Does he know what he has?" Leaning back in my chair, I put my hands behind my head. The chair teeters for a moment. "Or did his goons just grab it by accident?"

"I'm hoping he doesn't know. My list was in a binder on my desk, and that's part of what they grabbed."

For the second time in two days, I get a rush of well-being and a crystal-clear image forms in my mind. A leather-bound notebook with gold edge protectors flashes before me. Spinning around in my chair, I look out the window in order to hide my surprise at the clarity of the vision. *I'm going to have to find out why my visions sometimes get clearer.* The sound of screeching tires drags my attention to the street below. There's nothing surprising there, just a truck, with only the word "mentalist" visible, stopped at the intersection.

It doesn't stay there long, only enough for the driver to deftly back up to make a right-hand turn. My heart stops for a second when the van drives over the curb and almost clips the side of my building. I breathe a sigh of relief when it finally vanishes down the street.

Turning my chair around, I look back at Johnson. I suddenly feel tired, so I cover up by asking, "I suppose this binder is special enough that it caught their attention, and that's why they took it in the first place?"

"That's right. It's an antique made of leather with gold edging. Why?" He cocks his head to one side, "Is that important?"

"No, not necessarily. It's just a hunch. When did they steal it?"

"Less than a couple of hours ago. Look, can you…" He's impatient.

"Hmm…" I take a quick glance at my office clock. "They've probably arranged to meet Paggett back at his warehouse. I know for a fact he doesn't like having evidence at his home. Let me see if I can find your files before Paggett sees them. Five thousand for recovery? A thousand if I can't?"

Getting up, I rush around the desk. He nods grumpily.

"If you'll excuse me, Mr. Johnson," I hustle him out of the office. "I want to get your property back as quickly as I can. I'll be in touch."

312 OD—September 4—10:10 pm

The song finished on an up-beat and was replaced by the blare of a commercial. I reached up to tap off the radio in my ear, but hesitated. I had never heard this ad before.

"The Great Marani and her troupe are performing at the Centre Stage Club for the next week. They're such a hot act that most of the shows are sold out and tickets are running at $100 each, and…"

I tapped it off at this point. "$100. Sheesh, am I ever glad I'm not into that voodoo-hoodoo stuff! I'd hate to have to shell out that kind of coin for anything."

Paggett's warehouse is located in one of those small industrial parks surrounding most cities. This one has been gobbled up by the growing city and is now encircled by low-income tract housing and duplexes.

I know exactly which warehouse is his, because I had the misfortune to have visited it once before. When I was just starting my agency, one of my cases was looking for a missing person. He couldn't be found for a reason. He was a police informant, and Paggett had found out about him.

This was before I had created the tenth commandment—*locate a second exit or defensible position before proceeding into a room.* I wish I had coined it before; I could have saved myself some bruises.

It's providential that I'm coming back to this particular warehouse. Pulling my car off to the side of the road near the back, I turn off the engine. The houses on the other side of the road are all dark, and hopefully no prying eyes will bear witness to my actions. I slip on my tight leather gloves.

My right pants pocket bulges slightly with my lock-pick tools and miniature wire cutters. I gently close the car door.

To break into the building, I can use the same exit I had previously found. Paggett hasn't discovered it, because it's still there when I walk around to the south side and see the large floor-level fan spinning lazily. Squeezing into the housing of the fan, I lay there with my back firmly against the mesh while the blades tickle my nose. My timing has to be just right as I roll, and a blade sweeps by my face. Another brushes against my shoe, and I breathe a quiet sigh of relief. Now it's just a matter of squirming through the interior housing and into the dimly-lit warehouse. I unlock the door beside the fan housing for an easier exit.

My senses don't detect anyone in the building, so I have lots of time. This won't be a walk in the park, though. Paggett will be coming here soon to take a look at what his goons have stolen, so I'm not taking any chances. Winding my way through the maze of boxes towards the north side where the shipping and receiving offices are located is no mean feat.

Paggett's office is on the second floor, so I race up the wide corrugated metal stairway. The heavy, steel door has a standard tumbler that poses no challenge to my lock-picks. Due to many hours of practice, I know how to pop the lock. I love it when they use exactly the same locks for every door. Yes, it makes it easier for the workers, but no one ever thinks that if someone can pick one lockset they can pick them all.

I don't even have to search for Paggett's office. Nothing has changed in his office since my previous visit five years ago. There's his desk with a canvas bag plopped down on it. Once I open the bag I see Johnson's ledger sitting right on top of the rest of the stolen documents.

Grabbing the bag, I make my way to the door, then stop. I know I'm only supposed to get the binder, but this opportunity is too good to pass up, so I backtrack to Paggett's desk.

Thanks to movies, most people normally search for the safe in one of the walls. Paggett thinks he's smarter than everyone else. Sitting down in his black leather chair, I turn to face the window. The oak credenza is a not-so-obvious hiding place. The center door swivels up to reveal the safe.

I'm not the fastest safecracker in the world, but I'm fast enough. When I put my mind to a task my psychic sense helps. A flash of three numbers floating in the air in front of the safe appear in my mind. Most safes use a "four turns right, three left, two right, then left to zero to unlock." Sure enough—it worked.

There's a stack of Paggett's private papers. Scooping the whole batch up, I dump them all into the bag.

Something else catches my eye. Pulling out a black ledger, I start flipping through the pages. What a list! I recognize quite a few of the names. There are judges, lawyers, police officials, and even a couple of high-level politicos!

It isn't just the names that are interesting but the record of numbers beneath them. Paggett is meticulous. He has cross-referenced all the payoffs and bribes to the bank accounts into which they were deposited. This is a bonus that the police will dearly love to get their hands on. I squeeze it into the bag, but then I can't fit in Simon's ornate binder. I have to carry it in my hand as I head out the way I came in.

No sooner has my foot hit the main floor of the warehouse than my psychic alarm goes off. Someone's unlocking the front door. Ducking behind the nearest pallet of boxes, I fumble to keep the bag and binder in my grasp.

The main lights come on. From my hiding place I observe a pretty brunette with nicely shaped legs saunter in. I don't recognize her, but I do know whom she's with. I had the pleasure of meeting Slim Jim, Terry, and Brik the last time I was here. Since the brunette is leading the way, she has to be—Paggett's little sister. Lori.

"Slim and Terry, you stay here," she instructs, "while Brik and I go up to the offices for a minute. Paggett wants one of you to bring some papers back to him."

I look up and see the open door that I neglected to shut. A sick, hollow feeling invades my stomach.

Lori and Brik disappear from view, and I hold my breath while planning my escape. I have to make it to the other side of the warehouse where the unlocked door is waiting for me before Lori and Brik come back to the top of the stairs. From that vantage point, they could easily see me.

I clutch the bag of files closer to my black, leather bomber jacket and sidle to the next pallet, then to the one beside it. Sweat drenches the underarms of my shirt. Maybe wearing the jacket as camouflage wasn't such a good idea. I make it about halfway to the south wall when I hear Lori's voice.

"There he is!"

I look back and see Lori at the top of the stairs pointing directly at me. Brik is on his way down to join his cohorts. Slinging the bag of files over my shoulder, I dodge left between a pile of boxes then move left again. I hope that the maze of boxes will confuse the terrible trio enough to allow me to make it to the door and escape.

"Split up and surround him!" she yells.

My talent can't provide me with an indication of where my pursuers are in relation to me, but it does throw up STOP signs where I shouldn't go. Changing direction, I move away from these images.

"Slim, he's to your left! Terry, go right! Brik, turn around! He's behind you!" Lori fires off one direction after the other.

I move left, right, left again, and then stop. My psychic alarm is screaming, and the STOP sign is flashing urgently. I don't look around the pile of boxes. Slim Jim's right there. Turning around, I race back the way I had come, always moving away from my pursuers.

WHIRR-CRACK—the distinctive railer sound rings out.

Something whizzes by my ear and shatters the side of the box right in front of me.

WHIRR-CRACK—another shot.

I don't wait to see where the stainless steel railer ball lands. Quickly, I duck around another pile of boxes. The shooting stops.

"Slim! He's right in front of you!" Lori screams orders through the cavernous building. "No! Go left, not right, you idiot!"

I envision STOP signs indicating Terry and Brik, but I have no choice. Slim is getting closer and closer. And I imagined myself getting boxed in—something I don't want to happen—can't let happen.

Trotting to the left past a long row of boxes, I find the unlocked door right in front of me. It's no more than three long strides to freedom, and I waste no time. I skid the last little bit when the bag of files catches on the edge of a pallet and is yanked out of my hands. My pursuers are coming fast.

I hesitate for a second, then leave the bag and clutch Simon's ledger to my chest as I barely stop to open the door before racing through the opening. Slamming it shut behind me, I look for something to block it with.

Thank God. Four teetering three-meter high stacks of pallets are next to the outward-opening door. Grabbing the side of a stack, I rock it back and forth a couple of times. It topples into an impenetrable barrier.

I hear Slim Jim and Terry's frantic struggle to open the door. But the makeshift barricade won't hold them for long.

My escape route beckons to me, so I waste no time. I run through the back lot until I reach the spot in the fence where I had cut the chain link on my way in. The chinging sound of the chain link hitting the post echoes noisily in the night as I run to my waiting vehicle.

A mixture of grunts makes me stop and look back. The bright light from inside the warehouse frames my pursuers.

WHIRR-CRACK.

WHIRR-CRACK.

DING - one of the steel balls ricochets off the post beside my ear.

I slide across the hood of my 20-year old Sol-Ray 7.2 and take shelter behind the car.

Slim and Terry are professionals. They wait for a target before shooting.

I don't give them one. Swinging open the car door, I slide in, trying to keep my head down.

I pray my mechanic is as good as he says he is!

———•◆•———

CHAPTER 4

312 OD—September 4—10:22 pm

"Some idiot left the door unlocked!" Lori made her way into the offices with Brik dutifully following behind. "Jonny's going to have a fit!"

Going directly to his filing cabinets, she opened the top right-hand file drawer and pulled out the first two files as Jonny had told her.

"Miss. B-b-b-behind you."

Lori looked up and saw Brik pointing to the desk in front of the window. She couldn't believe her eyes. The safe was open and, worst of all, empty. She dropped the file folders onto the desk.

"Follow me," she ordered as she ran out the door.

Lori made it to the landing in record time. "There he is!" she yelled, pointing at the dark shape behind a pile of boxes.

After glancing up at her, the thief bolted

and ran around a stack of boxes.

Terry and Slim Jim both started heading towards where the crook had been. When Lori saw this she called out, "Split up and surround him!"

"Slim, he's to your left! Terry, go right! Brik, turn around! He's behind you!" Lori couldn't get the orders out fast enough.

"That's weird," she muttered. "No matter which way the boys move this guy seems to know in advance."

The thief came to a dead stop before almost running right into Slim Jim's arms, then ran back in the direction from where he came. It was unbelievable. "Slim! He's right in front of you!" She could feel the frustration building in her voice. "No! Go left, not right, you idiot!"

"Damn," she muttered after seeing Slim miss the burglar with two shots.

The intruder made it to the back door and slammed it behind him. Lori cried out in frustration as she watched her three bodyguards struggle vainly with the door. She raced down the stairs to look for another exit when she spied a canvas bag on the floor beside a pallet of boxes.

Picking up the dirty grey bag, she reached inside and pulled out a handful of papers. Lori glanced through them. "Well now… Could this have been what our thief was toting away?" She handed it to Terry. "Take this to the car."

"What do you mean, you couldn't stop him?" Paggett screamed. His cigar fell out of his mouth and plopped onto the oak desk, the lit end exploding in a small shower of sparks. He picked up the stogie and batted out the tiny glowing embers threatening to set the papers on the desk afire. Pointing his cigar at them, he yelled, "You three are supposed to be the best in the organization. And you couldn't even stop one single rotten little thief! I equip you with state-of-the-art, fully automatic, 24-shot rail guns and unlimited ammo and you only got off four shots! And you…" Paggett stopped and directed his cigar at Slim. "…YOU… didn't even wing the bastard!"

"It's not their fault." Lori tried to defend them.

"Don't give me that bullshit, sis!", Paggett spat as he spun around and glared at her. She took a step back and sat heavily on an ornamental cane chair. The chair creaked and almost tipped over. "I told you to lay low and what happens? You get mixed up in the middle of a damn robbery. What if he had been carrying a railer? Did that thought ever cross your mind? Just because you've never been caught during your escapades doesn't make you invulnerable!"

"Look, I didn't know anyone would be there. What was I supposed to do?" Lori hung her head. "I tried to stop him."

Paggett couldn't help it, and Lori knew it.

Whenever she used that sorrowful tone of voice her elder sibling couldn't stay mad at her.

"That's okay, sis. At least you're alright. Just don't ever do that again. Okay?"

Lori kept her smile hidden. She watched Jonny begin pacing in front of the desk as he puffed furiously on his cigar.

"So, whoever broke in, got all the stuff from Johnson's as well as the stuff in the safe. Did they get anything else?"

"No, B-b-boss. It looked like this was the only room that was hit."

Paggett stared at Brik until the short, heavy-set bodyguard started to shuffle his feet nervously, then shifted his attention back to the others. It was obvious to Lori that he didn't think his men knew about all the contents of the room—Jonny'd have to check it for himself to verify that only the safe was hit.

"Did any of you get a good look at this creep?"

"I never even saw his face, boss," Slim Jim muttered. "I got two shots off at him but missed. Miss Lori was yelling to us where he was at, but by the time we got around the boxes he was gone."

"Yeah," Terry agreed. "He was like some kind of rabbit—always one step ahead of us."

"Would you be able to identify him if you saw him again, sis?"

Lori shook her head. "I don't know. Maybe. It's hard to say. I saw his face a couple of times when he looked straight at me, but I never saw it clearly enough." She paused for a moment while recalling the chase. "It was sort of weird, though, how he constantly slipped away from the boys. Like, for example, I'd call out *Slim, he's to your left*, and a second or two later, he'd turn and head away. At one time he was moving straight towards Slim when he stopped, turned around, and ran off in the other direction."

"He must've heard Slim," Paggett remarked.

"Slim was standing still when the guy turned around," Lori shrugged her shoulders. "It was kinda weird. The path was clear ahead of him, and Slim was right around the next row of boxes and could have easily grabbed him… if he would have kept going. Terry was coming on one side and Brik from the other. There were all these boxes. How did he know? It didn't make any sense. He seemed to twist around and move towards Brik in order to get away."

Lori wasn't surprised to see the puzzled look in Jonny's eyes. She was just as mystified as him. "What did he get away with?"

"Mostly routine family business and some of my private papers plus the stuff that some of the boys brought in last night. I've got to find some way of getting that stuff back."

"I can help you!" Lori didn't bother trying to hide the excitement in her voice.

"No way!" Paggett shouted.

Lori squirmed in her seat at the vehemence in Jonny's reply.

"You are NEVER... I repeat NEVER... going to

get involved in the family business again! Look at the mess you've caused already! It's bad enough that I've got a rap sheet with them, but now you're known to the cops, too. They think you had something to do with deSalle's death…" he froze in mid-sentence and shook his head, "and deSalle's people are probably thinking the same thing."

Lori countered, "They have nothing on me. I have an air-tight alibi."

"Humph! Some alibi! You were in the bathroom next door. You were supposed to be using the damn facilities, but they won't find your fingerprints anywhere on the sink or toilet, will they? Shit! A routine check will blow your alibi all to hell, Lori! It's not a matter of IF… but WHEN."

Lori felt faint and gripped the arms of her chair more tightly.

"I have to make sure that they don't find you, sis." Paggett yanked the cigar from his mouth and pointed it at her. "You're going to get lost out in a secluded place in the country."

"Huh?" Lori was aghast. "The country? I can't go someplace without people. I'll go crazy. I need my shopping… my freedom… my stores… my… my…"

"Okay, okay," Johnny interrupted her. "It's against my better judgement, but if you can't do the countryside, then you'll do someplace with lots of people."

Lori stared at him in silence.

Paggett swept his arm in an all-encompassing

gesture. "Go back to MallWorld and lose your-self. It's big. You'll have your shops and stores. There are lots of people to blend in with. Cut your hair differently, get it coloured, put on glasses, whatever it takes. You should be able to hide right out in the open."

"How long do I have to stay hidden?" She cocked her head and stared into his calculat-ing face.

"Forever..."

"What?" she gasped.

"... unless I can find a scapegoat to stick with deSalle's ghosting."

"What am I supposed to do at MallWorld? Where am I supposed to stay?"

"Don't worry. I'm going to get Angel to hide you and the boys. Just make sure that you pay for everything with cash—no credit cards." He flipped the edges of a small notebook on his desk and reached for the up-link. "Angel owes me a few favours. He'll arrange the accommoda-tions. The four of you would look too conspicu-ous at any of the hotels in MallWorld."

"Wouldn't I be less notable if I were alone?"

"If you think I'm going to let you go any-where without the boys, you're freaking nuts!" Paggett stood up angrily. "DeSalle's goons are looking for any excuse to pin his ghosting on me. If they get their hands on you, they'll be able to get to me."

Silence.

"You'd give yourself up for me?" Lori could

hear the surprised tone in her voice as she watched her brother's stocky form approach.

"In your dreams, baby sis." He put a hand on her shoulder and stared into her amber eyes. "I promised dad I'd take care of you. And if that means not letting you do anything stupid, then so be it. I need you out of the way for a while. Just trust me on this, will ya?"

Lori wriggled from under his concerned stare.

"I hate it when other people tell me what to do." She stood and faced him. "Dad wanted me to be his *little princess* and NOT follow in the family business. But I did anyway."

Paggett broke eye contact with her defiant posture and looked out the picture window. The moonlight highlighted the Paggett family crest etched in the plate glass. "Look, sis, in this world you always have someone you have to take orders from or report to. Believe it or not, even *I* have a boss."

When he turned back toward her, she merely stared at him. She never thought of him having to answer to a superior.

"Now, as your big brother and boss, you're going into hiding. End of discussion."

312 OD—September 5—2:19 am

"Miss Lori. Umm..." Terry's normally soft voice boomed in the confines of the back seats of the limo. He along with Slim and Brik were crammed into the rear-facing seat thereby leaving the main seat to Lori.

"Yes, Terry?"

"I was wondering. Why didn't you tell the boss about the bag you found?"

"Just helping my brother, Terry." Lori patted the smooth leather arm-rest nervously and averted her eyes. She pondered what to disclose of her quickly forming plans.

Brik broke in, "B-b-but it's the b-b-boss's b-b-business."

She sighed. Her voice took on a devious lilt. "Like it or not, I am in the family business now. If Jonny won't let me be an active member, I guess I'll have to be an invisible one."

"Huh?" Slim broke off watching the sparse traffic to gape at Lori, who countered with her own stare.

"I plan on doing whatever I can to help Jonny." Her finger tapped gently on the armrest. "If that means 'on the side' then so be it. I'm going to examine those papers to find out what's happening. I don't know if anything will come from them, but it won't hurt to try. If I draw a blank..." she hesitated at the thought of failing, "...then I will give them to Jonny."

She looked up into his troubled face. "Until then, I plan on being a 'silent partner' in the family business."

Lori waited for the usual concerned reply she had come to expect and, more often, appreciate.

"We've got a tail, Miss." Jo deWitt was glancing from the road to his rear-view mirror and back. "We picked them up as soon as we left your house. They're the third car back—inside lane."

"Are you sure they're following us?" Lori asked as she turned to peer out the back window.

"Yes, ma'am. They keep dropping behind other cars, but I've spotted them after each turn we've made. They're pretty good. I've almost lost them a couple of times, but they keep hounding us." He slowed the car down to a veritable crawl. Horns blared as outraged drivers were forced to manoeuvre around them. The car following them slowed, too.

"Police?" Lori craned her neck to find a better angle.

"Probably," Jo replied, "but I'm not sure. Cops normally use a helicopter, but I haven't seen one."

"Can you lose them?" Lori turned to look at Jo.

"I think I can. Hang on."

The light ahead turned red. Jo raced through it. Lori spotted the police cruiser on the side street as it turned on its lights and siren and raced after them. The unmarked car sidled in behind the cruiser and continued following.

"What are you doing?"

"I've got an idea. I want them to follow me for two… more… blocks."

Jo spun the wheel of the car and barely missed the corner of a building, then raced into a long alley. When he was almost to the end, he stopped, leaving the limo blocking the exit of the alley onto the street.

The police cruiser's siren trailed off into an almost deafening silence. The police car's doors opened. Two officers scrambled into position behind their vehicle's muddy doors.

For eternal seconds each vehicle's occupants caught their breaths while planning their best move. One of the officers slowly approached, his foamer gun firmly aimed at the back of Jo's head.

Jo's window whirred down, and he placed his hands in plain view on the steering wheel.

The officer kept his foamer trained on Jo as he called out, "What's the bright idea, jackass?"

"What do you mean, officer?" Jo's face was the picture of innocence. He didn't want to feel the foamer's hardening gel any time soon.

"Racing away from us. That's the idea."

"Actually, officer, I never went faster than the speed limit…"

"And the red light?"

"Sorry about that. I was… distracted. I slowed down, but when I saw the light I sped up to get through. I thought I'd made it in on the yellow. Didn't I?"

"You entered on the red." The cop lowered his foamer slightly.

"Okay." Jo pointed to the right side of the car while keeping both hands on the wheel. "Is it all right if I reach into the glove box to get my license and registration?" Jo asked with a child-like air.

The police officer's jaw gaped. He obviously wasn't expecting co-operation, so he hesitated before nodding.

Lori saw Jo's grin as he leaned over to get his documents and passed them politely to the waiting hand. By now, the second officer had approached on the other side of the car with his foamer drawn and pointing at the dark side window. His partner went to the cruiser to write up a ticket.

Lori leaned forward slightly to whisper, "Jo, what are you doing?"

"Just setting up a little diversion. I'm going to get the cops to help us out."

"By giving us a ticket?" Slim asked.

"Yep."

The police officer returned and thrust the ticket through the window at Jo. "Next time, wait for the light to change," he ordered.

"Thank you officer, I will. May I go now?"

"Yeah. Get out of here."

Jo drove slowly and cautiously into the intersection and turned right. The traffic flow was very light. When he turned the next corner, he could see the lights of the cruiser still in the alley.

"We've just lost our tail." Jo proudly called into the back of the car, after five minutes of careful driving and observations in his rear mirrors.

"Huh?" chorused Terry and Slim.

"Our tail was behind the cruiser. They

couldn't get out of the alley in time to keep track of us. For the cost of a ticket, I lost our tail."

"Pretty slick move, Jo." Slim grinned.

"That's why Jonny pays me the medium bucks." Jo shot a smile at Lori through the rear-view mirror.

312 OD—September 5—3:00 am

Lori's limo slowed down then stopped in front of the least run-down of the buildings on the block. A shaft of light stabbed into the dark when the car door opened. Scurrying noises could be heard as denizens of the dark retreated further into the recesses. A shadow detached itself from the buildings and moved closer to the light. A human shape slipped quickly, quietly into the waiting car. The beam vanished with the solid thunk of the car door.

"All right, lady. Your brother wants you lost, so let's get lost."

Lori looked the speaker up and down. If she had seen him in a crowd, she wouldn't have noticed him. He was average in height, weight, and build. He would have blended into any setting and vanished.

"My name's Angel," a mischievous grin lit up his handsome face as he added, "and I'm here to *guide you.*" It was obvious that he had refined this line and thoroughly enjoyed delivering it. There was an expectant look in his eyes as he searched their faces for a reaction.

He wasn't disappointed. They shot curious glances of disbelief at each other.

Lori was the first to recover, "Okay, Angel. Exactly *where* in MallWorld are we going?"

"Shhh. Ears everywhere. I'll guide your driver."

Lori nodded. She knew the logic in this. MallWorld was the perfect place to get lost.

312 OD—September 5—4:12 am

Jo deftly manoeuvred their black BFM S-I limo into the underground parkade. It was a tight fit, but each of MallWorld's parkades had specially reserved areas for limousines, SUV's, and other over-sized vehicles. He was muttering, "I don't see why we have to park so far from the apartment and hotel lots", as he shut off the engine and pocketed the keys.

"Because they've got cameras that tape our car tags," Angel commented while scanning nearby stalls. "And they're sent to the mall's police station. Jonny wanted us to hide you, so we don't want them knowing where you're at." They cautiously exited into a quiet area of a parkade near the World Place Apartment Complex. "Your brother told me to hide you until his men find whoever they're looking for and 'lose' him permanently." Angel guessed that Lori was the target that had to be hidden.

Lori didn't enlighten him.

Angel opened Lori's door while Jo continued

grumbling under his breath. Jo exchanged a brief, frustrated look with Lori.

She stepped out of the car and, surrounded by her guards, walked the short distance through the brightly lit parkade into the elevator that would eventually take them into MallWorld. They could hear a slight murmur that increased as they neared the main floor. It rose in intensity until it was almost deafening. Lori rubbed her ears for a second. She had been here often enough that she knew she would adapt and eventually filter out the noise of the crowd.

Suddenly, an intense light filled the rising glass-walled elevator as it passed the demarcation line between the parkade and the mall itself. Lori stared out at the riot of colour that assailed her eyes. Flashing storefront signs advertised everything from aardvarks to zithers. Glass-fronted elevators afforded them a dazzling view of the cavernous ten levels of the mall. There were numerous open walkways connecting each side, and winding escalators and stairways leading to different levels. It looked like a hamster habitat gone mad.

DING.

"Follow me." Angel was first out the door and into the teeming sea of humanity. Even in the early hours of the morning, the mall was crowded with people. Slim Jim was right behind him, a lucky break for Lori and her entourage, as Angel virtually blended into the crowd and only Slim's height provided a sort of beacon that the others could home in on.

It wasn't far to the World Place Apartment Complex. Lori was more than happy to pass through its doors and into a zone of relative silence, a blessed relief to her ears.

Angel led them past the ancient, green-skinned security guard, who lifted his eyes from his newspaper to mechanically glance at the group parading past, before returning to his reading. It was hard to tell if the guard was truly looking at them since one eye was focused at the ceiling. The elevator doors sensed their approach and opened. They rode in silence to the eighteenth floor, then proceeded towards the far end of the hallway. Angel stopped and opened the door to 1818. He handed the key to Lori.

"This is your suite. There are two bedrooms—the one on the right is the biggest." He looked at Lori and her three guards and added, "You may want the one on the left. It faces away from the street so it's quieter and, anyway, your three friends wouldn't fit in it. There's clothing in all the closets, but I don't think it'll fit any of you."

With a nod from Lori, Terry brought her luggage to the smaller room while Slim and Brik lugged the other suitcases to the larger one.

Lori took in the entire low-class apartment in a single glance and asked, "Is this one of Jonny's hide-aways?"

"Nah! It used to be my grandmother's condo." Angel looked around reminiscently. "When she died, I sort of inherited it, then MallWorld expanded five years ago and engulfed the building, making it part of their complex." He fingered dust on the television set. "Jonny sometimes uses it as a safe house for `visitors'."

Jo dropped Lori's small maroon suitcase on a floral couch near the door to the smaller bedroom.

"And speaking of safe, if you do any shopping, try to keep as low a profile as you can. Make sure..."

"Yeah, yeah, I know. Jonny gave me the drill." Lori couldn't keep the exasperated tone from her voice as she plopped down beside the suitcase on the sofa and droned, "Make SURE you pay for everything with cash. Only make SMALL purchases. Yadda, yadda, yadda."

She looked at her three bodyguards who were busy unpacking. "Oh! I almost forgot... and don't get yourself NOTICED."

"I was going to say keep an eye out for the crowd control cameras."

"Cameras?" Lori slumped further down into the plush armchair. She thought she knew the mall inside-out.

"Yeah. The mall cops use them to spot pickpockets and low-lifes like me." He grinned as he surveyed the large dusty room with its fifty-year old, antique furniture. "They also have face-recognition software to spot run-aways and any high-profile criminals, so you have to be especially careful."

"How do we know where the cameras are?" Slim inquired as he walked back into the room from checking out the kitchen. He slipped a stale Christmas candy cane into his pocket from a tiny well-worn wooden sleigh on the coffee table.

"Look for bluish lights. They don't think we know it, but the blue gives a better picture for them to check and makes it easier for us to spot. They're all around the food courts and cross corridors. You can also see them spread throughout the hotels. The cameras cost too much to have them all over the mall, so they're only in key spots. If you know what to look for you can't miss them." Angel's voice had an *I know what I'm talking about* confidence in it. "I'll brief your boys on them… they'll be able to spot 'em easy for you."

CHAPTER 5

312 OD—September 5—9:58 am

This is one of those times when I wish I had a perfect photographic memory as my talent instead of these fuzzy visions. Mind you, I'm not knocking my ability. It has done wonders for my career. It's just that right now remembering what I saw is a lot more important.

I'm still shaking a bit from my narrow escape. I only got a few quick glimpses of the ledger on Pagget's desk. I was planning on bringing it with me and wasn't concentrating on memorizing the damn thing.

RINGGGGG

I was so focused on jogging my memory that I almost jump out of my skin when my office uplink rang.

RINGGGGG

"Damn." It dawns on me that since Rosie hasn't answered on the first ring, that it's my private line. The portable in my ear is still turned off.

RINGGGGG

I desperately start shuffling the piles of papers on my desk in a frantic attempt to find the stupid up-link. Don't get the wrong idea—my work space is not a mess. It just looks that way to outsiders. I have what I call an "open" filing system. I'm one-hundred percent familiar with every piece of paper on my desk and where it is in its spatial relationship in my work-place. My worst bad habit is covering up the desk up-link because I depend so much on the one in my ear and rarely use the desk unit. I know I should keep my files electronically, but I love the feel of paper files.

RINGGGGGG

"Finally," I move the last pile, "there you are." Lifting the receiver, I gasp out, "Hello?"

"Jack. Where were you? In the shower?"

"No, I just couldn't find the up-link."

"Ah, the famous Jack Valencz filing system."

I lean back in my chair and put my feet up on the corner of my desk, careful not to disrupt things further.

"What do you want, Phil?"

Phil Harris is in the PI business, too. He was my mentor and partner, and I learned the art of "urban camouflage" from him. Today, we have more of a loose association –he helps me, I help him. There were occasions when we competed for the same cases, but since I hit it big, we no longer travel in the same circles. He takes the low-rent stuff.

We share the same birth date, and even though he's only a year older than I am, he looks fifteen more. I keep telling him to get out of the business. He doesn't listen. It's wearing him down.

"I just wanted to know if you have any spare jobs kicking around?"

Whenever Phil asks me that question, I know that the rent on his one-room office in MallWorld is coming due. His place isn't much to look at. As a matter-of-fact it looks quite a bit like Humphrey Bogart's office from "The Maltese Falcon"—only much neater. Phil's a neat-freak. He even files scraps of paper. When we shared an office, my filing system used to drive him crazy. The only reason he's located at the mall is because of the large amount of foot traffic in front of his door.

I take my feet off the desk and look through a stack of papers. I'm hoping to find something that I can class as pending so I can pass it on to Phil. Nothing.

"Sorry, Phil, I've only got one case right now, and it's just a paper-chaser."

"Need any help?"

It sounds to me like the rent isn't just due, it's *overdue*.

"Sorry, bud. All that's left is the paper-work." I risk a quick glance at the mountain of red tape on my desk. Could I risk letting him put the papers in the filing cabinets lining the north wall of the office—and take a chance on never finding what I'm looking for again? "I wish I could be of more help to you. How about I pass on whatever comes up next?"

"Thanks, Jack. I appreciate whatever you can throw my way."

I can tell from the sound of his voice that he isn't thrilled about begging for help. Even though he isn't at my level anymore, Phil still has his pride. He resents having to ask for help.

"No problem, Phil. Always happy to pass along anything I can. Yeah... Okay... Bye."

As happens whenever I talk to Phil, I tend to reminisce about the good old days when he and I used to chum around. Leaning back in my chair, I put my feet up again.

Our first case was when we foiled one of Jonny Paggett's truck hijackings. We would've nailed Paggett on that one, but the judge disallowed a couple of pieces of crucial evidence. He got off with a "slap on the wrist" fine instead of jail time. What was that judge's name—Bryer? Bryce? No... Bruce. Judge Robert Bruce.

My feet slam down on the floor, and I almost jump out of my chair.

Wait! Hold it a second! That name rings a bell. It's one of the names in Paggett's ledger. Visualizing the sheet in my mind is easier. There's tomorrow's date next to the name and an amount of $10,000 followed by a list of numbers that could possibly be a bank account. The one underneath becomes clearer. It's the chief of police, and the district attorney's name is under his. Putting my mind to it, I've soon written five names and amounts from the sheet. It's a short list of "who's who" in municipal and federal politics. Now I have just one small problem.

The list is in my handwriting, not Paggett's. Any self respecting defence lawyer would shoot holes in it as evidence. As is, it's worthless. There's only one thing that I can do with it.

312 OD—September 5—2:10 pm

It's amazing how ninety percent of my cases seem to lead me to MallWorld. I hate this place. It's too crowded, too big, too busy and did I mention, too crowded?

MallWorld is so large it has its own security force overseen by the City Police Services. Unless you know what to look for you can't tell a mall cop from a real cop. Mall cops are assigned foamers instead of railers. Mall administration's worst nightmare is having trigger-happy security guards spraying hollow stainless steel projectiles through throngs of shoppers while chasing a shoplifter—very bad publicity.

The only reason I'm even at the mall is to bring the list of names and amounts to Constable Mariyan Kraemer. She's my private contact on the police force. Thankfully, she's neither a mall cop nor a beat cop. She works in the forensics lab on a normal nine-to-five shift. Everyone seems to like her, and because of that she's got contacts throughout the force. She'll be able to find someone interested enough in my list to get the investigation rolling.

The desk sergeant knows me from my numerous other visits. He doesn't bother to ask for I.D. before handing me a visitor badge and unlocking the security door.

My leather shoes make a soft tapping noise on the tile floor as I walk the short distance to her lab.

I don't want to disturb Mariyan, so I wait a few seconds before knocking gently on the plexiglas window. Before she gives me any notice, she closes the lid to the centrifuge and starts it working.

An infectious grin appears on her face when she sees me. "Come on in," she mouths.

I walk around the corner and through the lab doors.

"How are you, Jack?"

"I'm taking it one day at a time, Mariyan. How 'bout you?"

She shrugs her shoulders and points to the main lab table. "The same, only one case at a time. I meant to call you. Good job on bringing in Paul Dunne. Some of the guys wish you worked for us instead of in private business."

"I tried the academy route, but couldn't take all that happy-happy-joy-joy camaraderie."

"Huh? What the hell are you talking about?"

"Sorry, Mariyan, it was just a joke—a bad one."

"So you couldn't finish training."

The real reason is that my talent was over-loaded while I was at the academy. I kept zoning out in class when I concentrated too hard on a subject and had a vision. The exams were the worst. The stress of studying brought on more flashes.

But I can't tell her that, so I use a half-truth instead. "I couldn't take the teamwork. I'm a lone wolf—always was, always will be, I guess. I just don't play well with others."

She shrugs. "What can I do for you today, Jack?"

"I've got something your colleagues might be interested in." Taking the sheet of paper from my inside jacket pocket, I put it in her eager hands.

Her hazel eyes scan the sheet and widen in surprise.

I put my hand on her shoulder. "Before you get too pleased, I should warn you that I wrote it."

"Where did you get the numbers?" She runs a gloved finger down the page.

Shifting one of the lab stools closer, I sit down. "I saw them in Jonny Pagget's ledger."

Mariyan nods. "And I presume you don't have the original in your possession?"

It's my turn to nod.

"The original would sure help us."

I nod again. The centrifuge whirs to a stop.

"I don't suppose you could get your hands on it?"

I get a mental flash of an orange tabby cat in a room packed with chairs. This tells me that the list isn't in Paggett's cavernous warehouse anymore. It's someplace where there are lots of people.

A different image shimmers in my mind. Surprisingly, this one's much clearer and more detailed. Like the ones I had at Mexicali Rosa's and in my office. A street map appears showing the sprawling MallWorld complex, and a small red arrow pointing to one of the apartment complexes.

"Jack?" Mariyan is lightly touching my knee. "You okay?"

Bringing myself back to the lab, I grin at her and say, "Yeah. I think I might be able to find the original."

"Great. I'll bring this to a detective friend of mine. This is right up his alley. Can I tell him you'll get the ledger soon?"

I shrug as I shift my posterior in the chair. "I haven't got a clue. I have to get my hands on it first."

"Oh." She's trying to find out where I saw the ledger. "Then I'll tell my friend you'll do your best. He'll be interested in the numbers on here anyway. This will at least tell him who he can't trust in the D.A.'s office."

Sliding off the stool, I head to the door. "I'll get back to you."

Mariyan reaches for the centrifuge as she calls over her shoulder, "Later."

The guy handcuffed to the bench by the desk

sergeant looks up at me without making eye contact. Do I know him? His face isn't ringing any alarm bells. Shrugging again, I continue on my way then stop with my hand frozen on the exit door. Three things come to my attention.

"What the hell?" the desk sergeant cries out as he tips his pop can upside-down. "I just opened this!"

At the same time, I hear a scream of outrage from outside in the mall.

The third is that I wish I wasn't so paranoid about people getting close to me and discovering my hidden talent. And that's because the only other person at the front desk is the prettiest lady I've had the pleasure of laying eyes on in a long time. She pauses while talking to the grumbling desk sergeant and looks around. Her gaze passes over me. The biggest hazel eyes I've ever seen look directly at me. I wish I had the nerve to strike up a conversation. Suddenly, a vivid image forms in my mind… of her in a wedding gown standing next to me… on top of a wedding cake! Wow!

I toss my badge to the sergeant and make my way towards the exit, but the opening door slams into my out-stretched hand. I'm startled out of my daydream by the pain, and the assault of noise coming from the mall. Stepping around two cops, I join the wandering throng. I see the reason for the cry of outrage—one of the mall patrons is standing just outside the police station, and he's drenched from head to toe. The janitor robots are busy scurrying around him and cleaning the floor. It seems to be a losing battle, as the more they clean up the droplets of pop on the floor around him, the more he angrily brushes gooey liquid off his suede jacket.

Sitting down on one of the benches just outside the police station, I stare vacantly at the mixed crowd of mutants and normals milling past. My hands start to shake slightly as I ponder what's been happening to my visions. This is the third time that it's *flared* up on me. Strange. Normally, I get blurry images of things that I have to interpret and make sense of. I've gotten quite good at interpreting the dream-like images. These things are different. They're clearer and much more precise.

Hey! I'm not complaining. It's great that my flashes are becoming lucid and specific. That makes my job a hell-of-a-lot easier. I can live with that. What I need to figure out is why now and why not all the time? Is my psychic sense somehow evolving?

It can't be location-based. The first vision was at the restaurant, the second at my office and the third here at MallWorld in the forensics lab. All three places are within the city and in the west-end, but that's the only connection they have.

Sitting back on the bench, I clasp my hands behind my neck, and stare up at the ceiling. I haven't heard of any unusual sunspots lately. There haven't been any storms or electrical activity either, so they're not weather-related.

I think back to how I was feeling when each of the flashes occurred. Let's see. I was in the middle of a fight at Mexicali Rosa's. Maybe they're based on adrenalin? But, I was calm when talking to Simon Johnson in my office, and again just a few moments ago. Hmmm… that rules out my emotional state being a factor.

How about my health? I haven't had any bouts of Zorzut or Dresden flu recently, so it can't be that. My health has been the same the past while. Maybe I'm coming down with something and these flare-ups are a sort of early-warning system. Nah, that's just grasping at straws. But I remember feeling tired each time, really tired, more than normal. Maybe it's like a battery boost? Each vision gives me more energy rather than decreasing it. Nah… that's the opposite of what should happen.

None of the three instances happened at the same time. One was in the early evening at the cantina, the other was in the morning in my office, and the latest just this afternoon.

Maybe people are getting to me? Maybe I'm too close to some of these nut cases and its throwing my talent into overdrive? Paul Dunne was at Mexicali Rosa's and may still be here at this sub-station. I was alone with Mariyan just now when the third flare-up occurred. Neither Paul nor Mariyan were in my office when I had the second flash. Only Simon Johnson was there.

Thinking of Johnson's name causes me to flinch. Suddenly, a fourth clear flash pops up. Paggett's shaking hands with Johnson. They're partners? No, not shaking hands. They're squeezing hands—hard. Not partners, rivals! Both are in the same business. This explains why Paggett's trying to take over Johnson's operation. Now I also understand why I saw that grey haze around Simon. He's as much a crook as Paggett.

My hands come back from behind my neck, and I lean forward with my fore-arms on my knees.

"I have to be more careful about whom I trust," I mutter to myself. I don't even draw glances from the passing multitude. People who talk to themselves are a-dime-a-dozen these days. No one pays them any attention.

The second commandment in my agency handbook—*don't trust anyone, especially your friends* enters, unbidden, into my mind.

That beautiful brunette from the police station comes out and stands a few meters in front of me. She's looking around, probably trying to spot her boyfriend who's obviously late. I heave a sigh. Looking at the brunette, I think to myself, that I'd never leave someone who looks like that waiting alone anywhere.

Our eyes meet for a split-second, and I get a butterfly-like feeling in my stomach before she looks away then vanishes into the crowd. Any chance I have to meet her disappears.

"Do you know the lady?" A raspy voice intrudes.

Sighing wistfully, I tell him, "I only wish."

Shaking my head to come out of my daze, I

see two hefty individuals in expensive suits exchanging glances with each other. Before I can say anything else they too vanish into the crowd.

I go back to my psychic dilemma. Anytime… anywhere… with someone… or alone…

This is driving me crazy. There has to be a connection somewhere, but what is it?

CHAPTER 6

312 OD—September 6—11:17 am

I'm still in a bit of a fog as I get to my office. I've been re-playing the past couple of days over and over in my mind and driving myself crazy. I don't understand why my psychic sense is acting up.

Pausing for a second, I admire my door. Though it's not spectacular—just a plain light oak door, the ornately engraved brass plaque reads "Finders Keepers Detective Agency-Private Investigation—Jack Valencz". It fills me with pride every time I see it.

I put the key in the lock and walk in.

"Hi honey. I'm home." The coded greeting tells Rosie who I am.

The contralto voice of the brunette robot replies, "You only have one message, sir."

This particular Rosie 4000 voice is better than the other ones available. It's the sweetest and most melodic of the choices that came with the equipment, and the voice fits the brunette version I have. The other model, a buxom blonde, had no imperfections. It was too perfect for my tastes.

"Playback."

"Hi Jack. It's Brian from Triple-B Bail Bonds. I need you to call us ASAP!"

It's not often this particular company calls me. Manny's Bonds is the company I primarily deal with. I've dealt with Triple-B before, but I don't much care for the types of characters that they post bond on, low-lifes that no one else will touch.

"Thank you, dear." The code phrase puts Rosie into ready mode as I walk into my office.

My leather jacket lands on my "coat rack" (exercise bike) next to the door and I sit down in my high-backed armchair. The small bar fridge is conveniently placed to the right of my desk, and I pull out a bottle of Grample's apple juice. Taking a couple of gulps, I reach for the up-link.

"Triple-B Bail Bonds," a high-pitched nasal voice announces.

I've been to their offices once before and recognize the voice. She's a blonde they hired, obviously for attributes other than typing and office skills.

"Hi, Peg. Can I please speak to Brian?"

"Soytanly. Whom can I tell him is calling?"

The misuse of whom causes me to cringe. Unconsciously imitating her accent, I drone, "Tell him it's Jack Valencz returning his call."

"Soytanly. One moment please," the reception-ist drones back.

The up-link clicks, and my ears are assaulted by an old 20th century rap song.

I wince. I didn't like it the first time I heard it on the oldies up-link station, still hate it. I don't mind a lot of music. Rock from the same time period is what I prefer uploading directly into the personal player in my right ear. I've got mine set to give me the current time between each song. I like this better than the old-fashioned time devices that are the current fad. Having to look at your wrist to know what time it is seems too time-consum-ing. The high level of cosmic radiation from the depleted ozone layer also makes these out-dated pieces unreliable and prone to inaccura-cies. Although you have to give them credit; they are better than the holo-watches. None of those survived the solar storms of 2105 A.D, or as it's now called Zero O.D.

Keeping the receiver far away from my ear while still being able to hear it is quite the juggling act.

When the overly-loud music cuts out in mid-word, I quickly bring it back to my ear in time to hear a monotone voice, "Hi Jack, Brian here."

"Hello Brian. What can I do for you?"

"I'm glad you called back. I've got a case for you that you're going to *love*."

My interest is piqued, as Brian doesn't know me well enough to be familiar with what I do and don't like.

While idly drumming my fingers on the desk, I cautiously ask, "How so?"

"Do you remember the first case I sent your way?"

My hand clenches tightly around the bottle, and I take another swig of apple juice as I lean forward.

"How can I not?" I groan. "That's the one where I got my butt handed to me by Jonny Paggett's goons. Why?"

"Well, I haven't got any paper on her yet, but I need you to find her. You're the first one I thought of when I heard."

"Brian. *Who and what* are you talking about?"

"Lori Paggett."

The mouthful of juice I'd just taken chokes me, and I fumble the bottle and almost drop it. The name is very familiar.

"Okay, and…?"

"One of my contacts told me they want to talk to Lori. The cops went to Paggett, but he denies knowing where she is."

"Yeah. He's not the kind to turn in his baby sister."

A chuckle sounds over the up-link line.

"He's too smart to have hidden her himself. One of his cronies probably stashed her. That way he can say he doesn't know where she is and not be lying."

I open my mouth to agree, but Brian doesn't give me a chance.

"You heard about deSalle's *exit*, right?"

"Yeah," I'm not sure where he's going with this, so I play it close to the vest. When I heard about deSalle's ghosting on this morning's ear-radio broadcast, I suspected that Paggett had something to do with it.

"Well it looks like the boys in blue want to talk to Lori. She was at deSalle's that night. They let her go, but now they want to ask her some more questions. 'Course she's no where to be found."

I finish the sentence for him. "...and this is where I come in?"

"That's where you come in. You're the best when it comes to finding people."

I grin at the compliment. *Thanks to my talent.*

"I know you work for Manny, Jack, but... my contact is really anxious to talk to Lori. How about it? Do you want the job?" He sounds a little too anxious.

Thoughts of getting back at Paggett by arresting his sister flit across my mind. A blurry scene of a small white fish swimming in the midst of a huge aquarium packed with black fish fills my mind.

"Well, Jack? Yes or no? Look, I'll even sweeten the pot. How about... double your going rate, IF you find her within twenty-four hours?"
"

I think I know *exactly* where Lori is. When I was talking to Mariyan, I had a flash of Paggett's ledger and MallWorld. Lori obviously took it when I dropped it leaving Paggett's warehouse.

"Yeah... I'll take it." This makes me sound a little distracted. Brian is smart enough to figure out that I've already got a lead.

"Later." Putting the up-link receiver back on its cradle, I toss the empty container of juice into the reprocessing basket across the room.

There's no way any bail bondsman would pay double my normal fee for a normal job, let alone this one. There's no warrant out for Lori's arrest, so there's no reason for Brian to find her.

Another image, this time of a tug-of-war competition, comes to mind. It doesn't take a genius to decode it. Brian is working for deSalle's people. They want Lori, probably to trade for Paggett's man who killed deSalle.

312 OD—September 6—2:20 pm

"… and did you know that it was never intended to become this big?" No one, especially Lori, could miss the excitement in Terry's voice as he eagerly read the promotional pamphlet detailing MallWorld's expansion. Terry had been regaling her with MallWorld facts for the past two days during her forced imprisonment.

Lori was bored. Really bored. She was bored of walking through the food courts and eating fast food. She was bored of the entertainments available. She couldn't believe it, but she was even bored of shopping. And it had been slightly more than a day since she had arrived at MallWorld. She missed her own familiar suite at home. She missed her sense of freedom.

"I'm sick and tired of this! I want to do something different!"

"We can't, Miss. Your b-b-brother wouldn't like it." Brik looked at her over the rack of lace nightgowns she was examining when she blurted out her exasperation.

It wasn't that there was nothing to do in MallWorld. It was that she was tired of being confined to one place—albeit huge—and having to look over her shoulder for potential pursuers.

———·◆·———

MallWorld learned well from its smaller predecessors. It had taken care to hire away dozens of senior executives from other "world's largest" -styled malls, their lavish salaries paid for by MallWorld's financial backers, who had already exceeded their fiscal expectations and actually recouped their total investment in less than a single year of MallWorld's operation.

Those original investments had been considerable, since MallWorld's creators were determined not merely to expand what others had done, but to exceed them in every respect. The children's castle in FantasyWorld is made of real stone, not cheaper fibreglass. The main street is actually three massive thoroughfares connecting the East and West Atriums, with each street built to represent three separate ethnic groupings—Western, Indian/African, and Oriental. A standard-gauge railroad winds its way around the interior of MallWorld, with two replica steam locomotives—granted they have sound dampeners so as to not deafen the mall patrons.

There is another train line being built that will extend from MallWorld to the international airport. MallWorld provides fifty thousand full-time jobs and over twenty thousand summer and seasonal jobs for students. The ride attractions in FantasyLane are spectacular, with most being custom designed for an enclosed area. Again, sound suppression is prime consideration. Some of them are so adventurous that thrill-seekers from around the world have been known to come just for the experience, with many pale by the time they exit the rides.

In addition, the mall has a spectacular ScienceWorld section, with a moonscape attraction simulating 1/6 gravity. NASA uses it as their training simulator. There is an underwater walk-through aquarium with eight different species of sharks swimming around the patrons in WaterWorld. One of the most featured pavilions is IndustryWorld which features exhibits from every major industry in the world. The Planes-R-Us area is particularly impressive, allowing children (and adults) to pilot simulated versions of over fifteen different aircraft—from single-engine crop-dusters to sub-orbital super-sonic transports.

Visitors find characters in realistic costumes—gnomes, trolls, and all manner of mythical creatures from European, Asian, and African history, even Roman legionnaires fighting Huns—and the usual marketing areas where guests can buy replicas of everything MallWorld has to offer.

One of the smartest things the investors did was to build luxury hotels *within* MallWorld. Guests fly in from all over the world to stay at the large comfortable inns, which are designed for three different levels of expense and grandeur, from one that might have been decorated by Cesar Ritz, down to several with more basic amenities. Guests at all of them share the same physical environment, and can take time off to bathe in the many pools surrounded by white-sand beaches next to the wave pool and water slides in WaterWorld.

There is also a busy multi-level casino as well as a 4-storey bingo complex in GameWorld. This is something other malls have tried, but not to this extent. All in all, MallWorld has been an instant and sensational success, and it rarely has fewer than twenty thousand guests, and frequently more than fifty thousand.

A thoroughly modern facility, it is controlled by six regional and one master command center, and every attraction, ride, and food outlet is monitored by computers and vid-cams.

Other malls have tried to expand and copy MallWorld. They soon reached a stage where local economics dictated that this is as large as they could get. No other mall handles money

94

in the quantity that MallWorld takes in. On a good day it is normal to pull in ten million dollars in cash alone and far more than that from plastic. Every day an armed guard contingent with heavy police escort travels from the different theme areas of the mall to the Mall's own bank.

MallWorld is a multi-storey structure. Under the main concourses is a subterranean city where the support services operate. The employees eat their lunches there. People and things can move from place to place quickly and unseen by the guests. Running it is the equivalent of being mayor of a not-so-small city—harder - since everything has to work all the time, and, most importantly, that the cost of operations has to be less than the mall's income.

One thing that wasn't included in any of MallWorld's promotional brochures was the fact that the mall was segregated into two distinct stratas. The bottom floors were inhabited by mutants and the upper level by normals. Many of the middle floors catered to both levels of society. These tended to be the more lucrative stores. They didn't restrict their clientele. They catered to everyone.

———·◆·———

Even with all that MallWorld had to offer the senses, Lori was still bored. She couldn't stand forced confinement, even in such a stimulating place like MallWorld. She'd had enough of it three days ago during her last shopping trip. Now after two days she felt her sanity draining away.

Such a huge number of people aren't meant to be in close proximity for long periods of time.

"We could go ice-skating or bob-sledding in IceWorld, if you like?" Slim offered over his shoulder as he glared menacingly at anyone who came near the little group.

"Nah." Lori tried to suppress a yawn.

"How about RodeoWorld?" Terry eagerly pointed to his ever-present entertainment guide. "There's a gymkhana starting in about an hour. We could just make it, if we caught the train."

"Nah." Lori shook her head and continued to mechanically flip through the sweaters on the shelf. She stared vacantly into space, her eyes not even focused on what she was doing.

"There's a magic show at the Centre Stage Club. You like that." Slim moved to block a group of Oriental shoppers from getting too close.

Lori threw up her hands in frustration. "I've seen it, done it, and got the hologram-shirt." Finding a nearby sofa, she plunked herself down. "I'm tired of being cooped up in this place. I want to go outside," she pouted.

"We can go for a walk in the botanical gardens of NatureWorld, if you want a breath of fresh air?" Terry stood shoulder-to-shoulder with Brik in front of her. Neither dared break protocol and sit next to her—unless invited to.

"That's not the type of fresh air I want, boys." Lori looked up at her jailors. "I want the fresh air of not being forced to stay in one place. I want to be able to go where I want to, when I want to, and with whom I want to."

"We have to stay put until the boss tells us otherwise." Terry's wrinkled face looked like a puppy dog with an *I'm sorry, but there's nothing I can do* expression on it.

"With the cops and deSalle's people looking for you, it's not safe out there." Slim growled, while guarding the perimeter of the little group.

"I just wish Jonny would find someone to pin the ghosting on, so we could get out of here." Lori pounded her fist into the sofa's padded arm. She couldn't hide her exasperation.

"It takes time to find a patsy." Terry's eyes brightened and he lost the pouting look on his face. Suddenly, like a little boy getting a much sought-after toy, he pointed excitedly at his MallWorld guide book. "We haven't been to Bingo-Magic in GameWorld yet. How about that?"

Lori sighed and pushed herself up off the sofa. "Okay, okay." She knew that Terry didn't understand how the confinement was fuelling her boredom.

CHAPTER 7

312 OD—September 6—2:35 pm

Did I already mention that I hate this place?

MallWorld is the entertainment magnet for visitors to the city. But, it's so damn big it almost needs its own zip code!

When I was talking to Mariyan earlier, I received a two-part mental image. The first was of a cat in a room crowded with chairs. The second element was a mental street map with a bright red arrow. I'm still a little uneasy about the clarity of the second half of the flash, but it was nice to have a positive location instead of the usual fuzzy image which I would have to interpret and hope I was correct. I wish my talent would level out at the heightened ability. It would make my life a whole lot easier. I wouldn't have had to call in Phil to help me locate Lori.

The security guard is dozing off behind his

desk as I walk up to him. He looks like a green marble statue with a thatch of sparse white hair poking out from beneath his hat.

"Ahem..."

His feet thud to the slate grey tile floor, and he almost leaps out of his chair. "What?" he exclaims, and the beefy face under his uniform cap turns dark green. His face and the tightness of his uniform around his mid-section are proof of too much sitting and too many doughnut shops.

I pull a picture out of my jacket pocket and slide it across the counter. "Excuse me, but, have you seen this young lady?"

He squints, then fumbles a bit as he takes a pair of glasses out of the desk drawer and puts them on. One eye focuses on the picture while the other one stares at the brim of his hat. "Nope. What's it to you anyway?"

Shrugging, I thought this might happen. Lori is a pretty lady, and therefore note-worthy. The guard is obviously protecting the guests.

The ninth commandment in my handbook comes to mind—*never tell a lie, they're too hard to keep track of.* "I'm a private detective. She's wanted by the police for questioning. Someone told me she might be here."

Another set of pictures comes out of my pocket. "How about these guys?"

"Hey!" His good eye lights up. "I remember these guys. I was working the 11 to 7 shift yesterday when they came in. There was a young woman with them, but I can't remember what she looked like. And there was someone else." He pauses.

"Who might that someone else be?" I pocket the mug shots of Slim Jim, Terry and Brik.

"I don't think I can tell you. He's an owner."

"He's not in any trouble." I try to ease his conscience. "The lady's not in any trouble, either. The cops just want to ask her a few questions. No big deal."

"Oh, okay. You're not going to do something stupid like kicking in the door or anything, are you?"

"Nope." The truth gets stretched a little bit. "I just need to talk to her. If she doesn't want to come with me, then I'll just tell the cops where she is, and they can talk to her."

"The owner's unit is 1818, but I don't think anyone's there. I saw them leave a little while ago, the woman and her three friends. They went into the mall, probably to do some shopping."

Turning my head sideways, I look out the doors into the crowded mall. Shuddering at the thought of having to go into that madhouse to try and find them makes me hesitate. Talk about a needle in a haystack. The odds would be better at finding the needle.

Thinking back to when I saw the ledger in Jonny's warehouse, I concentrate on it. A binder laying in a rowboat surrounded by thousands of other boats appears in front of me. Blinking the image away, I stare at the security guard for a second. The ledger isn't upstairs. It's somewhere in the mall!

"Thanks, friend." A grimace stretches my lips. "Now comes the hard part—finding them."

He laughs. I've made his day. "Good luck," he calls to me as I walk towards the door to the mall.

There are two ways of finding someone in MallWorld. You can either make a circuit of the mall or you can sit in one spot and wait. You're not guaranteed to find who you're looking for either way, but the chances are about the same. I need to lure lady luck to my side.

I bring out my up-link dialer and make a quick call.

"Phil's Detective Agency."

Phil won't ask any awkward questions. He'll be happy to get the money and won't wonder why I'm looking for Lori.

"Hey, Phil. It's Jack."

"Er, hi," his voice is slightly hesitant as he tries to figure out which Jack is calling. Up-links sometime distort voices.

"Jack Valencz."

"Oh!" A tone of hope fills his voice as he asks, "You've got something for me?"

"Yeah. You free for a few hours?"

312 OD—September 6—2:50 pm

As it turns out, Phil isn't in his office. He's having a late lunch in one of the fast-food places on the Indian/African Main Street near the Atrium Food Court—East.

"Hey, buddy." He gestures to the appropriate

seat. "Come and join me."

I squeeze into the small space and look around. There aren't really that many people eating. Most of them seem to be just sitting and waiting.

Noticing that there's nothing in front of Phil, I ask, "How's the food?"

"It's great." He shrugs, then gestures to the back of the restaurant. "The service needs work though. I ordered fifteen minutes ago, and the burger's still not here."

Putting a spin on an old cliché, I tell him, "Maybe they're out breeding the cow?"

"Ha, ha." He grimaces. "Funny man."

My elbows take up most of the small table as I cross my arms in front of me. "I need your mind off your stomach and on a case. It's not much, but I'll make it worth your while. Interested?"

"Always. What do you need?"

Lori's picture comes out of my pocket along with the mug shots. "The four of them are loose here at the mall. I need to find them."

Phil glances at the pictures. I envy his photographic memory.

"There are no warrants out on them. I just need to find them for Triple-B…"

Phil interrupts me. "Since when do you work for those sleaze-bags?"

I put a hurt look on my face. "You know me better than that. They want Lori, the lady in the picture. I want to make sure they don't get her."

"Got it. So, what's the plan? The old divide-and-conquer?"

There's not much room to lean back due to the tight fit in the chair. I bring him up to speed.

"The security guard said they probably went shopping. Are there any stores near the mall railway station? I doubt that they made it as far as NatureWorld or AmusementWorld since they left on foot. Look, I'll head east towards WaterWorld and meet you at the hospital. Could you circle out that way and check out IceWorld, NatureWorld and RodeoWorld?"

He shakes his head. "There's a lot of people to see and places to look in. The odds of finding them aren't good, Jack."

"Yeah, yeah. But, that's why I want you to back me up. I have to find Lori in order to be able to protect her. You have your portable up-link, so call me if you spot them. I'll either hop on the Mall railway or hoof it to your location. Okay?"

We both get up at the same time. The table wobbles.

Phil walks towards the rear of the restaurant and tells the cook, "Forget my order. I've got to run. Sorry."

We then head off in opposite directions.

312 OD—September 6—3:00 pm

As I've mentioned before, MallWorld is huge. It's ten city blocks wide and about forty long.

That's why it has its own railroad. Only teenagers and tourists roam the mall aimlessly. Locals know where they're going and park nearby. The residents of the FamilyWorld, MallWorld, and World Place apartment complexes tend to shop near their homes. The guests of the East Hotel and the West Hotel wander the mall attractions and use the railway system. It's one of the better ideas the MallWorld people implemented.

Even though I've committed Lori's picture to memory and will never forget her henchmen, I occasionally pull out her photo to check her features. Suspecting that I might have to track her in MallWorld, I brought along my omniculars. I flip a tiny switch on the side of my regular glasses to convert them to binoculars and start scanning the crowd. The omnis automatically adjust focus as I look from right to left. With their range of 100 meters, I can quickly look at a lot of people. The only problem I've ever encountered while wearing them is that when I look at my feet they're blurry. I try to not look down when I have them on.

As I pass across the Oriental Main Street near the doors to the Centre Stage Club I get a vivid mental flash of Lori and her friends. They're being chased by a huge Bingo dauber. The only over-sized dauber I know of is part of a matched set which straddles the entrance to BingoWorld.

My talent is useful to a degree, but I don't rely on it totally. After all, a major part of my work is observation and deductive reasoning with a sprinkling of guesswork and sheer luck.

It doesn't take me long to get there, but surveying the sea of faces is harder than I thought. The omnis re-focus very quickly, but there are just so many people that it's too hard for them to home in on any one person.

There. A familiar face. Slim Jim is easy to spot anywhere since he's a head taller than most people. Beside him I see the stocky figure of Brik and between them a woman with short dark hair. It can only be Lori. Terry is bringing up the rear.

Just as I'm getting ready to bring the omnis down from my face, I stop.

Slim has turned and is staring directly at me. His mouth is moving as he points towards my position.

"...up there..." are the only two words I can make out.

That, and the fact that they all turn to stare in my direction, tells me that I've been discovered.

Trying to keep them in my sight, I race down escalators towards them. I know they're running. I only hope that I'm faster than they are.

Try dialling a 14-digit number on an up-link while running. It's virtually impossible. *Why the hell didn't I choose the hands-free voice-activated option when I bought this damn thing?* I keep getting the incomplete message error tone. Finally, I stop to correctly punch in the numbers to Phil's up-link which I know by heart.

The music from my ear plug radio stops the moment I tap on my up-link. It only rings once before Phil answers, "What?"

"I found them," I yell short of breath. I race towards where I had last seen Lori. "They're outside of GameWorld… heading west… towards the I-Max Experience." Phew!

"Got it." Phil's unmistakeable baritone booms on the tiny receiver, "I'm by NatureWorld. I'll head towards the hospital and catch up with you. I'll call you back in ten minutes."

"Just hurry." I yell into the receiver and tap the up-link again to end the call.

Slim's head towers above the crowd and is easy to spot. They're heading towards St. Theresa's, nestled between GameWorld and the I-Max Experience Theatre. Slim's head ducks into the church. I'm not far behind.

Old habits die hard. Quickly dipping my fingers into the bowl of holy water at the entrance, I make a hasty sign of the cross, leftovers of a Catholic upbringing.

I spot Slim and the others, but something's wrong. They're struggling with someone. At last, I catch up to Slim and Terry in one of the pews. Each is grasping the arm of a young girl with short dark hair. She's not Lori.

They release her as I get near them. In retaliation, she stomps down hard on Terry's foot and storms away.

"What's up?" Slim looks down at me with a big ugly smirk.

I'm breathing hard. "You son-of-a-…" Then I remember where I am. "Where's Lori? She's in danger."

"Yeah, right," Slim sneers at me. "And I'm the pope. We ain't telling you nothin', jerk!"

They sidle out of the pew and walk down the aisle towards the main doors. Terry's nursing his right foot.

Dejectedly, I slump down in the pew.

"Damn," I mutter to myself. "Oops, sorry," then I look around expecting to see some priest or nun glaring disapprovingly at my choice of expletives.

"Where can she be?"

A fuzzy vision creeps into my mind of the lever of a huge slot machine being pulled over and over again. Ka-ching!

My up-link rings. I scramble to get it out of my jacket pocket. *That does it! I'm getting the high-end model with all the bells and whistles.*

"It's me." Phil's voice seems to boom alarmingly in the quiet of the church.

"I lost them in the church," I whisper, "but I've got a hunch they're in GameWorld. I'm heading there next. Where are you?"

"I'm just getting off the train next to the elementary school by the hospital. I should be there in about ten minutes or so."

"Okay. Meet you in the casino… Yeah… Bye."

312 OD—September 6—3:25 pm

Phil meets me at the doors to the MallWorld

casino. He'd worked with me often enough in the past not to question my hunches.

"I think they're in here," I whisper, and lightly tap the door, then signal him to go left. "Slim and Terry were here before they led me on that wild goose chase. They were about as subtle as bulls in a china shop."

"I'm amazed they came up with something like that. They're definitely not the sharpest knives in the Paggett drawer," Phil chuckles. "Jonny does all their thinking for them."

"I guess I wanted to find Lori so bad, I screwed up and fell for it. She'll be harder to see now that Slim isn't with her."

"That's okay. Brik is visible enough to act as a beacon. Let's do it, partner."

I know Phil enjoys working with me. He feels indebted to me ever since our first case together. He got caught, and I had to rescue him. Ever since, he's been looking to repay the debt.

A blast of noise assaults us when I open the door. The mall is loud enough when you first come into it, but after awhile your eardrums get used to the steady drone. The noise level in the casino is about ten times that of the mall. Eight stories of slot machines make a hell-of-a-racket. Add the shouts from the crap and blackjack tables, and… well… you get the picture.

I head off along the right wall. My eyes scan every face I see. No luck. Taking out Lori's picture, I concentrate on it. Faint pictures of stop signs appear to my right and straight ahead, so I turn left. Each time I reach another set of mental stop signs, I turn where there are none. It's not the best of systems, but it usually works for me.

After about ten minutes of double-checking every red-head in the casino, I finally spot the broad back of Brik standing behind someone playing one of the slot machines. I sidle to his right. Sure enough—it's Lori. I've etched her picture in my mind, and her profile is unmistakeable.

"Hello, Miss Paggett."

Brik snarls as he turns to stand between Lori and me. His right hand shoots inside his jacket.

Putting up my hands, I shake my head. "Whoa there, muscle boy. I'm not here to hurt the lady. I just want to talk. Okay?"

Lori turns in her seat. Paggett's ledger is open in her lap. She's been studying it between spins of the slot machine. Softly, she reaches out to put a hand on Brik's arm. It's amazing how a gentle touch can affect a short, stocky mass like Brik's.

"What do you want?" Her unworried amber eyes look away from the spinning reels and eye my cheap suit. I must look pretty seedy to her.

"Triple-B Bail Bonds hired me to find you and bring you in." I expect her to bolt but not to shrug.

"The cops never charged me with anything. You can't arrest me." She calmly returns to the ledger page where her left hand is resting.

Her reply is almost missed. A psychic image forms in front of me of someone wrapped in a skull-and-crossbones flag, standing behind the Triple-B sign and pointing a finger at me. I shake the picture away.

"I don't know why they're looking for you, but I figured I might as well take the job and find out." Plopping myself down on the stool next to her, I glance at the slot machine—a losing hand—then back at Lori. Brik snarls. She closes the ledger and touches his arm again. He stops in mid-growl.

She jumps a little in her seat when I mention, "Some dead black guy's friends got Triple-B involved. Know anything about it?"

Lori hesitates too long.

Brik's face is unreadable, her's isn't. My theory must be close, so I continue. "I'm guessing here, but the only dead black guy I know of is Sharrah deSalle. If his people are behind Triple-B's search for you, then I presume they think you had something to do with his death. How's my guessing?"

"Remarkably accurate," she puts a brave smile on her face, "if what you're saying is true."

I've hit the nail on the head. "And if I found you this easily… maybe someone else will…"

"In other words, I'm in danger?"

I nod. Brik reluctantly pulls his glare away from me and starts scanning the crowd looking for deSalle's men.

"I would say that wherever you're staying now

is no longer safe."

"You know a safe place?"

"Only one." Looking first at Brik then smiling at her, "but neither of you will like it."

Lori cocks her head to one side. A look of horror dawns on her face. "No!" she whines.

Shrugging, I tell her, "Lori, Lori, Lori. It's the only way. The police are the only ones that can protect you from deSalle's men. If you don't come in with me, they ARE going to find you. They will NOT just want to talk to you." Her face shows that she knows my next comment. "And they will NOT be gentle."

She sighs reluctantly and murmurs, "Oh, alright. But you damn well better know what you're doin' or my brother will find YOU!"

I pause, trying to avoid a picture of that ever happening. Deciding to push the envelope, I tell her, "Okay, first we have to get you arrested. Let's see, what can you confess to?"

Lori smirks at me then casually reaches for the button to cash out. The clinking of the coins falling into the money tray soon fades. She scoops up handfuls of coins and drops them into a plastic bucket.

"That's not going to help you, Lori," I tell her. "Money can't buy what you need. C'mon, bare your soul."

"Oh, but I wasn't planning on buying my way out of anything," she coyly replies. "I have another use for it."

"I don't…" Brik's throaty growl interrupts me, but when I glance over at him I see that he's glowering at something behind me. Turning around on my stool, I see a burly individual striding purposefully towards us—obviously he's not a typical gambler. This guy means business.

In the split-second that I observe him, before Brik blocked my view, I note two things about our visitor. He's got a scar across the bridge of his nose, and he's got something black hidden in his right hand—a railer! Definitely BIG business!

But where the hell did he come from? My psychic sense didn't warn me of any impending danger. And how on earth did he get a railer through the casino's security gates?

As I jump to my feet to grab Lori's hand and pull her from her stool, she hefts the plastic container a few times then, with all her might, throws it directly into the face of a passing security guard. He doesn't have a chance. A shower of coins descends on him. The coins hitting the ground act like an electric current passing through all the players in our vicinity. There's a mad rush of players converging on the free money.

The guy coming at us freezes less than three meters away. He quickly puts his railer away and glares at us over the mass of people scrambling after Lori's coins.

The security guard pulls his foamer and levels it at her. "You shouldn't oughta have done that, lady," he growls. "You bought yourself a mess of trouble."

"That I did," she tells him as she holds out her hands to be handcuffed. She looks at me, "I believe you'll know where to find me in about an hour or so. Make sure I'm released into your custody."

BOOK Two—Kathee's Story

CHAPTER 8

312 OD—September 3—9:45 pm

The stage was quiet between acts. Jugglers had just finished a performance and the audience was expectant of the première act of the evening.

Kathee Maran's assistant Beth made small talk. "Well, Boss, how does it feel to be back home after all these years?"

Shrugging her shoulders, she replied, "A city is a city, and a stage is a stage. One is the same as another, I guess." The rest of what she was going to say was cut off by the announcer.

"Ladies and gentlemen! For your amused entertainment and enlightened edification, the management of the Centre Stage Club is proud to present, for the third straight week, the mental machinations, the mystifying mental talents, the telepathic tap-dancing of the all-knowing, all-seeing, all-revealing, the greatest mentalist on the planet, the one-and-only, the Great Miss Marani!"

On the Emcee's cue Kathee grasped the hand of her assistant, Beth Armstrong, and walked confidently onto the darkened stage just as she had for the last twelve years. It may have been a different city, a different nightclub, even a different voice, but the spiel was always the same. After all, why should it differ -- she wrote it.

Her floor-length purple gown brushed the floor of the stage. Even though she was half a head shorter than Kathee, Beth easily matched her strides. Kathee's hand remained on Beth's forearm as she led her to her seat.

Beth whispered throatily in her ear, "Are you ready for this, Miz Marani?"

That question and Kathee's answer have become a ritual for them since the first performance. "Let's bring it on, Miz Armstrong."

Stage performers are a superstitious lot as anyone can tell by the centuries-old adage "Break a leg". Beth and Kathee have their routine. Holding Kathee's hand high, Beth led her to the centre of the stage. The only point of illumination was the sole spotlight centred on the large throne-like chair in the middle. Bowing to her first, then to the darkness of the audience, Kathee regally sat down in her usual place.

Kathee's free hand reached up to casually flip the long blonde hair of her wig behind her back, and she began, "Ladies and Gentlemen, I could say to you that my telepathic powers tell me that there are four birthday or anniversary parties being celebrated among us tonight, but that wouldn't be truthful. Since there is no such thing as telepathy, the ticket office manager gave me this information." She smiled to the hundred or so laughing, applauding patrons. "Would the various guests of honour at these functions please stand so that the rest of the audience can give you the accolade you so richly deserve?"

Their chairs rattled as the designated celebrants stood. Once the clapping slowed, Kathee waved them back down into their seats.

"Thank you. Thank you. Believe me, you all deserve that applause." At their respective tables their friends nodded and drew out the accolade. "Jon and Mary are celebrating their fifth wedding anniversary." It took a moment for the small spattering of applause to abate. "And I hope Geoff and Lara are enjoying their fiftieth wedding anniversary." A larger and more prolonged applause.

"Mr. Simmonds is celebrating his fifty-first birthday." A loud high-pitched squeal emanated from his table and assaulted everyone's ears. They're lucky. The shriek also grated across Kathee's psychic band. The normal response to this type of noise was for the audience to cheer. They didn't let her down.

"And finally, a Miss Cyndi Jones is *purported* to be celebrating her thirty-second birthday. At least, that's what it says on her driver's license and what she's told the management of the club." Muffled giggles and snickers followed. "But I see differently than you do. I sense that this is a fabrication, an untruth, a falsehood, a lie if you will. I propose that our Miss Jones is actually thirty-nine tonight."

A gasp of "She's right!" broke the silent darkness.

Kathee heard "Oh's" and "Ah's" as well as "How'd she know that?" mixed in with the round of applause. She smiled again and sat back in her throne.

She'd been able to hear a constant droning of voices in her head since she was 14. Imagine being at a party surrounded by a hundred people all talking at the same volume. That was what she heard every day. She occasionally tuned in to someone's strong surface thoughts of people who come within ten feet of her, especially when they were excited or agitated.

When Kathee mentioned birthdays, she heard Cyndi think of her real age. Frank, the club manager, had indeed given her the dates as she had told the audience. She loved it when someone told the management a different date than the one they have in their minds. It made her mystique that much more profound, and her act became that much easier.

A hushed silence slowly filled the club while everyone waited expectantly for her next trick.

"Ladies and gentlemen. I would like to have one of you volunteer to assist me. How about our *young* 'fabricator', Miss Jones? Please come up, Cyndi."

A few words of encouragement accompanied her as she shyly came forward.

The clicking of high heels drew slowly closer. A very smartly dressed lady, obviously nearer to thirty-nine than thirty-two, climbed the three steps to the stage. She nervously approached. Her red leather heels matched the mini-skirt that was cut a little too high on her mature frame. Little rolls of flesh peeked out around the edges of her outfit. Definitely too tight.

"Come, come, my dear. I'm not going to hurt you." She was hesitant, but Kathee reassured her as she motion for Cyndi to stand beside her throne. Cyndi's body language showed she didn't trust Kathee.

"So when are you planning on going to the Motor Vehicle Licensing Department to have that error fixed?" Cyndi blushed as Kathee grinned up at her amid the laughter of the crowd.

Cyndi smiled apprehensively and looked like she was about to bolt off-stage.

Taking hold of Cyndi's wrist locked her in position. Cyndi pulled away slightly, but Kathee's grip was stronger. She shook her head.

"Uh, uh! You don't get away that easily, my dear." Reaching over, Kathee patted the hand below the captured wrist. "You have a little work to do."

Cyndi frooze in place.

Kathee released her wrist and picked up a length of black silk draped over the arm of her chair.

"Would you please fold this into a blindfold for me?"

Cyndi fumbled with the material but finally got it arranged correctly.

Kathee turned to the audience. "I'm going to ask Cyndi to blindfold me."

Cyndi's hands shook as she brought it near to Kathee.

"But first…"

Cyndi frooze with her hands and the smooth silk band almost touching Kathee's face.

Peeking under it at the audience, Kathee grinned mischievously.

"I want Cyndi to try to look through this material and verify that I won't be able to see a single thing through it."

Cyndi covered her eyes.

"I can't see nothin'," she blurted out, moving her head to look around, and Kathee verified that with her telepathy.

"Thank you, dear."

That simple phrase eased Cyndi's tension. She smiled half-heartedly at Kathee as she lowered the folded material.

Cyndi grinned weakly while the audience found her misfortune hilarious.

"I think it's time to let Cyndi off the hook. Don't you, folks?"

The audience applauded.

"Okay, Cyndi. Will you fasten the blindfold securely behind my back? Tie it tightly now, but not too tightly, please." A sudden thought flashed through her mind, "And while she does this, folks, I should let the skinny balding man with his right hand on his date's ass, and an Ozone Daiquiri in his left, know that his wife has de-bunked his alibi and has just come in."

Kathee can't actually see the activity, but she heard a distant commotion as the audience broke into uproarious laughter.

She can sense that the spectators are intrigued with her talent as they turn back to the stage.

It took three attempts for Cyndi's hands to stop shaking enough to adjust the silk blindfold around her head. Cyndi's red leather outfit clashed with Kathee's purple velvet gown.

Kathee almost gagged at the smell of Cyndi's cheap perfume as she leaned over her.

"Thank you, Cyndi, for your assistance. You've been a great sport. Folks, will you give her a big hand!"

Breathing in the smoke-filled air, Kathee heard the rapid clicking of Cyndi's high heels as she escaped from the glare of the spotlight.

"Now that you've been assured by our *young* Cyndi..." Kathee had to pause for a couple of seconds to let the laughter die down. "...that I can't see, I would like you to take any items out of your purses, wallets, or pockets. My assistant, Beth, will hold up your objects for all to see, and I will attempt to correctly identify it by reading her mind. Are we ready?"

The audience murmured as Beth made her way down the stairs onto the main floor.

Beth went into her spiel. "Hear me, O Great Marani. What am I holding? It's an item of minimal sentimental value…" Laughter interrupted her. "As I said, minimal sentimental value to our guest."

Everyone waited eagerly. Kathee strained her ears to hear what the whispered voices were saying, but they were too far away and soft for her to make them out.

"It is an implement of sorts, made famous by the FOOT soldiers of the American army." Beth over-emphasized the word "foot". People started to suspect.

Murmuring.

Beth deserved credit. She was great at what she did. As an entertainer, she was more the main part of the act than Kathee was. Whenever she concentrated on an item Kathee could clearly hear her voice through the constant chattering of spectators assaulting her mind. Ever since the day Kathee first met her, she could make out occasional words from her. Now, after years of practice, she could perceive full sentences. Beth's holding a pair of toenail clippers.

The pleasure in her voice is almost tangible as Beth finally comes up with the perfect clue. "I don't want to CUT your time short, but we have to CLIP right along."

Hearing some snickering from the audience as well as a nervous cough, Kathee knew it was time to wow them.

"Is it…" Pausing for dramatic effect, Kathee moved forward slightly in her seat, adding to the tension.

"…a pair of…" Another moment of hesitation passed. This time she got nothing but silence and the scrape of a chair being moved. The natives were getting restless.

"I see a pair of toenail clippers." A polite spattering of applause graced her un-inventive pronouncement.

"Clippers with the initials B.M.K. engraved on them? And they seem to be broken."

"Correct!" Beth announced while brandishing the clippers triumphantly over her head. An enthusiastic applause broke out, especially from the owner's table.

"How'd she do that?" "Wow!" and "That's amazing!" or whatever else came to their minds.

The murmuring in her head intensified. Kathee forced a smile as she sat back in her chair. This is the part of the job that she hated. The roar, the noise—it hurt her brain. If it weren't for the applause and the thrill that it gave her, she'd have quit the business years ago.

The mental cacophony eased off at the same time that the ovation died down.

"As you can see, ladies and gentlemen, my act is a little different than run-of-the-mill mind reading. You will note that Beth never passed the initials B.M.K. or its condition to me."

The audience whispered. They were probably

nodding to one another.

"How do I do it, you may well ask?"

"Yeah, how?" A lone drunken voice from the back parroted her question.

She loved audiences. They could be so predictable.

"Ah… that would be telling my secret. My job is to keep you guessing, ladies and gentlemen. Your enjoyment tells me how well I am doing my job, and how much I will get paid."

The audience roared with laughter.

Beth moved over to the next victim. I heard her sopranic mental voice call out "Time piece. To Bill—Bunny hugs—Love Bunny."

"Now WATCH this. For our next TIMELY item, I have a PIECE of personal jewellery up for your consideration."

Kathee knew Beth was holding the watch far above her head so that the entire audience could clearly see it.

"Hmmm." The throat-mike in her velvet choker carried the sound of confusion easily through the room.

"This one's a little tougher." Years of practice had made it easy for her voice to sound perplexed.

"I'm getting a strange image in my mind. I see a… a… a DVD player?"

The crowd laughed.

"I see the clock stuck on a flashing 12:00."

Again the audience chortled.

"Hmmm… this can only mean that it's a wristwatch."

The wave of mental noise caused her to grimace, but she still managed to put her "smiling face" mask on for the audience. Then, she waited another few seconds for the clamour and applause to die down.

"I have a question for the owner of the watch."

In her mind's eye, Kathee imagined the spectators hunching forward in anticipation.

"What are bunny hugs, Mr…?"

Her ears and mind are assaulted by an irritating squeal of surprise. She didn't need her special talent to know that the wristwatch belongs to the birthday boy.

She finished her question, "…Mr. Simmonds?"

A baritone voice called back from the center of the room, "They're hugs from my wife, Bunny."

There was a wary tone in his voice. Obviously, he was someone who didn't like being put on centre stage.

The psychic murmuring and the applause lessened, but then the murmuring changed, becoming clearer, and Kathee suddenly heard words more distinctly.

I wish she didn't have that stupid pet phrase engraved on the watch.

Startled, Kathee moved forward in her chair.

Did I really hear that spoken or just in my head? Two years working on the Solara assembly line had ruined her right ear, so she wore a small hearing aid. But she never responded to voices that she heard, because she didn't know if they were vocal or mental. Many people thought she was totally deaf, because she didn't answer them unless she was looking directly at their lips. She could hear them alright, but she didn't want people to know that she could pick up their thoughts by showing a reaction just being near them.

Kathee's head turned slightly to the right so her unencumbered ear was to the crowd.

There was a disturbance at the bar. People yelling. It was hard to make out. Sounded like…

"My wallet's gone!" and "Hey! Mine's vanished too!" and "Pick-pocket! That son-of-a-bitch! Find him!"

When is this over? I need to talk to the boys… gotta nail that cop with Tony's death before he gets too cocky.

Kathee forgot her smiling mask for a few seconds as she gasped in surprise. *I'm hearing someone's thoughts clear as a bell! Criminal thoughts!* Her hands started shaking. All the moisture from her throat had found its way to the palms of her hands, so she wiped them on the arms of her chair. She felt weak for a moment.

The audience was still tittering about "Bunny Hugs" and the commotion at the bar. They were not reacting to her discovery.

"For my final trick of the evening…" She had to wait a while until there was dead silence in the club. Everyone waited expectantly.

"We're going to do something a little different. I would like my assistant, Beth, to hold up one of Mr. Simmonds… I presume you do have one, sir… a business card?"

"Yeah, I've got one," the baritone voice replied. "Hang on a minute."

"Before you give it to my assistant, I would like you to write something personal on the back. A favourite colour, or what you are buying your wife for Christmas, or an associate's name. Something that no one else can know about. When you're finished I'd like you to give it to Beth and she will bring it to another table and show it to an audience member."

Beth's footsteps echoed as she purposely walked across the room.

"I assume that whomever Beth shows the card to is not someone you know, correct?"

A different voice, unsure of precisely what to say, replied with, "Un huh, that's right."

Kathee read the card in her mind.

"Well now, Mr. William K. Simmonds, what is it exactly that you import and export…Oh yes, textiles go out and clothing comes back. Business is good, I hope?"

Pausing for a couple of seconds, she debated adding his personal up-link number. Everyone gets this life-time number when they buy their first up-link, and it was used to connect to satellites and transmit calls anywhere in the world.

Kathee decided that if he had gotten it printed on his business card, then he won't mind it being said aloud. "…and can we still reach you at 780-555-4238-9035?"

"She's nailed it!" the unsure voice called out.

The audience produced another polite but jaded applause.

A wheezy voice, just barely audible to Kathee, whispered, "Sir, Mr. Paggett sent me to get you."

Mr. Simmonds had obviously heard enough revelations for the evening and had business to attend to.

Time for the big finish, so Kathee added, "You wrote an address on it and a man's name. Kevin at 715-32…"

"That's okay," she heard Mr. Simmonds' now-familiar baritone voice break in from the audience.

The room erupted into wild cheers and fervent applause. The mental noise forced her back into her chair. A weak smile was all she could manage as she tried to cope with the hubbub.

CHAPTER 9

312 OD—September 3—10:00 pm

A six-foot hammerhead shark swam in a lazy loop, almost keeping pace with Simmonds, as he strode impatiently back-and-forth in the middle of one of the three-meter wide glass tubes that traversed the Shark and Dolphin Habitat at MallWorld.

He didn't want to be here. His guests were waiting for him back at the club. No sooner had that mentalist finished her act, when he had been called away by one of Paggett's boys. As he thought about it, he was happy to be out of the spotlight.

"There's something surreal about walking among nature's perfect predators," he murmured to the creature swimming less than a meter from him.

As it turned, the shark seemed to pause and listen to him. Its un-blinking stare never wavered.

He stopped in his tracks, while an involuntary shiver ran down his spine. Staring intently at the shark, he muttered aloud, "Sheesh! It can't understand me. I must be losin' it."

The shark continued its languid spiral.

He took in a deep breath and glanced down at the black lettering on a brass sign on the railing.

Do Not Tap On Glass

Wincing at the thought of the thousands of gallons of seawater being kept from gushing through the walk tubes by sheets of glass, he looked down towards the far end of the tube to the bright red exit sign. He tried to guesstimate how long it would take him to reach safety if the glass should break. The answer was "too long".

He edged a little closer to the exit.

"Hey Bill," a raspy voice called out.

He tore his gaze away from the sign. Jonny Paggett was walking down the centre of the tube towards him. His ever-present cigar dangled from the corner of his mouth. It was lit.

Simmonds looked up at the large red 'No Smoking' sign just above the *Do Not Tap On Glass* sign and grimaced. It said *No Smoking* in the twelve main languages spoken throughout the world.

"Paggett, can't you read?" he gestured angrily to the sign with his right hand.

Paggett reluctantly took the cigar out of his mouth with his left hand while reaching into his jacket pocket with the right. He pulled out a small ceramic tube. Its hollow end was just large enough for the lit end of the cigar to fit into.

After five seconds, he pulled out the cigar and jammed it back in his mouth.

"Satisfied?" he grumbled as he tapped the un-lit end of the cigar with his forefinger.

Simmonds shrugged then looked back at the hammer-head which had continued swimming in its gentle circles.

Without taking his eyes off the shark, he snapped out, "What the hell is so urgent that it couldn't wait for MacDonald's regular monthly meeting? My girlfriend dragged me to the Club, and I had to leave the rest of my guests. This better be damn important!"

Paggett shuffled his feet, whispering, "I need another favour."

"You interrupted me for that? Oh, there's no need to whisper," Simmonds spoke in a normal voice. "That's why I like this place for my *discussions*."

Still, Paggett nervously glanced all around, as if searching for hidden recording devices. Simmonds knew that wherever Paggett was and whenever Paggett was doing *business*, he made sure there were recording devices. Paggett had quite the extensive audio collection of his deals. Others in the organization knew about Paggett's paranoia and made sure that they minded what they said when around him, speaking in code, or simply jamming the listening devices.

"Cops would need omniculars to read our lips here" Simmonds continued, "and even though it's hard to tell they're wearing them, we'd still know they were watching us. I make sure no one close to us wears glasses of any sort. The Snooper devices have become so small they're barely discernible. But they're not invisible and undetectable. Don't worry. I have this area regularly swept by my boys, and," he paused for a second while staring down at Paggett, "I know *I'M* clean."

Paggett looked worriedly at Simmonds.

"I know you're recording us, Paggett."

He jumped a little at being discovered.

"But that's okay," Simmonds smiled down at his diminutive associate and patted him brotherly on the back. "You're paranoid and can't help it. I always have a scrambler on me. All you're getting right now is… well, static."

Paggett glanced guiltily down at the nondescript pin on the right lapel of his white sports jacket.

Simmonds now knew where the recorder was located.

"Okay, Simmonds," Paggett snarled defensively, "Then let's get down to business. I want someone ghosted." He took a second to glance around. "But I don't want our usual deal."

Simmonds shook his head. "You know I don't do business like that. We do a ghosting, you owe us. Plain and simple. That's how it's always worked."

Paggett puffed angrily on his un-lit cigar.

Grumbling when he couldn't get the hit of tobacco he wanted, he reached up, grabbed the cigar, and almost threw it away. His addiction kicked in, and he kept his hand clenched.

Simmonds grinned in satisfaction. He knew perfectly well that smoking was Paggett's release valve. *He must be right frustrated by now,* he thought.

"Who do you want ghosted? I'm guessing it's your friend deSalle?"

Paggett stirred slightly at the mention of his rival's name.

"Who told you?" His gaze darted from side-to-side as if seeking an invisible informant.

"It doesn't take a genius," Simmonds reassured him while he glanced at the shark swimming by. It had been joined by another. The new-comer could have easily been its twin. "I know that deSalle's men are trying to muscle in on your zone. You want him stopped. One plus one equals two. Simple math."

Paggett glared up at him.

"How about this?" Simmonds ignored the sign and tapped his finger on the glass above the sign. "We ghost deSalle, and you let us in on some of your action. How does that sound?"

Paggett sputtered, "Are you nuts? I'm not letting you muck your fingers into my business."

"I need to get something out of this, my friend. I'm not running a charity. Just be glad I'm giving you a choice—a future favour or a piece of your action. Which is it going to be?"

Paggett puffed hard on his un-lit cigar again without a fix, then sighed dolefully in resignation, "Okay, okay. What action would you want?"

Simmonds shrugged. "I don't know, yet. I was sort of looking for something Bunny could get her hands into. What do you have that she could handle? It's got to be real easy to learn."

"Uh… well, the cops were getting too close, so I had to close down some of my houses. The girls are free-lancing now through their uplinks. There's no real place for me to slot her in except as a working girl. I suppose you don't want her doing that?"

Simmonds frowned. "Anything else?"

Now it was Paggett's turn to shake his head, "Nope."

"Well if you can't help me with Bunny, then I guess I'll have to settle for a future favour. You're not getting my work for free, Pal."

"All right," Paggett snarled. "deSalle's throwing a big bash right now at his place. How soon can you get someone to do it?"

Simmonds didn't answer right away. He was trying to see who the two people walking towards him were.

He finally realized what Paggett had asked him. "Oh, yeah. As soon as possible. We can get it done tonight."

Two men had stopped a respectful twenty paces from them. Simmonds recognized Frank Langelli, one of Pharen's couriers who worked the numbers for the entire south side of the city. He didn't know the other guy, but something told him that he wasn't a cop if he was with Frank.

Paggett turned to see Simmonds making a come here motion with his head.

"Excuse me sir." Tall Frank looked down at both Simmonds and Paggett. "The boss told me you might be here."

"What does Pharen want now?" Simmonds asked in a guarded voice. Pharen was not a confidant. He knew where Simmonds liked to have business meetings and often sent Frank there if he couldn't find him at the club or get him on his up-link.

"Actually, nothing," Frank looked from one to the other before continuing, "We have some information for Mr. Paggett there."

"For me?" Paggett was surprised. He didn't swim in the same pond as Pharen, so couldn't imagine what he would have for him.

"Let's have it," Simmonds urged. In the back of his mind he was wondering how the hell Pharen had known that Paggett was going to be meeting with him, here.

"My friend, Paul Dunne, has something you'll want to hear, Mr. Paggett."

All eyes turned to look at Paul. He squirmed uncomfortably at all the attention and, reached up to stroke his beard. Simmonds noticed Paul's nervous habit.

"I was collared this evening in Mexicali Rosa's by a PI named Valencz—Jack Valencz, I think."

"I know the guy," Paggett admitted, as

Simmonds looked at his watch and asked, "If you were arrested at dinner and it's now only a little after 11:00, how'd you get out so fast?"

"My lawyer."

"The judge let you go?" Paggett asked incredulously.

"When the lawyer got through spewing all this bull the judge released me with just a warning."

"Amazing!" Paggett exclaimed. "That's some lawyer."

"Yeah," Simmonds laughed. "I want his name."

"Anyway, Mr. Paggett, I was sitting in the bar when this Valencz character shows up and tried to arrest me. He fought the entire bar of muties and almost beat them all…"

Simmonds sneered at the term "muties". He made no pretence at liking them and generally called them "freaks". They were a fact of nature, that he knew, but he still didn't like anything that wasn't "normal" in his eyes. The members of his ghost-squads were normal-looking, if a bit on the beefy side, and they didn't stand out in crowds too badly. Not like a run-of-the-mill "mutie".

Paul was still talking, "…and he jumped around like some kind of Kung-Fu hero. It was like he had eyes in the back of his head, and he knew exactly what they was about to do before they did it!"

"Martial arts experts can make it look easy." Paggett agreed.

"Yeah, but not like this. Not like this guy

was." Paul started miming some of the moves Jack had performed. "These two muties were coming up behind him..." he showed them being on both sides but slightly behind him with one guy a little ahead of the other. "He stepped backwards and..." he motioned with both arms coming up to deliver close-fisted blows, "...nailed both of them. They went down like cows with sledge hammer headaches."

"He was good," Paggett said.

"Good, hell! He didn't even look to see where they were! He just nailed them both!" His head shook with disbelief. "It was amazing and damn scary to watch—both at the same time. The muties finally managed to gang up on him and threw both of us out of the bar. But... he was totally amazing!"

"Ah, you were drunk. He must have looked at them first. You just didn't see it."

"No sir!" Paul was adamant. "I watched him the whole time—never took my eyes off of him. Believe me, it was hard *not* to stare at him. It was... it was... it was like he *knew* what was going to happen before it did. Almost like he was psychic."

The look of disbelief creeping across Paggett's face was easy for Simmonds to see. He knew it must match the one on his own.

"There's no such thing as psychics. That's just an urban myth, but I'll check Valencz out anyway," Paggett placated his bruised messenger.

Paul turned to leave, but Frank put out a

hand and held him back. "There's just one more little thing I need, Mr. Simmonds."

"What?"

"I've got a little favour to ask. "My Comp-u-link was stolen this morning, and I need it back. There's lots of stuff that I can't let the cops see," he hesitated for a second, then added quietly, "...or my boss."

"Where was it boosted?" Paggett tried to puff on the cigar clenched firmly in his teeth.

"I was here at the mall in the East Food Court, I think. I'm not sure. I remember using it after breakfast, but it was gone by lunch-time."

"Maybe you left it someplace where a light-fingered-Louie could lift it?" Simmonds asked.

"No. I always make sure I put it back on my belt," he patted the empty leather case.

"Did you trip or something?" Paggett came up with a possible scenario. "It might have come out then."

"Yeah, I did trip once, but someone caught me before I hit the ground. I remember feeling it in its case just then."

"I'll put the word out on the street to look for it. What model was it?"

"It was a standard 2212 with a red lightning bolt decal on the face plate. It should be easy to spot."

Paggett nodded agreement. "We'll keep an eye out for it," he assured Frank.

Paul and Frank turned and walked down the tube towards the Shark Exhibit exit.

Simmonds turned to Paggett, "I'll see about getting a squad out to ghost deSalle."

"Yeah, okay. But give me a couple of days to sort out alibis for the guys."

CHAPTER 10

312 OD—September 3—10:00 pm

"Bravo!"

"Amazing!"

"Fantastic!"

"Encore!"

The ovation continued as the curtain came down on Kathee's final bow.

"You did great," Beth called out on her way to her dressing room. "That was a primo performance!"

It was hard to smile when her brain was on fire, but Kathee managed a weak one anyway. "Thanks Beth." She grabbed a white towel from the stage manager's desk and wiped the perspiration from her brow. She didn't care if she messed up her glitter mascara. Once she was finished, she draped the towel over her weary shoulders.

There was a mixture of relief and worry as she closed her eyes for a second or two. The questions in her mind came rapid-fire.

What happened? Why did my talent flare up like that? Could this be what great-aunt Prudence talked about when she told me that her power got stronger twice in her life? Could that be happening to me? Am I causing it? Solar flares? Nah. Why the change?

Kathee's glasses were on the manager's desk. Thankfully, she didn't have to grope around too much before she found them. The world came into sharp focus when she wore her glasses, which helped a little bit with the headaches. *Ah, feels better already.*

Kathee looked down at her hands. They were still shaking from what she heard on stage.

What the hell was that all about?

The ends of the towel were being squeezed almost to shreds as she tried to get her emotions under control and stop the tremors.

She'd never heard anything that clear before—not even from Beth, and she'd had years of practice receiving thoughts from her. Kathee thought back to when she first started hearing voices, right after she turned 14. She had begun to notice that sometimes she could hear people, but their mouths weren't moving. Weird. She never told anyone except her great-aunt Prudence. They talked a lot—in secret. When she was about 10, Prudence had told her that soon some strange and wonderful things might happen to her, but no matter what, she had to keep quiet about it. She shouldn't tell anyone about her new abilities. Kathee didn't know what she was talking about, but she listened and had dismissed it as an old lady's ramblings.

Great-aunt Prudence was a prim-and-proper no-nonsense school mistress type. She couldn't imagine how useful this talent could be. Actually, Kathee paid for her entire college education, including room and board, by playing poker. Yes, yes, technically, it was cheating. But, it wasn't her fault if people got excited when they had a good hand, and their minds broadcasted what they were seeing. She could have taken all of Beth's money, but that wouldn't have been ethical. And Beth would never have forgiven her and become her friend and partner. The biggest pot she ever raked in was over $30,000 dollars—just enough to pay for one term of school.

Her thoughts were interrupted as a horde of fans surged backstage and clamoured for her autograph.

This was the part of her work she loved the most. Their eyes glowed as they stared at her in awe and shyly, even after trampling over twenty other fans, asked for her signature on their programs. Kathee made it a point to talk to each fan for a short moment. It made them feel more like friends than fans. It was a small sacrifice on her part, but it did wonders for them and her.

After about fifteen or twenty minutes of this, she managed to satisfy the last of her admirers and wearily made her way to her dressing room. She was almost as wrung out from the autograph session as from the entire act. She was looking forward to her after-show ritual of a long soaking mineral-water bath followed by eight hours of uninterrupted sleep.

"Kathee! Wait up a minute."

She turned around and saw Beth walking quickly towards her. She was being trailed by a pretty blonde who looked vaguely familiar. *Where do I know her from?*

"Kathee, I want you to meet someone." Beth stopped just in front of her, almost out of breath.

Kathee hadn't seen her this excited before.

"This is Bunny."

"Hello Bunny," Kathee politely exchanged greetings while racking her brain trying to recollect where she knew this lady from. "How are you?"

"Fine," she shyly replied with a slightly nasal whine. "Your act is just amazing! My husband and I just loved it."

Now she knew where she'd met her. It was at the doughnut shop the other day.

————•◆•————

The 10-year old was singing "Mommy, mommy! Mommy, mommy..." gratingly over and over again while her mother was buying donuts.

Kathee winced as she remembered that shrill nasal voice cutting through her psychic band like a knife. Ever so politely, Kathee shushed the child as she walked to her seat in the shop.

The young girl ran and complained to her mom who was, by the glare she shot at Kathee, none too pleased with her child being chastised by a stranger.

"That's alright dear. Let's go outside where you can sing all you want to me, and no one will be *rude* to you."

Kathee thought she had been quite civil under the annoying circumstances.

"Excuse me, ma'am," she stopped her before she reached the door. "Your daughter does indeed have the right to sing to you all she wants. It's just that out in public isn't the right venue for her… singing." Kathee should have called it for the screeching it was.

The mother's voice was just as nasal and whiney as her child's. "My daughter can sing whatever she wants whenever and wherever she wants." She looked down her nose at Kathee and snorted, "and where no one can tell her to shut up!"

Boy the fruit doesn't fall far from the tree.

"I didn't tell her to shut up…" was all Kathee managed to get out before the lady hustled her smirking brat out of the now hushed donut shop.

The woman's face turned beet red, and Kathee thought the woman was going to explode.

"Yes, you did!" she screeched, just as the shop door closed.

She reminded Kathee of fingernails scraping down a blackboard.

Behind her back, Kathee couldn't resist muttering a parting shot under her breath, "Lady, both your voices are grating and shouldn't be inflicted on the rest of the world." She turned to see one of the other patrons smiling at her and softly applauding.

——·◆·——

Beth cut short Kathee's musing. "Bunny and I were in school together way back in grade four."

It was obvious that Bunny hadn't recognized her. Kathee was still wearing her blonde wig and a little of her glitter mascara, even though it must have looked like a sparkly smear across her eyes by then. She bet her face must have looked like a raccoon's.

Kathee made sure that she was looking directly at Bunny as she spoke. Some people think completely different thoughts from what they're saying. So, she had to be especially careful to read their lips, instead of just their minds, or she'd sound like an idiot when she responded. Or scare the hell out of them.

"My husband was one of your..." she searched Kathee's messy face for a word, "...victims tonight."

A memory of Bunny's squeal of delight caused Kathee to wince. She covered it up with a nod. "If I remember correctly..." being the show-off that she was, she couldn't resist the slight pause for dramatic effect before proclaiming, "... the wrist watch with the bunny hugs message."

Bunny gasped, "That's right!" Her eyes were wide with child-like amazement.

Kathee made an off-handed gesture of dismissal. "It's all part of the act."

Beth was almost quivering with excitement. "Bunny would like to hire us for a private gig!"

Feigning disappointment, Kathee declared, "I'm sorry but we don't do those." Kathee was surprised that she had to remind Beth about that.

"I know, but can't we do it just this once?" There was an almost desperate quality to her voice. Beth stared at Kathee with a mixture of hopefulness and contriteness in her face.

"But we…"

"Bunny!" a voice cut in. "There you are!"

Turning around, Kathee saw Bunny's husband walking purposefully towards them. A cold chill ran up her spine when she looked at him.

Why am I getting this threatening vibe? Kathee thought. *He doesn't look intimidating, what with being a lot shorter, and, from the look of his jowls, a lot heavier than me. His hairline is receding, and he obviously dyes his hair. No one has hair that black.*

"Honey, I'm glad you're here!" Bunny rushed forward with hands out-stretched as if to defend us from him. When her hands lightly contacted his chest, he stopped dead in his tracks.

Grrrrrr.

What the? I must have imagined that. I've never heard growling in my mind before.

"She's going to perform a private show for us," Bunny gushed out the entire phrase as if it was a single word.

"Uh, I never…"

"She is?" The surprise in his voice was quite evident.

"But, I…"

Again, Kathee was cut off. *This is getting monotonous.*

In a single breath Bunny blurted out, "Beth asked Kathee to come to our house and perform an exclusive show for all of our friends and isn't that just the most wonderful thing you've ever heard and all our friends will be so jealous of us…" She stopped to take a breath.

Before she could continue, Kathee quickly interrupted. "Wait a minute!"

All eyes turned to look at her.

"Slow down a second, lady. I haven't agreed yet to perform for you."

A look of utter disappointment washed quickly over Bunny's face.

It didn't take a mind reader to decipher the look of anger that Mr. Simmonds turned on his wife.

You stupid bitch.

"Uh, I haven't said that I *wouldn't* perform. You just caught us off-guard, that's all. Uh, Beth, would you check our booking schedule to see if we can clear up a date to accommodate this nice couple?" Kathee's forceful mediator voice was working. The stress ebbed from Mr. Simmonds' face.

"Oh, will you?" Bunny jumped up and down in excitement. "Pleeeassse? Please, please, please? Can you come to our house tomorrow night? It's William's birthday. We came here tonight and ran into Beth! And she works with you! This is so great! Please say you'll come?"

Kathee almost missed her last plea. As soon as Bunny mentioned the word "work" Kathee heard that voice again.

Work? Damn, I almost forgot. I gotta get the boys to ghost deSalle. Paggett will owe me big time.

It had to be Simmonds' thoughts. The vehemence was almost palpable. Kathee definitely didn't like this guy!

Her attention turned briefly to a shadowy form at the end of hall-way exiting the stage door.

A wave of fatigue washed over her and her shoulders slumped. She sighed tiredly.

I need my bath and sleep to recharge.

Bunny flinched when Simmonds barked her name.

His tone silenced her. It was obvious that she'd had previous occasion to fear this pitch in his voice.

Kathee pasted a smile on her face. "That's okay. There's no need to beg. We'll be happy to perform for you tomorrow night."

Now it was Kathee's turn to flinch as Bunny's screech of glee sliced through her eardrums and echoed in her mind and soured her fake smile.

Simmonds was staring directly at Kathee, and

there was no way to hide her reaction. But Kathee breathed a sigh of relief when he began to smile at her while rubbing his ear. He had fallen victim to Bunny's squeal many times before and was sympathizing with Kathee.

"I have one condition to our performance, though. I'd like our entire troupe to perform for you."

"Troupe?" Simmonds wasn't sure what she meant.

"All the acts that you've seen tonight—the card magician, jugglers, and hypnotist—they all work with me. I figure that if you're going to make your friends jealous you might as well go all out."

Bunny hopped up and down, clapping her hands in bobble-head glee.

"But, it's going to cost you a little more. I have expenses, mouths to feed… you know."

Turning to place her hands on Simmonds' shoulders, Bunny begged, "Please, honey? I won't ask for anything more. You can even consider this an early Christmas present! Pleeease?"

He sighed in resignation.

312 OD—September 4—9:15 am

The news director continued his reporting with, "So Inspector Kelly, what is your department going to do if they can't find little Gregory? Will you call in the Finders Keepers Detective Agency again to help you out?"

It didn't take a genius to figure out from

the inspector's tone that this was his least favourite topic. Kathee could tell he obviously didn't want to broach this issue, and it showed in the tone of his voice when he responded with, "We only use Finders Keepers when ALL other avenues of Police investigation have been exhausted."

Kathee snickered. *Finders-Keepers, cute name for a detective Agency.*

"Why the hell are we doing this again, boss?" Derek, also known as Mesmero, interrupted from behind.

"Yeah, Kathee. We *never* do private gigs," Frank, one of the Juggernauts, piped up from the third seat of the Solara 3500 van.

Before answering, Kathee reached over and flicked the news broadcast off. She sighed and glanced back at Derek and the rest of the troupe.

"I know we normally don't do jobs like this. I don't suppose telling you guys that it's because the lady of the house is an old friend of Beth's is enough of a reason?"

Ann, the Card Manipulator, proclaimed from the second seat. "Nope. Definitely not good enough. Spill the beans, boss."

"Okay, okay." Kathee shrugged. "When Beth introduced me to Bunny, I had no intentions of doing this private party." She looked over at Beth, who was nodding agreement.

"Yeah. You surprised me when you agreed. I thought for sure you'd say no in your normal, polite manner, and that would be that."

"You're right," Kathee shifted as best she could in the seat, "but I noticed something when William Simmonds showed up."

For a few seconds, the interior of the van was totally quiet.

"Bunny is terrified of her boyfriend," Kathee proclaimed.

Beth leaned slightly towards Kathee. "I didn't get that feeling."

Kathee smiled self-consciously. She knew Beth considered their act more of a comedy routine than a true use of Kathee's talent. She was aware that Kathee could read her surface thoughts, and she had trained herself to more easily send these thoughts to Kathee. She didn't understand how or why, but she was happy to be earning a paycheque from it.

"William was angry when he called out her name, and she flinched. It wasn't just a normal flinch either. From her reaction, I can tell that he's hit her more than once. She cringed like he was going to reach across and slap the notion out of her head."

The troupe exchanged worried glances with each other.

"Don't worry," Kathee reassured them. "If anything happens, I'll pull the plug and get us out of there before you can say 'Boo'."

There was a small collective sigh of relief. The rest of the trip was made in silence.

Boss—the turn! Frank's frantic thought had Kathee automatically hitting the brakes just as he shrieked, "Boss, you're missing the…"

"Damn." Kathee uttered her usual response as everyone braced themselves, and the van screeched to a halt on the side of the road.

"Sorry, guys." Kathee relaxed her death-grip on the steering yoke and looked back at a few perturbed faces. "I got a little distracted for a moment. Thanks for the heads-up Frank. Now let's get this road on the show."

I could swear you braked before Frank yelled out.

Kathee could hear murmuring in the back as they re-settled, but in the rear-view mirror Derek and Frank were wearing puzzled expressions that made her uneasy. But their lips weren't moving.

Huh. She put the brakes on before Frank even… and she wasn't lookin' or anything'… how'd she…

Much as she hated to do this, Kathee realized she had no choice. They were starting to suspect something. She took a deep breath and concentrated on a scenario where Frank yelled at her to brake, she saw herself slamming on the pedal, and the van screeched to a stop. She imagined this with all her might, then looked back in the mirror to see if the replacement memory hit its mark.

Derek's baritone mumbling calmed her fears.

"Thank God *someone* was paying attention in this car. Stupid women drivers."

She could feel sweat beading on her brow as she took in a long deep breath and let it out quickly. Her hands were shaking slightly, so she gripped the wheel a little tighter as she looked around for a way to back up the van and trailer.

God, I hate doing that, but I must be getting better at it because I'm not as wiped as I normally am after I plant a false memory. This one was a snap.

When she was in her early twenties, Kathee discovered that another aspect of her talent was the ability to implant thoughts or change someone's memory of events. The first time it came in useful was when she had to sneak back into the dorm and the monitor caught her. Was she ever surprised when a blank look took over the monitor's face, and she let go of Kathee's arm and walked away. Kathee thought she was going to get reprimanded the next day, but the monitor never mentioned it.

I don't like how I feel after doing this, and I apologize to you, Derek. I know it's an invasion of your privacy, but it's just a tiny one. Please forgive me.

Thankfully, the van was easy enough to manoeuvre, so Kathee had no trouble backing up to the right-hand turn that would lead them towards the Simmonds' estate. The van bumped twice as it went over a curb and onto the moving slidewalk. Kathee lightly scraped an edge of a nearby four-storey office building with the van.

There goes a layer of paint from the car.

This time Kathee didn't need to see him to know that this was Derek's thought booming clear as a bell in her mind.

Her grip tightened on the yoke. *Why am I hearing them so clearly?*

Just then, their thoughts faded into the murmuring she was so used to and that tired feeling came back.

Huh? Why'd it stop?

CHAPTER 11

312 OD—September 4—9:45 am

A wall of tall pine trees was broken only by the occasional glimpse of a high stone barrier behind it. A twelve-meter gap between the trees and fence turned out to be a well-manicured lawn devoid of any shrubbery.

The murmuring in her head cleared up enough for Kathee to hear *"No cover for a covert assault"* from Bill Simpson's thoughts.

Kathee smiled to herself. Bill wasn't always a juggler. He started off as a cat burglar. He was quite good, too. That was, until he met and married Ann, the troupe's resident card manipulator. *There's nothing like a good woman to give a man religion*, Kathee thought.

But the murmur in her mind became less distinct. *What is going on with my talent?* Glancing up through the sun roof, she offered up a quick plea. *Great-aunt Prudence, I wish you were here.*

"Oh… wow!" whispered Beth as she stared off to her left at the short access road leading to an antique, ornate iron gate.

Kathee lowered her window to push the button on the narrow intercom pad.

A surly voice growled from the brass speaker. "Yeah?"

"Uh… hi," Kathee started to have second thoughts. "It's Kathee Marani and company. We have a private show scheduled for Mr. Simmonds this morning."

"Yeah, I know," the unfriendly voice replied. "C'mon up."

The gate rolled noiselessly inward. Kathee put the van back in gear and drove in. Scanning the lay-out of the estate, she silently agreed with Bill. It would be difficult to approach this place undetected with all of its wide open spaces. The driveway was lined with meter-wide boulders spaced just sufficiently apart to prevent vehicles from straying off the path.

A long lane curved gently left towards the front of a gleaming white, 2-storey mansion. Two huge boulders were situated at the edge of the front steps framing the only site along the road wide enough to park a vehicle.

They weren't alone.

Four guards armed with wicked-looking assault railers were standing, with fingers on triggers, at each corner of the steps into the mansion.

Bill whistled, "Fort Knox doesn't have this much security! What the hell does this guy import, anyway? Rare gems?"

"Maybe he's into Ion Dreams?" Anne suggested.

"God! I hope not." Kathee shivered as the image of her kid brother's tortured face distorted by the drug's deadly chemicals flashed into her mind. She turned and took a silent moment to look at each member of her troupe, "My little brother died five years ago of an Ion Dreams overdose." She shook her head. "It wasn't pretty. The docs tried everything, but by the time they got to him, well nothing could save him."

There was dead silence in the van.

"If he's into the Ion Dreams market, then his guards probably also have full-metal rounds in their railers," Bill remarked in an absent-minded tone. They're illegal, but… like… he wouldn't care about legal anyway."

Kathee didn't tell them that it was her brother's death last year that had spurred her to begin her crusade against the drug lords who got him hooked in the first place. *God help Simmonds if this is what he's into.*

One of the sentries took a step forward and motioned with his railer for them to get out of the car.

The guards stared silently at them as they unloaded their equipment from the van. The sight of the guns didn't worry them too much. After all, anyone who had anything worth protecting could afford their own personal security force. And from the look of Simmonds' place, he had enough money.

312 OD—September 4—9:55 am

"Wow!" Anne and Bill exclaimed simultaneously.

"This place is huge!" Derek said, while staring across the great room.

"It's damn near bigger than the Centre Stage Club," Beth whispered in awe.

Derek craned his neck back and looked up while muttering, "Cripes! It's almost three-storeys high!"

"You could hold a circus in here," Kathee remarked.

"Including the high-wire act," Derek joked. "I'd guess it at being about twenty meters wide."

A deep baritone voice chimed in. "Actually, it's twenty-five meters."

The troupe turned as one and was confronted by the owner of the house.

"Greetings. I'm glad you were able to find the place. We've set up a stage for you over there." He pointed towards a wall of massive 3-storey high windows at the far end of the room overlooking a beautiful valley. "The changing room is just to the left of the stage. Unfortunately, it's the only room is available. I hope you won't mind sharing."

Kathee stepped forward. "That'll be no problem. When you're on the road as long as we've been, you learn to make do. The juggling team, The Juggernauts, will need an open area to warm up. Do you have a large dining room?"

"Hmmm! I guess they could use the living room. I'll have someone move the furniture out of the way."

"Oh! They can move whatever out of the way, then move it back when they're finished," Kathee promised.

"No bother," Simmonds shook his head. "We have servants for that." He snapped his fingers and four of his guards slung their railers over their shoulders and headed to the doorway to the right of the stage. "It's right over there."

A high-pitched squeal erupted at the far end of the room as Bunny emerged from a large gold door to their right. She was wearing a frilly pink robe that was more appropriate attire for a centerfold model than a housewife.

Kathee cringed slightly at the sound, and then felt a flush hit her cheeks when she noticed that Simmonds was looking directly at her.

"Sorry," she muttered to him.

"No problem. It grows on you. By now, I'm used to it."

"You made it! You made it!" Bunny gushed as she embraced Beth. "I'm so glad! How was the map I drew you? Did you get lost? How long did it take you to get here? How soon can you set up? When can you start? Can you stay for lunch? Will you…"

"Slow down, dear," Simmonds rested his hand on her shoulder. "Give them a chance to get their bearings." He squeezed her shoulder with his meaty hand, and Bunny winced slightly.

I wonder how many bruises she's sporting?

"Let's let them set up their equipment. We've got lots of time afterwards to get better acquainted. Besides, our guests should be arriving shortly and..." Simmonds easily turned her around and gave her a slight push. "...you have to get ready for them."

Kathee frowned as she led her group towards their dressing room.

He's obviously the lord and master of his home, and he uses his strength to keep it that way.

312 OD—September 4—10:15 am

"That guy gives me the creeps," Beth whispered to Kathee while positioning her make-up case on the bathroom counter. "Are you going to take him down, too?"

"What?" Kathee dropped her case with a loud thump onto the vanity.

"He IS a crook, isn't he?" Beth's eyebrows arched questioningly. "We are here to shut down his operation. Right?"

Trying to put as much indignation as possible in her voice, Kathee blurted out, "I'm sure I don't know what you're talking about."

"C'mon, boss. I've worked with you too long to fall for that." Beth smiled conspiratorially. "We've been together since college. I can tell when you're lying to me. Fess up."

Kathee whispered, "How did you find out?"

"It wasn't hard." Beth sat down on the make-up chair in the powder room located next to their makeshift dressing room.

"What gave me away?" Kathee made sure her voice never got any louder than a whisper.

"The newspapers. The reports over the up-link."

"Huh?"

"They all pointed at you."

"My name was never published."

"Okay, not you—us."

"Us?" Kathee was getting more confused.

"Let me try this again." Beth looked over at the adjoining room then leaned closer to Kathee and took a deep breath before starting over. "Every time we were playing in a major city, the papers always seemed to carry headlines about some local gang lord, or the head of a crime organization, or biggie in the crime business being brought down by an unknown source or leak or some incriminating evidence that the police mysteriously got their hands on."

"Okay..." Kathee sounded a little hesitant.

"I kept track of reports from other cities. By using a worm search program, I found that these things mostly occurred when we were in that town performing at a venue somewhere."

"That doesn't prove anything! It could just be a coincidence."

"Nope. The worm figured it out. Using a correlation program I found that the criminals, whose names I got from the news reports after they were captured, all had been at our act two or three nights before they were taken down. This was just too much of a coincidence."

"But…"

"Don't worry about it boss," Beth reassured her. "The cops aren't using the same criteria in their worm program that I used in mine. They'll never figure out it was us. Er… you, that is. And don't be worried. I haven't turned you in for being a psychic. Why would I turn you in now?"

"I'm amazed." Kathee stared at Beth in disbelief. *I didn't know she could do that level of programming.*

Beth sounded almost too eager, and she nearly bounced up and down in excitement. "So, what are we going to do now? How are we going to bring Simmonds down?"

"What about Bunny?"

Beth shrugged her shoulders. "Bunny *has* to know what her husband is doing, so she's just as guilty as he is."

"But what if she doesn't know?"

"Then I'll commiserate with her. But I'll tell her that she's better off without him."

Kathee stared unblinkingly at Beth for almost a minute. Just as she was about to say something there was a knock at the dressing room door.

Kathee stepped out of the powder room and cautiously walked over to the wooden door and opened it. One of Simmonds' guards had his railer slung idly over his bulbous shoulder.

"The guests are here. Mr. Simmonds wants you to start the show..." The guard unconsciously reached up and touched the sling of his rifle as he barked out, "Now!"

312 OD—September 4—10:25 am

"Ladies and gentlemen!" Derek's booming baritone was the perfect announcer's voice, "For your entertainment today, I would like to present the amazing Miz Simpson! She will mystify you with her manipulations—tease you with tricks—astound you with antics! So without any further ado, heeeeeres Anne!"

An overweight lady dressed in a bright purple Mu-Mu stepped out from the right side of the stage. She was carrying a small box filled to overflowing with decks of cards. She put the carton down on the single chair in the centre of the stage. The only other furniture was a waist-high table in front of the chair.

"Thank you, Derek. And thank you, ladies and gentlemen." She paused until all the applause had died down. "I especially want to thank our host, Mr. Simmonds for his kind generosity in letting us perform here tonight."

Simmonds stood up and bowed to his applauding guests. His chest puffed out at the adulation.

"For my first trick, I'll need a volunteer. And... well... since Mr. Simmonds is already standing. Would you care to join me on stage, sir? Please?"

Simmonds' chest deflated slightly as he realized that she had set him up. His feet seemed to be a little reluctant to mount the three steps up to the stage.

Anne pulled out a deck of cards and slit open the seal with her thumbnail. She pulled the cards out and tossed away the carton. "My lovely assistant and husband, Bill, is going to bring out the prop for my first trick."

Kathee grinned from the sidelines. *I love this trick.* She moved a couple of meters closer to the stage. *She's cut the first five minutes out of her act.*

Bill wheeled a large 4X8 double-pane Plexiglas sheet out and positioned it a little over a meter from her and facing the crowd.

As she riffled the deck, she motioned for him to stand closer. "You're going to be very instrumental for this procedure. First, I want you to shuffle this ordinary deck of cards three times." She handed him the deck and waited patiently as he tried, in vain to move even one card. The deck of cards was now a solid block of cards.

"Hmmm. Maybe you're doing it wrong. Here, let me help you."

He gladly handed the deck over.

Anne cut the deck of now loose cards and riffled them on the table with practised ease. "They seem to be okay. Try it again." She passed him the cards.

But again Simmonds could only struggle clumsily with a lump and neither cut the deck nor shuffle them.

"Maybe you just don't have the knack. You seem to be doing it right."

A red tint climbed up Simmonds' face as his frustration grew.

Anne reached over and patted his hands. "That's okay, dear. Not all of us are cut out to handle a deck of cards.

Simmonds stopped trying to shuffle the deck and began to vibrate with anger. His jaw clenched tightly.

A startled gasp came from Bunny. She'd seen this anger before.

Kathee looked for the source and saw Bunny staring at her embarrassed husband with fear on her face. She brought the knuckles of her right hand to her mouth. Kathee looked at Anne and she, too, was looking at Bunny.

"That's okay, Mr. Simmonds. You've just fallen victim to the *Frozen Deck* trick. Thanks for being such a good sport. Let's give our victim a big hand!"

Kathee could see the tenseness slowly leave Simmonds' shoulders as he began the trek back to his seat.

Anne had pulled out another deck of cards and opened the package. She reached out and stopped Simmonds.

"Oh, no you don't. I'm not finished with you yet, dearie."

The tenseness returned. It seemed that he was about to refuse, then his shoulders slumped in defeat. He had obviously weighed his standing among his friends with what they would think of him if he refused to play along.

One-handedly, she cut the deck and put it back together. Then, she fanned them out on the table.

"I'd like you to pull out one card from this deck and show it to the audience." She turned her back on him and the crowd. "Once you've done that I'd like you to place the card back anywhere in the deck and tell me when you've done so."

"Okay, I've done it."

"Good. Now I hope you've memorized the card or else this trick isn't going to work very well. Did you memorize it?"

"Yeah," he volunteered suspiciously.

Anne scooped the deck off the table and turned slightly to face the sheet of Plexiglas.

"For this trick, I need total silence. Now, I will throw the deck against that wall and try to make your card stick to the glass."

Simmonds sounded a little sceptical. "Okay."

Anne wound up like a World League baseball pitcher and threw the deck with all her might. In a flurry of cards the deck hit the Plexiglas and scattered on the floor like rectangular leaves. A lone card remained.

"Would you please retrieve your card?"

Simmonds walked over to the glass and reached for a card now sandwiched between the two panes at about his shoulder height. He looked back at Anne with amazement.

"You'll have to turn the pane around," Anne told him.

He did as instructed.

Gasps of surprise were quickly followed by thunderous applause. The card that Simmonds had chosen and replaced in the deck was stuck between the panes of Plexiglas!

Kathee smiled from behind the curtain on the left side of the stage where Derek was standing. She gently elbowed Beth.

"I have to go… er… run an errand," she whispered.

Beth nodded knowingly. "I'll cover for you, boss."

I've got to be quick. Everyone was cutting their act by five minutes, and I don't blame them. I don't want to be in this armed camp any longer than I have to either.

She glanced up at the ceiling but couldn't find any signs of video surveillance cameras. That would have made her job much more difficult.

Making her way out to the dressing room was easy, but getting past the armed guard to Simmonds' office was going to be a little trickier. It was the same surly guard who had led them in.

Suddenly, she noticed that the psychic murmur she'd lived with for so long had died down. She could hear applause behind her.

Damn. I wish I was at the show, too. Everyone's having a blast except me.

Her jaw dropped. *My talent's jumped up a notch again. I've got to figure out what's causing this roller-coaster stuff! Okay, I might as well take advantage of it while I can.*

She concentrated and sent the guard a mental image of her turning left and walking into the dressing room. It worked flawlessly. Squeezing past him, she quickly slipped into the forbidden office.

312 OD—September 4—10:40 am

William Simmonds leaned back in his chair. His hands were still smarting from the enthusiastic applause he'd given to the card manipulator during her three curtain calls.

"Her act was stupendous!" he whispered to his wife. "Especially that *Levitating Card in the Cup* trick."

"I liked the *Card Between the Glass Panes* trick. How she..."

"Ah, you're prejudiced. You like it only because I was the guinea pig for that one." He put his arm around her shoulders and smiled. "But thanks anyway for the vote of confidence."

The curtains on their home-made stage ruffled, pulling his attention away from his wife. A large figure dressed in black stepped slowly onto the stage.

"I am The Great Mesmero! Today I will entertain you with a display of my world-renowned hypnotic talent."

His pronouncement was greeted by a polite round of applause—much less than Ann's curtain calls.

"Before we get started, I want to conduct

a little experiment. Please clasp your hands tightly in front of you and squeeze hard."

He waited while the forty or so audience members reluctantly complied.

After about a minute of silence broken only by an occasional cough or scrape of a chair leg on the oak floor, Mesmero continued. "Now, you may try to pull your hands apart." Giggling and mumbling ensued amidst a few worried looks. "You will notice that some of you can do this easily, some with a measure of difficulty and others not at all." He scanned his startled audience. "For those of you in the last group, don't panic. I will un-clasp your hands in a minute or two."

There was more than one relieved sigh at this assurance.

"The reason for this experiment was to tell me who will make good assistants for my next trick. So, will those who are still struggling please stand? I will assist you when you come onto the stage."

"He leaned his large black frame forward to get a better view of his subjects. "We've already punished our gracious host and birthday boy enough, so let's let him off the hook. But the lovely hostess…" he smiled broadly, "…who's desperately trying to hide behind her husband, looks like a good choice. How about it folks?" His next words were drowned out by cheers and hoots.

Smiling genially, he continued, "Well, there you have it. It's unanimous." He extended his hand towards Bunny and urged her towards one of the chairs on the stage. "Would you care to join me, Madame?"

Reluctantly, Bunny walked up the three steps—her hands still clasped tightly together.

"And how about you, sir?" he pointed to a beefy, red-faced man standing behind Bunny, "and the pretty brunette in the last row, would you both join our hostess on stage? And…"

He kept going until he had six nervously-stuck people coming towards the stage. While they were making their way up, Mesmero stepped down and began walking between the chairs, tapping one clenched set of hands after another until every remaining struggler in the audience was free.

312 OD—September 4—10:55 am

"The person that I am now touching," he paused to choose the perfect antic, "whenever you see me touch my nose you will hear a voice coming from beneath your chair." Mesmero removed his hand from Bunny's slight shoulder. "You sir," he touched the beefy gentleman's head, "every time I ask you your name, your tongue will refuse to work. You will not be able to speak your name, no matter how hard you try. And you, young lady," he put his hand on the pretty brunette's shoulder, "you will do your best to convince me that some of the people in the audience are on fire. You will get more and more frustrated with me the longer I ignore you."

Simmonds grinned. *This is going to be funny.*
He shifted slightly and sat straighter in the
chair. He felt a tap on his shoulder. Looking
up he saw one of his guards leaning down to
whisper in his ear.

"Excuse me sir, but there's an urgent call
for you."

"Who is it?" he grumbled. "I left instruc-
tions not to be disturbed while the show was
on."

"I believe he said his name was Mack."

A shudder ran down his spine. *Why the hell
is MacDonald calling me here?*

"Okay, okay." He looked towards the stage and
sighed. "I'll take it in the library. At least
from there, I'll be able to watch the show."

Making his way around his guests wasn't easy,
so he excused himself a number of times. Most
of the gentlemen realized he wouldn't be leaving unless it was business. Simmonds knew that
since they shared the same line of work, they
would presume that James MacDonald had sum-
moned him for some reason.

Simmonds grumbled under his breath all the
way upstairs to the library. He cracked open
one of the windows in the library so he could
hear some of the show while he took the call.

"Hello, Mr. MacDonald. What can I do for
you?"

"You know damn well what, Simmonds!" the
British voice at the other end shouted. "You
were supposed to get information on Knoll and

Eduardo for me! Where is it?"

"Oh yeah… sorry about that, but my guys are still working on it. So far we haven't found anything incriminating on either Judge Knoll or the DA. They're both as pure as snow."

"Pure as snow, my white ass!" MacDonald's fake British voice slipped for the last few words.

"I tell you these guys are like saints. They haven't even got a jay-walking ticket against them!" Simmonds paused for a second then quickly continued. "But don't worry, sir, we'll find something even if we have to make it up. You'll have their balls before your trial comes up. I guarantee it."

"I damn well better, if you want to keep your own, Simmonds!"

The up-link went dead.

"…now sing Jailhouse Rock just like Elvis when I call your name." Mesmero's faint voice drifted up from the floor of the great room.

A knock sounded at the door on the other side of the library.

"Yeah?"

Two burly individuals walked in. Both looked like they could be linebackers on some football team.

"What do you want, Jimmy?"

The shorter of the two cleared his throat then said, "Sorry to disturb you boss, but we need to ask you something."

Simmonds' voice was a little leery, "Go ahead."

"Thomas and I want to bring in a couple new guys into our ghost squad... if it's okay with you, of course."

"Sure. Who are they? What do you know about them?"

"They're brothers and they're both super strong."

"Super strong?"

"Yeah," Thomas excitedly piped in. "Sonny can bench press almost half-a-ton and Slugger can punch a hole through a brick wall."

"They sound like muties?"

"They are. They're like us, except they're both… green-skinned."

"I don't want any muties in my organization." Simmonds barely contained his revulsion. "I want everyone to look like they fit in with normal people. They're out!"

"But boss…"

Jimmy was cut off by Simmonds' shout.

Both Jimmy and Thomas seemed to shrink.

"Okay, boss," Thomas whispered in fear.

"Send them to Paggett. He hires muties."

"Thanks, boss." Jimmy sidled towards the door, anxious to leave.

As they exited, Simmonds felt a shiver run up his spine. *Muties… I can't stand them. They should be banished someplace where they can be with their own kind. Why are they so keen on being with the rest of…*

A noise coming from his office broke his train of thought. As he quietly opened the door a sudden stabbing chest pain hit and stopped his forward advance. *No one in sight. Good.* Shaking off the pain, he walked into his office and over to his safe. *While I'm here, I'll just check to make sure no one's tampered with this. Can't afford to lose any of those papers.* A menacing thought was shouting in the back of his subconscious, but he couldn't make out its warning.

The metallic door was firmly locked.

I'd better check to see if someone broke into the safe.

No sooner had he finished the combination and opened the door, a small pigeon sitting at the open window was startled when the window slammed shut forcing it inside where it momentarily fluttered around Simmonds' head.

"What the hell? Get away from me! Shoo! Shoo!"

The bird blundered into the open safe. It landed on the pile of papers.

BRRRRING...

"Stupid bird! You set off the alarms."

Out of the corner of his eye he spotted a movement by the door, but nobody was there.

"Must have been one of the guards checking the room," he mused aloud. But a horrible thought was surfacing and panic filled his ordered thoughts of the past couple minutes. "What... just... happened?"

CHAPTER 12

312 OD—September 4—10:00 am

Kathee wondered why the guards hadn't put their railers down while helping her set up for the show.

"Put it over there on the right," Kathee directed the guards as they carried her ornate, plush throne." She winced when they accidentally bumped it against a door jamb. "I want to keep this stuff SAFE for the act."

Stressing the word "safe" paid off and she was able to read one of the guard's thoughts. The psychic murmuring cleared up just enough for her to get a quick picture of exactly where Simmonds kept his safe.

Now I've just got to find some way of getting into it.

"Boss! Hey, boss!"

"Please, be careful with the equipment, okay, guys?" she begged the makeshift stagehands, then turned to face the members of her troupe.

"What's up, gang? Shouldn't you be getting changed?"

Derek stopped a couple of steps closer to her than the rest of the group.

"We've decided something and want to run it by you."

"What's up?"

"We want to get out of here as fast as possible."

"It creeps me out!" Anne piped up.

Bill added, "Yeah, boss. This place is more of a prison than a prison is!"

Kathee smiled then looked over her shoulder to make sure that the guards were far enough away not to hear. "Do you all feel this way?"

They nodded in agreement.

"Yeah, me too," she conceded. "What do you want to do?"

"How about we shorten up the show?" Derek suggested. "Instead of our 20-minute acts, we could chop them down to 15 minutes. That way we'll only have to be here for an hour."

"Sounds good to me. How about the rest of you?"

Almost as one they all agreed.

"Hey!" They were startled by William Simmonds' deep baritone voice.

"Okay guys," Kathee quickly distracted their guilty looks, "let's get this show going."

She turned to Simmonds. "How can I help you?"

He stood uncomfortably close and stared up into her face. "Why are you just standing around instead of getting ready for my show?"

A wave of strength washed over her. She smiled down at him. "We were going over some last minute logistics for your sh…" A heavy thump stopped her from throwing *show* back in his smug face.

One of the make-shift stage hands had dropped a costume crate.

"… and trying to find some way of keeping our COMBINATION of props and equipment SAFE," she paused for the briefest of moments, "from your heavy-handed assistants." She turned back to look Simmonds square in the eyes. Would he concentrate enough on the words "safe" and "combination" to help her?

22-85-36.

Kathee smiled. *Gotcha!* Stressing the word had paid off.

She now knew where the safe was and how to open it.

312 OD—September 4—10:25 am

The September sun streamed through the windows in Simmonds' office. A slight breeze gently riffled the thick brown drapes. The over-sized desk and chairs were made of dark, polished oak, while two large filing cabinets on the left side of the desk were a highly burnished stainless steel.

Kathee quickly made her way to the desk—more specifically, to the framed Renoir on the wall behind it. When Simmonds had thought of his safe she received a quick flash of a faded picture behind a line of numbers. This was the bigger of the two pictures occupying wall space, so she gently worked a gloved hand around the left side of the heavy wood frame until her index finger found a metal stop.

She fumbled with the unfamiliar catch and worried at her lengthening visit. Kathee cursed her poor dexterity. Why couldn't great-aunt Prudence have gifted her with nimble fingers as well as psychic abilities?

Okay, slow down. Take a deep breath. She finally tripped the latch. The spring hinges were so tight the picture almost clipped her as it swung open. In was only a matter of seconds she had the safe open.

Bingo!

Sitting on top of a pile of papers was a brown leather-bound binder that almost screamed 'Here I am'. This had to be what she was looking for. She couldn't imagine Simmonds feeling secure enough to keep his books on a computer, what with all the spammed viruses, Trojans and worm programs infecting the internet faster than the anti-virus companies could detect them. Computers were not a safe storage medium anymore, so most people kept a paper copy of all important work.

Just as she reached for the "treasure", a noise came from the doorway, and turning her head, she saw Simmonds walking into the room.

Freeze! She screamed into his unconscious mind.

Close the door! A million thoughts raced through her mind as she searched for a way to cover up her indiscretion while her victim stood immobile just inside the doorway.

Coo. Coo. A pigeon on the window ledge was a life-saver. A quick idea came to mind.

"Come here!" she ordered Simmonds' receptive mind.

Zombie-like, he tottered slowly towards the wall safe.

"You came in to… to check out a noise," she whispered to him. "You don't see anybody here. The pigeon on the windowsill catches your eye. That's what made the sound you heard. You decided to check out the safe to make sure the contents are okay, so you opened it. Everything was fine."

As Kathee murmured her orderly scenario, she visualized the events in her head and sent the images into his. She had to make him "see" this, remember the events, and forget her. Perspiration broke out on her brow.

"You closed the safe and locked it, and then you shut and latched the picture. You don't see anyone in the office." She paused to stare at his pock-marked, double-chinned face only a step away from hers. He looked adrift in a sleep-walker's dream. But she continued focussing her thoughts into his. "When you walk out the door you will not remember my being in here, and you'll go back to watching the performances."

Reaching into the safe, she grasped the ledger.

BRRIING!!!

"What the…" The noise brought Simmonds out of his coma-like state.

Kathee quickly brought him back under her control again. The blaring alarm had rattled her concentration. She could feel a cold sweat trickle from under her blonde wig, down her neck, and between her shoulders.

Just then the window slammed shut and the pigeon flew into the room disoriented by the alarm's vibrations. It fluttered quickly around the unfamiliar environment trying to find an escape from the noise but kept fluttering into perceived exits, one of which was the painting. It caught itself and flew off, but not before losing a couple of feathers in the process.

"Stupid pigeon," fumed Simmonds, waving his short, thick arms wildly over his head, but Kathee saw her chance. Before he could regain any more awareness of the situation, Kathee shot him another bolt of suggestions.

"The pigeon flew into the safe when you were looking in and disturbed the papers. It set off the alarm. You are alone in your office."

Rushing to the door, she slipped the ledger under her arm. No sooner had she closed the door than the guard came racing towards her. She stared at his hefty face and he instantly fell under her spell.

"You never saw me here. Open the door to check on your boss. When you see he's alone and okay return to your post, and forget you ever saw me come out of here."

She hated doing this. Planting one false memory was hard enough—two was something she had never been able to do very well. They tended to affect one another and sometimes the second suggested memory didn't take or didn't last as long. But her talent seemed to still be running at a better level, because planting the memories in Simmonds and the guard were almost, well… too easy.

312 OD—September 4—11:20 am

"And now, ladies and gentlemen, since the alarms have finally been turned off, we need a victim…er… I mean, guinea pig for the next portion of our act." Chuckles erupted from the spectator's. Bill Simpson, the shortest of the Juggernauts on stage, gestured towards Bunny in the audience who immediately shrank down in her chair. "Actually, no. Don't fret Miss Bunny. You've been picked on enough today." She sighed a relieved giggle. "So let's give the pretty brunette to your left a chance to be part of the show."

"Yay, Bev. Go for it!" A male voice called out in encouragement.

Bev was a little hesitant but moved slowly from beside Bunny onto the stage where juggling pins had begun whizzing back and forth in a game of catch between Bill and his cohorts.

"I can't catch worth a darn," she jokingly apologized from the edge of the busy stage.

"Hmmm… that could be a bit of a problem,"

said Bill feigning disappointment. "But, since you're already here, let's see if there's something else we can have you do." Bill stopped to scratch his head with one of the three pins in his right hand. "I know! Can you stand still?"

A blank look appeared on Bev's face as she turned to watch the hurtling pins being passed from one performer to another behind her. She responded with a nod. Her heavily moussed hair formed a stiff halo around her apprehensive face.

"Really, really still?" he added.

"Yeah, I guess so." She sounded less sure.

"All you have to do is stand right here." Bill walked over to the center of the stage and placed a juggling pin there. "And it's very important that you don't move once you get into position."

There were a couple of titters from the audience. A few of them grinned with what they thought was coming next.

Before Bev could move to get into position, George moved forward and stood over the pin. "Let me demonstrate what you're going to be doing."

Bill threw one of his clubs, just barely missing his partner's nose. Frank, George's brother, caught the club while his thrown club whizzed, almost faster than the eye could see, behind George's head.

"Here's why you have to keep perfectly still… ah… almost paralyzed," Bill explained to Bev.

George turned sideways between the two rows

of whizzing pins.

There were more gasps from the audience. Bunny emitted a squeal of fear.

The clubs were brushing his long hair, barely missing his head.

"This is how George combs his hair in the morning," Frank explained. "He'd do it himself, but he's all thumbs until he gets at least two cups of coffee into his system."

The viewers erupted into laughter.

Without seeming to look, George stepped out of the path of the flying clubs.

Again the audience gasped—this time in amazement.

"Would you care to step in, my dear?" Bill asked Bev. The clubs flew, lightning-fast, back and forth between Frank and Bill.

Bev paled slightly at the suggestion but smiled and moved forward to take her place.

The clubs were no longer flying as fast as before.

Bill pretended to doff a hat and motioned Bev to the centre spot of the stage, but she was frozen in place.

George moved quickly to stage left and rummaged through their trunk yelling, "Hold it! Hold it a second!"

The juggling ceased. Everyone looked at him.

He dramatically pulled out a piece of paper. "Ever since the last time we did this trick, our lawyer says that we need our `assistants', that's you, to sign this waiver. It's just in case one of the guys misses while we're doing this trick... like the last time."

Bev paled again, as a serious George handed her the paper and a pen. She laughed nervously as she mechanically signed her name without even looking at what she was holding.

While George guided Bev to her position, Simmonds returned to his seat.

"What was the alarm for, Dear?" Bunny asked him.

"Nothing. Just a stupid bird. It flew into the safe and set off the alarm."

"Into the safe?"

"Yeah." Simmonds rubbed his right temple with a knuckle. "I was checking it out and the window slammed shut, then the damn bird just flew into the safe. Anyway, everything's under control now."

Bill watched Simmonds talking to his wife out of the corner of his eye. He snuck a glance off-stage at Kathee attired in her royal purple dress and stage make-up, coming from the dressing room to take her place on stage.

312 OD—September 4—12:00 pm

"Boy am I glad that's over with!" Frank exclaimed, lifting the trunk filled with juggling pins into the troupe's trailer.

"Yeah, me too!" Bill agreed as he heaved a sigh of relief. He fitted a bag of props into a space just above the trunk.

"Let's get the hell outta here," Anne mumbled

as she gave Bill's hand a squeeze.

"Okay guys," Kathee wiped perspiration from her face. "Let's pack up—quickly—and split." No one seemed to notice her nervousness.

"Hell, boss," George spoke up. "I vote we toss everything into the van and repack once we're back at the hotel. All these guards and railers make me as nervous as a long-tailed cat in a room of rocking chairs."

"Yeah!"

"Good plan!"

"I agree!"

"Let's do it!" Everyone grabbed at scattered belongings, clothing and props.

Kathee smiled at her friends' eagerness. "Okay. Let's go!"

If there was a prize for the "world's fastest group packing", they were sure they'd get it, the way they furiously loaded their gear into the Solara 3500's spacious trunk and utility trailer.

"Thank you for doing the show, Beth." Bunny hugged her old classmate even as she puzzled at the activity around her and then at her husband who had joined her backstage.

"No problem, Bunny. We're just so sorry we've got to run. We wish we could stay for the party, but we've got to get set up for the late afternoon show at the Centre Stage Club."

"I… I understand." She stepped back to her husband's side.

Kathee couldn't help but notice the wary stare that Simmonds had fixed on her. Even

though she was dead-tired, she tried to concentrate enough to get any thoughts from him,
but... nothing. Her power surge seemed to have
gone away. She wiped the sweat from her efforts
with the sleeve of her jacket. The blonde wig
itched so much that she was forced to remove
it.

I know her... from the donut shop.

Kathee didn't have to look to know this
thought came from Bunny. Even her mental voice
was high-pitched!

"Okay, troupe," she yelled out while opening
the driver's door. "Everyone in the van. We're
burning daylight. Let's go!"

Once everyone had jockeyed themselves into
the van, she accelerated around the limos
parked in front of the manor and down the
driveway. Glancing in the rear-view monitor,
she noticed Simmonds nodding to one of his
men.

But there was an overly-long delay at the
gate. The guard dallied to assist its opening,
more so than when they first arrived.

Kathee glanced nervously at the rear-view
monitor to see a black limo pulling out of
the parking area. She hoped it was one of the
guests, but something told her she wasn't that
lucky. She guessed that it was probably one of
Simmonds' men sent to follow her.

The gate opened slowly. Kathee didn't wait.
She stomped on the accelerator pedal and
screeched out of the driveway with a flurry
of stone chips in her wake and her passen-

gers gaping at her new haste. The van barely squeezed through the opening.

"Whoa, boss, what's the rush?" Bill called out from the second seat, faking a G-force ride.

"We've got company." She powered through a screeching right-hand turn at the end of the lane onto the highway back to the city. She laid on the accelerator again. "I don't think our host wants to let us go all that easily."

"Kathee," Bill's voice warned, "there's no way this boat's gonna out-run anything he's got following us. It's built for a lot of things—but speed isn't one of them." Kathee and Bill looked at each other while sneaking worried looks at their perceived pursuers.

"I agree," Frank piped from the back. "We haven't done anything wrong. Let's… let's like find out why they're chasing us."

Kathee shot a glance at Beth, who was staring over her shoulder and frowning.

"Yeah, you're right," agreed Kathee, slowing down to the speed limit. We've got nothing to hide. I don't know why I'm being so paranoid." She hoped the rest of the group was buying her act, because the stolen dossier was becoming a lumpy burden inside her jacket.

312 OD—September 4—12:25 pm

The light turned red as the Solara 3500 approached. Kathee had no choice but to stop. A black limo pulled up behind her.

Kathee could see the driver on her rear-view monitor and a chill ran down her spine for the second time tonight. She'd have to think fast. She had never tried to implant a memory from a distance without first making direct eye contact. It might not even work, but she had to try anyway. She concentrated with all her might. It was an effort, because she was still weary from her performance. Her head felt like it was going to break open. The traffic light turned green, but neither car moved.

A scene came into focus as she stared at the monitor. She imagined them stopped at the red light. The light turns green. The limo stalls and the driver can't get it started again. The van drives away. Kathee visualized each detail with every fibre of her being. She pictured the motor refusing to turn over and start.

The light turned yellow.

She accelerated away. The limo didn't budge.

"He's not moving!" George called out. "Hah, he must have stalled!"

"Boss, I've got a suggestion," Derek whispered from behind her.

"What?"

"Let's not take any more outside jobs. Okay?"

CHAPTER 13

312 OD—September 4—12:05 pm

"I don't trust them any further than I can throw them," Simmonds whispered to his lieutenant, R.J.. "Since that alarm went off during their performance, I've been watching them."

"I have, too," R.J. whispered back through non-moving lips.

"Put a tail on them. Use Billy. He's the best in the business."

"Okay, boss." R.J. turned to leave then stopped and looked back. "Should I have them delayed at the gate?"

"Yeah," Simmonds nodded. "But not for too long. Don't make them suspicious."

Bunny moved closer to him. "That's weird." Her furrowed brow deepened on a see-sawing head.

"What, dear?"

"Someone moved the rocks."

Simmonds was a little confused. "Rocks?"

"The boulders lining the driveway. They're not in the same places they were before."

Simmonds looked to where his wife was staring.

"What the…?" he shouted.

The two-ton boulders were indeed moved. Their graceful arc was now ragged. Three of the massive rocks were out of place, not by much, but it was noticeable.

"How the hell?" He turned to the guards at the door, but both stared nervously at their boss' growling face. "Did you guys see anyone mucking about with the rocks?"

"No, boss," answered the two guards in unison.

The taller of the two added, "We would've seen any vehicle around them. No one's been here… except your guests. But no one could have..."

"Did any of their drivers run into the rocks?

"No, sir."

"Then how… the hell… did they… move?"

312 OD—September 4—1:00 pm

William Simmonds walked imperiously into the dimly lit surveillance monitor room and yelled, "Whitey, are you in here?"

A scarecrow-like individual popped up from behind the bank of monitors. He was as pale as a sheet of paper. It looked like he'd never been out in the sun in his life.

"Here, boss. Just re-aligning monitor three. It's been giving me grief all morning."

"Never mind that," Simmonds snapped out. "Did you see anything strange on the monitors when the alarms went off?"

"Uh, no. But I wasn't in front of them either. I was putting the new monitor in slot three and couldn't just drop it." He studied Simmonds' worried demeanor. "By the time I finished that and got here, the alarm was off and everything looked normal. Why?"

"I don't care about *normal*. Something's screwy! Show me the feed of my office from just before… oh, about five minutes before the alarm sounded. Hurry!"

Whitey's hands flew over the console, flipping switches to reset the monitors. "Coming up on the main monitor… now."

The image of Simmonds' office, as viewed from the door facing the desk, came into focus on a large central screen. The same image could be seen on a smaller monitor to its right. All the other screens continued to show the doors leading into the mansion and the garage. Simmonds' office appeared empty until the edge of the door appeared at the bottom of the screen. A blonde woman could be seen walking purposefully towards the desk.

"What the hell?" Simmonds blurted. "That's the so-called Great Marani!" He leaned closer. "She was supposed to be getting ready to perform her act. What's she doing snooping in my office?"

"It doesn't look like snooping." R.J. had just walked into the room. "It looks like she knows exactly where the safe is, boss."

Simmonds turned his attention away from the monitors to R.J. "How'd she know where it was?"

"Well, she *is* a mind-reader," R.J. offered. "Maybe she read your mind..."

"Impossible!" Simmonds' face blushed as he interrupted. "That's bullshit. No one can read minds."

"Then how'd she know how to do that?"

Simmonds spun around to look at the monitor. Sure enough, the Great Marani easily moved the picture out of her way. His mouth dropped open when he saw her work the dial in a precise pattern.

"Shit!" he yelled thumping his fist onto the console. "Mind reader my ass! Someone gave her the combo to the safe. That's the *only* explanation!"

"Then we've got a leak somewhere," R.J. assured him. "Somebody ratted you out."

"Wait a minute..." Simmonds couldn't believe what he was seeing. "That's me! But why aren't I stopping her? I'm just... standing there?" Pleadingly he spoke to the screen, "Why the hell don't I remember any of this? What's she saying to me?"

Whitey turned a dial on the console and the sound came up.

"...a noise. You don't see anybody here. The pigeon on the windowsill catches your eye. That's what made the sound that you heard. You decided to check out the safe to make sure the contents are okay, so you opened it to make certain it's there. It is."

The Simmonds on the monitor continues to stand there in mute silence.

"You looked inside the safe." His image turned to look into the safe, "And everything was fine. You closed the safe and locked it, and then you shut and latched the picture. You don't see anyone in the office." She paused to stare at him only a step away from her. He looked adrift in a sleep-walker's dream. But she continued. "When you walk out the door you will not remember my being in here, and you'll go back to watching the performances."

"What's she pulling out of the safe?" Simmonds asked himself.

BRRIING!!!

The sound of the alarm coming from the monitor startled him and he jumped slightly. The Simmonds image didn't flinch at the sound.

Kathee's soft, melodic voice was barely audible over the alarm. "The pigeon… safe when… looking in. It disturbed… pap… off the alarm. You… alone in your office."

"She's leaving," Whitey stated the obvious.

"Let me see the hall camera!" Simmonds ordered.

The monitor went dark while the digital CD-ROM whirred in the deck searching for the hallway camera's feed.

An image appeared of R.J. running towards the opening door, then abruptly stopping in front of the Great Marani.

Her voice was slightly louder now as Jimmy was able to filter down the sound of the alarm. "You never saw me here. Open the door to check on your boss." She waited while he obeyed. "When you see he's okay, return to your post and forget you ever saw me come out of here." Her commanding lullaby was irresistible.

"Follow her," Simmonds ordered.

"I can't boss." Whitey gulped nervously and moved as far from his boss as he could on the chair. He'd been verbally beaten down more than once by Simmonds. Whitey's pale face seemed to get even whiter whenever he had to deliver bad news. "The cameras only monitor the doors into your office, the office itself, the garage, and the doors into the mansion."

Simmonds mentally cursed himself for not getting every room in the house outfitted with security cameras. *That's a short-coming that I'm soon going to remedy,* he thought.

He snarled in anger, "Get that bitch! I want her ghosted!" He took two fast breaths. "No, wait! On second thought, put a tail on her, twenty-four seven. I want to know exactly *where she goes, what she does, and most of all who she talks to!* Hell, I want to know when she goes to the can!" He smiled at his next thought. "I'll ghost her entire organization!"

312 OD—September 4—1:30 pm

William Simmonds paced up and down in front

of his desk. This was one time when he wished that he'd partaken of that ancient twenty-first century smoking vice like Paggett. The nervous tension was almost unbearable.

"Where the hell is Billy?" he muttered. "He should've called in by now. It doesn't take that long to get back to the city."

R.J. stuck his head into the office. "Boss, Billy just drove up." It was obvious to see that he didn't want to incur Simmonds' wrath—better to let someone else have that pleasure—so he quickly finished with, "I'll send him right in."

"Billy?" Simmonds was confused. "Why isn't he still following her?"

It wasn't long before a very contrite Billy sheepishly stuck his head into the highly-tensioned room.

"Boss?" His voice was quavering slightly in fear.

"Get in here!" Simmonds commanded. His back was straight and almost vibrating with anger.

The vehemence in Simmonds' voice propelled Billy like a rock from a slingshot, where he stood soldier-straight trying not to wither under his boss' glare.

"What the hell are you doing back here?"

"I lost 'em boss." Billy's hand moved of its own volition to sub-consciously twirl the hairs of his sideburn in a nervous habit that Simmonds knew Billy'd never been able to break.

Dead silence filled the room. Whitey stood beside Simmonds' desk glad to be watching someone else in the hot seat.

Simmonds tried three times to speak but with no success. He finally managed to croak out, "You what?"

"They vanished, boss." Billy held out his hands in a begging posture. "I don't know how it happened."

Simmonds knew that his voice was threatening. "Maybe you'd better try to figure it out. 'Don't know' doesn't cut it with me, you little worm."

Billy gulped, "We were at a red light. I was right behind them. Honest. There was very little other traffic on the road..."

"Forget the traffic!" Simmonds stopped pacing long enough to thump his fist on the desk. "How'd you lose them at a simple stop light?"

"The strangest thing," Billy started to mutter.

"What?" Simmonds shouted.

"Sorry, Boss. It was the strangest thing. I saw them stop at the red light right ahead of me. Next thing I know they're gone, but I'm still stopped at the damn light. It's almost like I blinked and they vanished."

"Vanished? That's impossible!"

"I know, Boss. But that's what happened. It was like real weird. Actually, weird doesn't even begin to describe it. Spooky is more like it."

Simmonds continued to pace in front of Billy in silence for almost two minutes before he finally sat down. Billy was still standing at attention in front of the desk. Simmonds groaned in resignation.

"Relax Billy. It's not your fault you lost them."

Billy deflated like a rubber balloon losing all its air.

"It wasn't magic. At least not magic like a magician making an elephant disappear or something like that."

Simmonds could hear the relief in Billy's voice. "Huh?"

"Somehow that Marani lady can mesmerize people or make 'em see things the way she wants 'em to." He held up his hand to stop Billy from saying anything. "Hey, I can't explain it either, but it's true. We've got her on disc doing it to both R.J. and I or we'd never have known how she pulled it off. Gutsy babe, I gotta admit." He paused to look at his motley band guarding the room, then sighed. "Maybe I can get her to work for me…"

"What're we gonna do, Boss?" Billy broke in.

"Well, it shouldn't be too hard to find her. I'm pretty sure she's doing her act this afternoon at the club. Tell the boys to tail her round-the-clock, but this time," he looked squarely at Billy's round face, "put a *lot* of men around her. Maybe she won't be able to mess around with *all* of your minds at once." Simmonds spun around to face the barred window of the security room. "We may not be able to stop her without ghosting her, but we sure as hell can keep her from passing off my papers."

"What papers?" Billy asked, braving his boss' anger.

"I don't know," Simmonds mumbled, looking down at his Italian leather shoes then over at the view of his office on one of the monitors.

He was careful not to show weakness or confusion.

"Whenever I look in the safe now, I don't see anything missing! Everything is there just as it should be. There's… nothing… missing." He continued to stare at the monitor struggling to understand what was wrong with his memory.

"Maybe she didn't get nothin'," Billy suggested, mostly to break the embarrassing silence after Simmonds' admission.

Whitey jumped to Simmonds' defence. "Nope. The disc definitely shows her pulling *something* out of the safe just as the alarm went off. Sure as shit she got what she wanted."

Simmonds, mesmerized by his *paralyzed performance* could only mumble, "I just wish I could remember what the hell is missing. It's driving me crazy!"

"Don't sweat it, Boss," Billy tried to reassure him.

Simmonds looked over his shoulder and nodded with a grin.

"We'll have her so covered she won't be able to pick her nose or turn around without bumping into one of us. We won't lose her again, Boss."

Simmonds gestured to the monitor as he roused from his trance and leaned over the desk. He could feel his voice go as cold as ice, "If you know what's good for you, you'd better not."

He paused and stared at his men. "She should be easy to ghost. But MallWorld is Paggett's territory, and if he finds out we're searching for someone there, he'd want a favour in return. I don't want to owe him anything, so we've got to be discreet about this. Use body scanners to see if you can find her. And don't let her out of your sight this time!"

312 OD—September 5—1:10 pm

Kathee's room was dimly lit, and she was alone with her thoughts. She'd missed a couple of shows after her experience at the Simmonds' home. Her abilities had been overtaxed, and now she'd paid dearly for it with headaches and a general malaise that were hard to shake.

She also began to feel that she was being followed but try as she might, she couldn't detect any nearby threatening thoughts. Oh, why couldn't she get her great insights when she really needed them! She had them in the club the other night and a couple of times at Simmonds' house. It was frustrating not having control, though.

Meanwhile, the dossier was burning a hole in her jacket pocket. From what she had glimpsed, the information in it would bring down Simmonds' organization, as well as a couple of his associates. Her only problem was finding a go-between who would "appreciate" this properly before her "follower" came to call.

She muttered to herself, "Damn, I'm doing the same old thing, getting too caught up with these god-awful gangs. I should have just given Simmonds a mental nudge to go confess to the police. It would have saved me all this aggravation. Oh well, twenty-twenty hindsight is always too late."

"Kathee?"

She jumped a foot into the air.

"Sorry, Boss," Beth apologized from the dressing room door.

"Oh, it's you, Beth. Hi." She reached over to straighten up her makeup containers and brushes. "You spooked me." Kathee took a deep breath. "What's up?"

Beth quickly sat down on the little faux-leopard skin stool next to her friend. "I wanted to warn you about a gang of nuts roaming MallWorld."

"Nuts?"

"Yeah. Both Ann and I have been body scanned three times in the past couple of days." She looked worriedly at her friend. "It's almost like they're looking for something in particular. Maybe something that was stolen from them recently? Don't tell me you haven't been body scanned?"

Kathee's answer dripped with sarcasm as she twirled a pen in her fingers. "Nope. Haven't had the pleasure since I haven't been outside lately."

But a sick feeling hit her stomach as she now realized exactly what the *scanners* were after.

"When were you and Anne scanned?"

"Hmmm... I was scanned last night after the show, and Anne..." Beth scratched her head. "She told me she was scanned just this morning as she was leaving your suite. She also had that big white purse of hers stolen. Why?"

"Oh, nothing." Kathee felt a sudden chill. "I was thinking there might be some sort of pattern or connection between the two. Time of day, place, something. It was just a thought."

"Mall Security is watching for the scanners, so hopefully, they won't bother us anymore."

"Yeah, I hope they catch 'em before they get to me." Another shudder passed through her. She was the reason this group was harassing women. She had what they wanted, and they were searching anyone who might have any connection to her.

But they weren't nuts. They were William Simmonds' men. He'd figured out that she'd gotten the dossier and he was checking everyone with whom she'd come into contact. She had to get rid of it and fast.

Patting the dossier inside her jacket pocket assured her that it was still there, despite its weight constantly reminding her of its presence. She was making her way to the nearby MallWorld police sub-station. Hopefully, she could leave it with someone there, which would be the signal to Simmonds' men to stop harassing her friends. At least, she hoped they would.

312 OD—September 5—1:55 pm

It took Kathee a little while to work her way to the station. This place was huge, and more like a maze than a mall. She got lost twice.

She had ducked into stores and gone out their back doors. She doubled-back on her tracks and did everything she could think of to confound any possible tails. Now she wished she had paid more attention to those detective shows on her holovision.

She thought she had thrown off any possible tails. She was wrong.

Where the hell is she going? The cops?

We've got to tell the boss.

Two separate voices boomed in her mind just as her hand touched the door handle of her destination. Suddenly her talent had another boost.

Should I ghost her anyway?

That thought spurred her to action. Pulling the handle, she opened the door and stepped into the less noisy, yet bustling police office.

The room was nondescript. Lockers to the left… a cop sitting behind a desk… doors on either side of the desk leading to the bowels of the station… benches to the right complete with a prisoner handcuffed to one of them. She heard busy calls and conversations from deep behind wanted posters plastered on the walls. Like numerous other cop shops she'd been in before, this one had the same architect as all the rest.

The middle-aged cop sighed then glanced in her direction, noise from behind her having pulled his attention away from his paperwork.

While the doors closed, the noise level dropped dramatically.

The boss is gonna kill us.

As she stopped in front of the cop's desk, the door on the right opened and a bedraggled guy sauntered through the bowels of the busy police station. Probably an undercover cop or something, she surmised.

"What the hell?" the desk sergeant cried out as he shook his pop can upside-down. "I just opened this!"

Suddenly there was a scream of outrage from outside.

Looking around, Kathee's gaze passed over the undercover cop as he tossed a badge, with a large black V on it, to the sergeant and walked out.

Not a cop, just a visitor.

Thud! The opening doors slammed into his hand.

Kathee thought she saw him blush a little as he walked out. Before he left, though, a strange image grabbed her attention. A hand was reaching out and giving a pretty redhead in a lab coat a sheet of paper, while a voice said, *"Here you go, Mariyan."*

Kathee's mouth dropped open. That thought wasn't think-speak, as she called it. It had a totally different feel to it. Something indescribable. It felt more like a buried thought of some sort.

"Well, what d'you want, lady?" the desk sergeant queried impatiently. She'd obviously missed his first comments to her.

A name popped to mind. "Mariyan, please. She's expecting me."

"You and the rest of this damn mall," he muttered as he tossed Kathee a visitor's badge and plunked the logbook in front of her. Kathee quickly signed her name and handed over her ID.

His fat finger found the small button on his desk and the door on the right unlocked.

Kathee's hesitation triggered a sarcastic, "Down the hall, turn left, first door on the left. Don't go nowhere else!"

Not wanting to pull any more attention to herself, Kathee quickly rushed through the door and went to see this Mariyan. Her door had "Crime Lab" etched on it. Through the glass she saw a redhead in a traditional crisp, white lab coat. Most technicians wore coats in the colors of their particular precinct, and others in the large office wore light or medium blue.

Kathee's hand reached up to knock on the glass, but the redhead turned and saw her. She flashed Kathee a warm and friendly smile and beckoned her into the lab.

Glancing at her name badge, Kathee saw Mariyan—Forensics.

"Hi, can I help you?" She held out her hand and shook Kathee's firmly.

Reaching into her pocket, Kathee pulled out the dossier.

"I think you'll be very interested in this," Kathee told her as she concentrated and began to place a false memory into her mind.

Imagining the undercover cop she had seen earlier, Kathee repeated his words. "Here you go, Mariyan." Kathee hoped that by repeating what he had said, Mariyan will only remember him handing her something not Kathee. "I was never here. You got this from your friend."

With that Kathee walked out of the lab and out of the police station. She made sure she didn't make eye contact with anyone while she left and tried to be as inconspicuous as possible. The sergeant mechanically returned her ID as she dropped her badge on his desk.

The noise of the mall struck an almost physical blow to her senses. She looked around for her "followers". They were around—somewhere. She spotted two beefy guys in expensive suits over by the frozen gelato stand looking in her direction.

DAMN. LOOK AT THE BITCH'S SMILE. I BET SHE DITCHED THE BOSS'S PAPERS.

A group of red-maned tourists passed by, and Kathee was able to easily merge with their enthusiastic tourist chatter and slip away.

Maybe now they'll leave us alone, she prayed.

BOOK Three—Cliff's Story

CHAPTER 14

312 OD—September 3—7:00 pm

Cliff Bowen watched carefully behind dark glasses until his mark was in the perfect position. The tall broad-shouldered, middle-aged man with the horn-rimmed glasses was pushed and jostled by other pedestrians until he was walking on the narrow curb between the MallWorld railway system and the busy slidewalk. Cliff sped up his gait slightly, white cane in tow. He concentrated harder as the mark's foot moved towards a loose chunk of concrete curbing. This rail line near the Atrium Food Court East in MallWorld was Cliff's favourite spot, and he knew it like the back of his hand. He really enjoyed playing his "games" in this area.

Cliff reached out a mental hand, sweat dripping down his forehead. His prey was heading towards him. He caused a chunk of concrete to lift barely an inch off the ground, just as the toe of a polished shoe reached the same place in space. The result was utterly predictable, and for Cliff very lucrative.

The business man pitched forward off-balanced and fell into Cliff's grateful arms. Unobtrusively he lifted the man's wallet, pocket watch, and Comp-u-link from two different pockets without even lifting a finger. The newly acquired booty quickly found their way teleported to a large camouflaged pocket sewn into the back of Cliff's plaid sports jacket.

"What the hell?" the mark snarled before he got a chance to really see Cliff. "Oh, excuse me," he apologized as he noted the dark wraparound sunglasses and distinctive white cane.

"No problem, sir," Cliff replied pretending to fumble to get his own balance. "These slidewalks aren't the safest places, I suppose. It's fortunate you didn't land face-first on the pavement. I'm glad I was here to help."

"But, how could you see me… to catch… me. Oops! Sorry, I didn't mean for it to sound like that."

"Again, no problem. It's a common misconception. And, no… yes… no… yes."

"Huh?" The perplexed look on his face was priceless, and completely expected.

"No, I don't mind answering questions. Yes, I am legally blind. No, I don't usually need help or assistance. Yes, I can see some things—mostly shapes and shadows, nothing definite. As you can see…" The victim winced at the pun. "…I answer these questions often."

"I can't imagine not being able to see or see

212

well," the flustered man commiserated, brushing his jacket back into place on his beefy frame.

Shrugging his shoulders, Cliff continued, "If it's gradual enough, you get used to the diminishing sight. It's part of life, I guess. Like grandpa used to say… If you get bruised apples, make applesauce."

"You've got a good attitude."

The stuff Cliff had stolen weighed heavily in his secret jacket pocket. It was time to end this.

"Well, it's been nice talking to you, but I've got to head out," Cliff told him.

"Oh, okay. Thanks again for your help," he replied as he resumed his journey.

Swinging the white cane in a well-practiced manner, Cliff too continued on his way. Keeping his head straight, Cliff looked out from the side of his glasses and saw the mark pause to look back at him. Cliff had done his best "totally blind" impersonation.

Almost everything he had told the mark was true. He was legally blind and did have limited eyesight. It was not as bad as he painted it, though. At one time all Cliff could see was a very blurry, and very scary world. After numerous surgeries and laser treatments, his eyesight had improved dramatically, which meant he could still drive, but he was at the very edge of the legal limit. Distant items like street signs were impossible to read, so he seldom traveled to unfamiliar areas.

Fate had dumped this as well as other medical problems on Cliff. His money had run out a long time ago. He'd be dead by now if he hadn't resorted to crime to pay his medical bills. He'd honed his survival talent to a sharp edge and knew exactly what he could do with his telekinetic ability. He preferred to steal from gang members, drug dealers, and wealthy criminals whenever possible and didn't like boosting from common folk unless absolutely necessary. Well, he would if he had to. He just didn't like doing it too often.

The people he stole from could well afford to be robbed, he justified. They were living high-off-the-hog while he had to scrape by just to make ends meet and pay for his medicines. This reasoning helped dull his conscience along with the occasional stingray oil he bought on the black market for his telekinetic headaches.

Cliff's career as a pickpocket began when he was in his early teens. His parents were neither the best nor the worst—they were just… indifferent. They didn't praise his good grades in school nor chastise him for bad behaviour. He slowly slipped from a good student to one who remembered only what he wanted to, so his schooling went into a downward spiral. His friendships changed until he was hanging with an unruly lot. He got into trouble more and more often and soon had a juvenile offender tag, a label he proudly circulated to his peers.

He and his friends used to love to torment girls and the weaker kids in school. One of their favourite pranks was to try to unhook a girl's bra without getting slapped in the process. The winner would be the big man in the group.

As a gangly teen, Cliff didn't have the manual dexterity to accomplish this and usually got caught in the act. One day he was reaching for a bra clasp, knowing he was going to get slapped yet again, when something clicked in his brain. His fingers were still a good inch away from the clasp when, all of a sudden, the girl let out a squeal and turned to slap him. Cliff jumped back in alarm, and she missed him.

No one in the group was more surprised than Cliff. He became the "man" of the day. He was so proud of the honour that he didn't say anything about not actually touching the clasp.

Later that night, he tried unhooking one of his mom's bras that he had snuck out of her bedroom. He found that he could unhook it from further and further away each time he tried. It was like strengthening a muscle with exercise. The tiredness and increasing headaches seemed to lessen as he improved the intricacies of his talent. Now only the moving of heavy objects tired him. Small objects like wallets or watches were a snap.

He also discovered something else. Other than physically moving small objects short distances, he could make them disappear, teleport, then reappear about ten feet away, depending on their size. Smaller objects could teleport further while heavier objects went only short distances. Things weighing a couple of pounds would move about an inch, while a few ounces could be moved three feet. No matter how much he practised, however, he couldn't increase his range past this.

One day while trying to "boost" a purse he was caught. He had accidentally only moved the purse rather than teleport it. But the purse's owner took pity on Cliff and introduced him to "Fingers", a gifted pickpocket. Cliff wasn't yet fluent with his blossoming talent that had just recently manifested itself. But under Fingers' influence, his gift strengthened considerably, to Cliff's delight.

Manipulating small objects up to ten feet away became a snap. This included any type of dead bolt and the inner workings of alarm systems. Every new contraption that intrigued him was added to his collection. He practiced until he could by-pass anything that came his way. He was good at what he did—very good, in his own opinion. But he wished he had more of a nest-egg built up for when he had no more eyesight and was forced to retire. One of these days, he kept telling himself, he'd hit it big and quit.

"Bowen," the voice cut through the drone of voices in MallWorld like a hot knife through butter. "Bowen," it repeated, "hold up there a minute."

Stopping to look around, Cliff realized that he probably looked like a rock in a stream of humans. Everyone gave the blind guy a wide berth.

The voice was hard to pin-point, though.

"Behind you, moron."

Spinning around at the insult, Cliff's cane almost slipped out of his hand. Luckily, the strap was secure around his wrist.

These two plainclothes detectives were thorns in his side. He'd nicknamed them Mutt and Jeff after characters in a set of old comics his grandfather had passed on to him. They looked and acted more like goons than cops, giving the mob muscle a good name. Everyone who encountered them left with a bad taste in their mouths. These guys were thugs with badges.

Using his most polite voice and manners, even though he was tired and cranky, Cliff asked, "What's up, guys?"

His mind flashed back to an earlier time. Fingers was showing him how to pick an inside jacket pocket. They were on the road, and Fingers had lifted six wallets so far. Cliff knew how it was supposed to be done, but he couldn't duplicate Fingers' style and ease. A couple of uniformed and armoured cops stopped them.

"What are you doing here, Fingers?" one of them asked. "Got a new pupil?"

"Uncle Jim, why are these morons hassling us?" Cliff asked with a sneer of disdain in his voice.

It was a toss-up as to who was more surprised: the cops, that Fingers had a nephew, or Fingers, that Cliff knew his real name. But to give him credit, Fingers was fast on the uptake and he took advantage of the alibi Cliff had given him.

Before the cops could search him, Fingers rounded on Cliff and exclaimed, "There's no reason to be rude to the officers! They're just doing their jobs. We have to cooperate with the police whenever they ask." He turned back to the confused cops. "Sorry about my nephew's language, officers. I blame his parents for his bad manners. I'm trying to straighten him out."

Cliff didn't know if it was the tone of Finger's voice or his words that turned the cops from menacing figures to passing acquaintances. Either way it worked, and they let them go without searching Fingers and finding the money and ID's from the wallets.

"Why were you so nice to them?" Cliff was obviously puzzled.

"It's always best to be nice to the cops. You never know when you'll need a favor when push comes to shove. Remember Louie the Lip? He used to give the cops a hard time whenever they stopped him, and look what happened to him. It's always good to have *low* friends in *high* places."

Cliff's reminiscing was cut short when the shorter and meaner cop, Mutt, snarled at him, "Have you been working again, Bowen?"

"I don't know what you're talking about," Cliff shrugged. "Enlighten me."

"I'll enlighten you, smartass." The taller one, Jeff, snapped out a hand and smacked Cliff in the temple. His glasses snapped apart and pieces went flying.

The noise level in the vicinity dropped as a collective gasp went out. No one hits a blind man. No one.

Shaking his head, Cliff collapsed his cane into more of a weapon. The elastic band running through the hollow cane pieces acted to hold the pieces in the shape of a billy club. The cop wasn't going to get a second chance to hit him again.

"I haven't done any thing wrong," Cliff whispered through tightly clenched lips. "Go roust someone else."

"You're a known pick-pocket," Mutt growled at him.

"When I could see, yes," Cliff admitted as he responded to the accusation. "Since I've started losing my sight, I've gone legit and given up the business."

"Bull," Mutt snapped out. "Once a pick-pocket, always a pick-pocket."

"It's kinda hard to do when you can't see the mark, isn't it?" Cliff muttered and let his gaze drift off the cop.

The detectives looked at each other, and it didn't take a rocket scientist to know that even their limited intellects were beginning to get it.

The crowd was starting to mutter. Knowing that he'd won the round, Cliff decided to get even.

Beads of sweat broke out as he concentrated

on their jacket pockets where their badges were hanging out. He needed to picture the object he was going to teleport before he could move it. Both of their badge wallets landed in his hidden jacket pocket next to the Comp-u-link and watch.

A well-manicured hand reached out and rested on Cliff's cane-wielding forearm. The pieces of his sun glasses were thrust into his other hand. "Leave him alone," a sweet voice laced with steel rang out.

"It's none of your business, Lady," Jeff grumbled. "Back off."

"How about I make it my business then." She smirked wickedly and handed him a business card.

"Schwarz and Sons—Legal Aid."

"I'm sure we have a case of police brutality here. If this gentleman wants to press charges, I will represent him pro bono."

Mutt nudged Jeff. "I think we're done with Mr. Bowen."

"Ah, but is Mr. Bowen done with you?" She smiled evilly, but her voice was silky smooth as she asked, "Are you going to press charges?"

"No… I mean… yes, I'm done with them. They can go."

They slinked away amidst the murmurs of the crowd.

"Thank you."

"No problem, sir," she grinned as she slipped one of her cards into the breast pocket of his coat. "Call me if you have any more problems with those creeps."

Putting the pieces of his glasses into one of his pockets acted as a diversion of the tension he was feeling. "Thanks, again."

Her back was towards Cliff, so she acknowledged with a slight wave of the hand. As he passed by a garbage can, he deposited their badges from his hidden pocket the same way he had taken them.

312 OD—September 3—8:00 pm

It wasn't long before Cliff was sitting in his apartment where no one could see him remove the day's booty. He took the credit cards and ID from the wallet and mentally "tossed" them into the kitchen recycler. He may be a pickpocket, but he didn't believe in identity theft and running up someone's credit cards. That was much too risky for him.

The antique pocket watch and Comp-u-link were valuable only as something to be pawned, so he put the watch in his pants pocket. The standard Comp-u-link model 2212 had a red lightning bolt decal etched onto the faceplate. It was a pity that this made it more distinctive and wouldn't get him as much.

"Let's see what you've got on your Comp-u-link," he muttered as he flipped open the unit and began rifling through its directory.

"Hmmm… list of phone numbers, probably friends and relatives. What's next? Oh, here's a directory called Work."

Opening up the work files was a bit of a surprise. Cliff expected phone numbers not a list of names with dollar amounts and dates beside each one. Curious list. He reached for the delete button.

CHAPTER 15

312 OD—September 3—9:15 pm

"This guy's absolutely in the mob," Cliff murmured to himself. "There's just too much encrypted data here for a normal dude." He moved his finger away from the delete button. The information was too valuable to erase without seeing if someone else was interested in it.

There were also money amounts beside a lot of code names, names he didn't recognize, but which obviously belonged to old "buddies". Definitely, not a good sign.

"These have got to be bribes, maybe blackmail… something like that," he muttered aloud while advancing screens. "The amounts are too precise and even. I mean, why's there a $10,000 next to this name?"

A finger tap on the up button showed something else. "Now, these numbers are too small. Bets maybe? 5's, 10's, 25's, 50's, and 100's. This guy's obviously also a bookie." Cliff whistled softly as the information carried onto the next screen.

"Dates, times, and money. And, if I'm not mistaken…" He couldn't believe his luck. "This is a formula for calculating interest. He's a loan shark *as well* as a blackmailer and a bookie!" A sudden shiver went up his spine. "What *isn't* this guy into?"

Screen after screen of names, numbers and money amounts flashed before his eyes, while a cold sensation of dread crawled into his belly. It wasn't that he was afraid of the mob. It was more a feeling of how this had fallen into his lap. Stealing from the mob on a regular basis was what he did anyway. Whenever he got the chance to stick it to them he did. They were living large off someone else's misery and misfortune, so why shouldn't he give them grief and live off them? Cosmic karma was what he called it.

"Hey, what's this?" he marvelled when a new screen page flipped into view. "He's into money laundering too! Hmmm, looks like he's got rare gems stashed around town. Nice! I definitely need to keep track of this."

He downloaded the entire contents of the Comp-u-link into the printer's memory and hit start. A thirty-page printout promptly spewed out. A lot of it was garbled due to the encryption, but a fair portion was readable.

Grabbing the printout and putting it into a portfolio binder, Cliff put on his brown leather bomber jacket. His dark glasses were lying on the dining room table along with his white cane, but he decided not to take them with him. The blind guy persona was too noticeable, and the gangster and his associates would probably be on the lookout for it. Cliff would become someone else for now.

312 OD—September 3—10:30 pm

The guy that bumped into Cliff wasn't a pro. He was clumsy and his sloppy drunk act was a little too forced. Smiling genially at him, Cliff picked his pocket in turn. The amateur got Cliff's fake wallet that contained no money or ID. Cliff didn't care, as his money and ID were safely tucked into his sock, and he was holding the antique watch and Comp-u-link in his hands.

Shaking his head at his inept tottering down the alley, Cliff pulled the crook's wallet out of a hidden pocket and gently placed it on top of a nearby garbage can. The criminal would be back to look for it once he realized it was gone.

Cliff made a point not to steal from the poor, only from rich drug lords and their ilk. Hopefully, this would teach this doofus to pick his marks more carefully, or to learn to pick pockets more professionally. You couldn't really blame the guy. Cliff's thousand-dollar leather jacket was definitely out of place in this part of town. All his jackets had hidden pockets sewn into them because he never knew what he'd be wearing when he went out to "work." Cliff realised now that he should have worn something less conspicuous, but he wanted to get rid of this Comp-u-link and watch as soon as possible.

Suddenly, crowd noises from inside a nearby tavern drew his attention, while a neon sign of a rose and a sombrero cast colourful flickers across the mouth of the alley. The sun was setting, but here in the heart of the city, the towering buildings blotted out any sunlight much sooner, so the dark alley beckoned menacingly to passers-by.

Turning to the grimy window and peering through glass that obviously hadn't seen a cleaning cloth since it was installed, Cliff could see the start of a fight. One guy was standing between someone sitting at a table and about twenty or so muties. He didn't have a snowball's chance in hell.

But the guy obviously had some martial arts training because he took out three of them with practised ease. His frog-like leaps knocked out another bunch, and he seemed to be winning. Correction… he'd had lots of martial arts training! He was damn good. But he didn't have eyes in the back of his head. There was a guy coming at him with a bottle. Twenty-to-one odds didn't merit a cowardly attack.

Cliff's talent usually only worked when he was within ten feet of something, but amazingly the bottle vanished from the attacker's hand and created a dead weight in Cliff's hidden pocket. With shaking fingers, he pulled it out and dropped it onto the alley floor with a clunk and rattle as it rolled away.

That had to be a 'port of at least fifty feet! He'd never ever been able to teleport anything that distance before. This was too weird... but a good weird. If his talent had evolved, then he'd be able to expand his thefts. Imagine being able to 'port something from outside the house instead of having to break in and be close enough to touch it. This was too cool!

Glancing back into the building, Cliff saw the guy he had helped being overrun by the muties. *Oh well, I tried to assist him, but there's nothing else I can do for him.* Hopefully, they would only beat him up and not kill him.

It wasn't far to the garage where he kept his car, so he didn't waste any more time on this poor guy's fate. His main concern now, other than divesting himself of his ill-gotten booty, was to try out this new ability. Mentally picking up a rock, he teleported it as far away as he could to check out his new range.

Huh? What gives? It only went ten feet before it reappeared, which meant his power was back to what it had been before. *Must have been some sort of power spike.*

312 OD—September 3—9:35 pm

Frank Langelli was a man on a mission. He was standing in the East Food Court at MallWorld in the middle of a large group of other stocky men.

"It was somewhere around here that I last used my Comp-u-link. Then I noticed that it was gone by the train terminal over there." He pointed vaguely to the northwest, and as a man the group around him turned to look. "I bumped into a blind guy over there by the Oriental Food Store."

"So you want us to find this blind guy and ghost him.

"No, just find him. I need to talk to him. I tripped on something. It may have fallen ..."

The shortest member of the group inquired, "So you just want us to find the guy? You've got the finest ghost squad available to you and all you want to do is find this guy? That's a waste of our talents." He looked around for agreement.

"Yeah," another member blurted out. "Since when do we get sent out to find something? Someone... yes. To ghost him... yes."

"I don't care if it's a waste of time or talent," he scolded. "We don't need bodies floating around. We just need that Comp-u-link."

"What's so important about it?"

"The organization's database was on it," he sighed with a frown.

Two squad members whistled in amazement.

"Whose stupid idea was it to put all that info onto a Comp-u-link?" The short leader of the squad was dumbfounded.

"I was bringing it to another computer."

"We were transferring info because our snitches told us it was about to get hot around there. We had no choice but to re-locate." He avoided eye contact, trying to save tribal faith among the scum before him. "And as for more security, we didn't need any undue attention, so we went with one guy—me."

"So we're supposed to fan out and find one blind guy just so you can talk to him."

"If it fell out of my belt carrier when I bumped into him, he may have found it on the ground. The sensitive stuff is all protected, but there's enough un-encrypted stuff in it to be dangerous to us."

The short guy was shaking his head in puzzlement. "You had un-encrypted stuff on it," he mumbled. "That's not only stupid, it's idiotic!"

Frank, hearing his tone, knew he could do nothing except agree.

312 OD—September 3—3:10 pm

Thankfully, it wasn't far from Cliff's garage to MallWorld, and he'd pretty much memorized the entire route. Driving wasn't too hard, even with his limited eyesight. He just had to be attentive to motion and movement of vehicles and pedestrians, especially the all too frequent jay-walkers.

After parking his J-Cat in the MallWorld parkade off Avenue Bravo, Cliff headed up the elevator to the main floor of the mall. Mark's pawn shop wasn't far from the I-Max Experience theatre and the Oriental Main Street bazaar, so he grabbed a quick afternoon snack from one of the food boutiques.

Walking in MallWorld and watching the parade of humanity stream by was one of Cliff's favourite pastimes. He'd developed the ability to watch people without their knowing they were being watched. It was a lot easier when he was doing this from behind his dark glasses, but he could manage to do it without them. It was also his choice place to 'port small objects from the rich mob guys who frequented the mall. It was easy to spot them. They were pushier than the rest of the people. They thought themselves better than everyone else.

"You've got to take in this show, folks. The Great Marani's the best thing going on in the mall," the reedy voice pleaded. "Tell the booking agent at the Information kiosk over there that Joey sent you. He'll give you a discount for the tickets."

Cliff quickly spotted the owner of the voice. He was talking to attentive tourists, obviously too well-dressed for this level. Normals rarely came down into the mutant levels, but tourists didn't know better. Joey got a piece of the ticket price for "referring" customers to a particular booking agent. The price of the tickets they were going to buy would be slightly inflated to cover his commission plus the booking agent's cut of the tourist pie.

Maller's Pawn Shop was like many other pawn shops in that it had bars on all the windows—for obvious reasons. Antique musical instruments, such as 21st century electric guitars, hung in the front window. Mark had a soft spot for musicians. Not many pawn shops carried guitars since there was no real market for them.

The other thing that set Mark's shop apart was the large selection of garish neon signs in his front window. Mark was smart. Somehow, he'd guessed that there'd be a big demand for neon. Everyone was going retro and neon signs were about as retro as you could get. Mark was a genius. Cliff didn't know where he got his supply of signs, but he always had new novelty ones in stock. The neon bathed the front of the shop in dazzling light, and created a constant buzzing from inside the brightly-lit shop.

As he got closer to the shop, Cliff had to gingerly skirt two groups of kids. The "Furries" were composed of furred muties, while the "Colours" were teens with skin colors ranging the entire spectrum. It was clear they were up to something by the blustering and gesturing with home-made weapons. Cliff noticed that some of the furry kids were wannabes who wore their fur, while others, probably the leaders, had natural fur.

Mark's shop had the misfortune of being right at the edge of their respective territories. The bars on his windows weren't so much to protect his wares from looters, as to keep his shop from being broken into for makeshift weapons in the on-going conflict between the Furries and the Colours.

BONG!

A loud resonant gong announced his entrance into the shop. Motion sensors detected his presence, and the six video cameras all swivelled to follow his progress towards the back of the room where Mark was sitting in the cage. Most shops didn't have cages, but Mark also carried on a fair business in selling railers and foamers.

It cost him big-time for insurance and the special weapons certificate, not to mention the plasteel windows at the front of the shop. Cliff had asked him why he bothered. His answer was eloquent in its simplicity—money.

"Hi Mark," he called out when he got to the cage opening.

"Hey Cliff. How's it going?" Mark glanced away from the six video monitors and put the railer back on the rack before he looked up at his friend. "I haven't seen you in a couple of weeks. What've you been up to?"

Mark wasn't paranoid. He had the railer ready as a matter of course, having been robbed before by one of the mutant gangs that frequented the neighbourhood. The whitish scar midway between his dark brown eyes and his crew-cut light brown hair was a frequent reminder of the incident. He wasn't taking anymore chances.

"Oh… the usual, I guess. Someone gave me some stuff here that I think you might like to have. I don't need it, and I can sure use the cash."

Mark knew about Cliff's medical problems and was more than sympathetic, so he tended to turn a blind eye to all the "stuff" Cliff had been "given." Cliff figured Mark suspected he was a pick-pocket, but he'd never called him on it.

"I've got something you may be interested in." Reaching into his hidden pocket, Cliff pulled out the antique watch and handed it over.

"I don't know," Mark muttered as he examined the timepiece with the Pawn Broker's calling card—a jeweller's loupe. "It looks like a knock-off."

"A knock-off?" Cliff couldn't hide the disappointment in his voice. Counterfeit antiques were flooding the market. Only someone with a practised eye like Mark could tell the difference.

At least the guy I lifted it from also got hosed.

"Okay, then how about you give me what you can for it?"

"I guess…" he paused for a second, "since it's you, and you're my best pack rat… how about twenty?"

"Twenty?" Cliff couldn't believe his ears. "Twenty? Well I was sort of hoping I could get a lot more for it."

"How much?"

Mark almost choked when Cliff told him, "At least a grand?"

It took Mark a couple of minutes to stop laughing. When he did, he had to wipe the tears from his eyes with the florid handkerchief he always kept close by.

"A grand?" he managed to gasp, then started guffawing again.

Waving it away, Cliff told him, "Okay, okay. How about sixty?"

Still chuckling slightly, Mark responds with, "How about we split the difference and call it forty?"

Cliff hesitated for the slightest moment.

"That's more than anyone else will give you for it," Mark warned. "And I'm only doing it because you're a friend."

Knowing he'd never do better than that, Cliff quickly agreed to Mark's offer before he changed his mind.

"Got anything else? You normally don't come in with just one thing."

The fancy comp-u-link is what Cliff had hoped to get a hundred for, but now... he didn't know. A quick glance to his left showed a table of electronic equipment. There were at least twelve comp-u-links piled up there. *Mark may not be in the market for yet another one, even if it was fancy.*

"I've got a used comp-u-link," Cliff told him as he brought it out and placed it on the counter in front of him.

Mark glanced quickly at one of the two security monitors beside the cage opening. From the furrowed-brow look he gave him, Cliff guessed that he was looking at the table with the used communicators, blocked by Cliff's body.

"I'll be honest with you, Cliff," he started

off, "I've got a ton of these. There's just not that big a demand for these 2212's, ever since the new 2300's came out."

"I really need the money," Cliff pleaded with his little hurt boy tone of voice.

It didn't work.

"Look Cliff," his brown eyes were sympathetic. "To be truthful, the only good thing about this old model is the data it contained. And that's valuable only to the owner. What did you have on here?"

"Ah… you see… it's not really mine. I'm unloading it for a friend."

Mark was no fool.

"Oh, and I suppose this <u>friend</u> wiped it before he gave it to you?"

"Actually, he didn't. I erased it myself." Cliff wondered if the data could be useful after all. "I still have the information. I printed it out." Reaching into his pocket again, he pulled out the thirty-page printout from the comp-u-link.

Mark took the sheaf of paper and started flipping pages. A couple of times, his eyebrows arched upwards. Cliff had seen him do this before whenever he was interested in something. His hopes began to rise each time Mark's eyebrows shot up.

Mark started to mutter to himself and Cliff caught only the occasional word.

"Hmmm…possible…useful…garbage…okay!"

He put down the printout and looked at Cliff. His understanding eyes were now hard and calculating. "Have you looked at this stuff yet?"

"No, not really," Cliff lied. "It's just a lot of numbers and information. Not my cup of tea."

"You're right," Mark agreed. "But some of this stuff could be useful to certain people. How about you leave it with me…"

"But…" Cliff began, but Mark continued.

"…with me on consignment. I'd like to look over the information more carefully and flesh out a couple of ideas that I might be able to use someone like you for. Okay?"

"I guess so, but how much can you give me for it?"

"What I'm thinking may not pan out. If that's the case, then I'm out the money."

"Can't you give me something on account?" Cliff pleaded.

"Okay, okay. You win," he conceded. "How about I loan you the grand you wanted. If this pans out and I get what I expect, you'll get more. If it doesn't, then you'll pay me back with the next batch of stuff you bring in. Deal?"

"Deal."

"Come back tonight and we'll talk more."

312 OD—September 3—8:17 pm

Fortunately for Cliff, MallWorld was open twenty-four hours a day. Most shops stayed open as well, but a small minority, usually the mom and pop operations, closed down every night. Mark's pawn shop was one of these. As far as Cliff knew, Mark was the only employee of Maller's Pawn Shop, and he put in twelve hour days.

Mark's shop was closed when Cliff got back, but a gentle knock on the door always opened it for him. Cliff was one of Mark's favourite clients and after-hours visits were common.

"Hey, pack-rat!" a voice called out to him. "Come on into the back."

The aisles were neat and tidy even though the items on the tables were jumbled. Mark was sorting out some of the stuff on the *Breathing Aids and Cosmic Ray Shields* table.

"Hey, yourself," Cliff called back as he wound his way to Mark past the *Portable Read/ Writers* and associated books and the *Food Purificators* tables. "I wish you wouldn't call me 'Packrat`."

Being that Cliff was almost a hand taller, Mark had to look up at him and grinned mischievously as he responded with, "Sure, Packrat. Whatever you want, Packrat. Your wish, Packrat, is my command, Packrat."

Cliff knew a lost cause when he heard it, so he let the name-calling drop.

"What have you got for me?" Cliff was hoping that Mark found the stuff from the comp-u-link to be profitable enough that he didn't have to repay him the grand.

Mark smiled. "Well, now. Aren't we anxious? Keep your shorts on and help me sort some of this stuff, then we'll go into my office and talk."

It was not hard work—just mind-numbing. Cliff sorted out the small shields by model number. There were only four models and the printing was fairly big, so it wasn't too difficult. After about five minutes they were finally finished and heading past the *Comp-u-link and Data Pad* table and into Mark's office.

This was only the second time Cliff had been in there in the past three years since he first met Mark. The wall of *Personal Defence Weapons* always gave Cliff the creeps. In his younger days before his talent had developed, Cliff was on the receiving end of a couple of these weapons. Some of them hurt—real bad.

Mark motioned Cliff to sit on the edge of his desk while he plunked down onto the only chair in the tiny office. Cliff leaned back and rested against the wire mesh of the cage.

"I've got a proposition for you," he told Cliff. "If you're interested."

"Spill it."

"I did get some interesting bits of information from the papers you left. Quite a bit, actually."

Cliff's interest was piqued.

"It seems that your *friend* works for some people who are into gambling in a big way. They run quite a few gambling parlours and are definitely on the wrong side of the law, if you get what I mean?"

"I get it," Cliff replied. "So?"

"How would you like to make twenty-five grand?"

For Cliff, that was a hell-of-a-lot of money. More than enough to keep him going for a few months. "What do I have to do?"

Mark had a curious look in his eyes. Cliff had never seen that look before, and he wasn't sure what it meant.

"Okay, I'll be frank with you," he said. "I know you're a petty crook and that the stuff you bring me is hot."

Cliff's mouth barely had time to open in protest when Mark shook his head to shut him up.

"I'm guessing you're a pick-pocket because of all the small stuff you bring in."

"What if my friends only want to pawn their small stuff?" Cliff tried to protest innocence through his guilt.

"Bull feathers!" Mark's outburst stunned Cliff. He'd never been so blunt before. "It's okay. Your secret profession is safe with me."

Shrugging in surrender, Cliff says, "What's on your mind?"

"Well, it seems that this guy's comp-u-link that you boosted shows he's in charge of a good chunk of the illegal gambling in the city, if not the region. I would like to liberate him of some of his working capital."

"Sounds intriguing. What would I have to do?"

"Do you think you can make your way into a secure establishment, crack a safe, and bring back a sack full of money?"

Cliff considered the risk. "To be honest, I'm not sure. It depends on the layout of the place and if I have enough cover. I'll have to see once I get there, I guess."

"Have you ever done anything this big before?"

"Nope." Cliff didn't want to tell him the truth—that he'd broken into many a home. "You guessed right when you said pick-pocket, but I'm always willing to expand my field of expertise."

Mark pulled out a blueprint from a drawer and unrolled it across his desk. "This is a schematic of the building." He pointed to a corner of the plan. "This is where a Pharen's office is."

"I don't suppose you know exactly where his safe is, do you?"

"It's actually right about… here…" his finger tapped what should be an outside wall. The office was separated from the other outer wall by the reception area. Cliff would have easier access from the side of the building. That was good.

"…next to the reception area… on the second floor."

"Hmmm."

"What's wrong? Don't think you can do it after all?"

"No. I can do it." Cliff reassured him. "It's just the second storey makes it a little harder."

Mark drummed his fingers idly on the blueprint. "What else do you need to know?"

"Anyone working there at night?"

"They all leave by 8pm."

"How about security? Electronic or biologic?"

"All the rent-a-cops leave with the afternoon shift. You'll only have vid-cams and alarms to worry about. I suppose that won't be a problem?"

"Nope," Cliff assured him, then decided to be a little more truthful. "I've broken into the occasional home before, but not into a business. Should be just a matter of scale."

"Anything else?" he inquired.

"I'll probably do a run-through first to check out the lay of the land. You should get your money by the end of the week."

"No, whatever money you get, you keep. All I want is the papers in the safe."

Cliff's felt his jaw drop open. "Huh? Are you nuts?"

"Nope," Mark comforted him. "My contacts want information only, and they're willing to pay handsomely for it. Your cut is whatever you can get out of the safe."

Cliff's eyes widened. "What if there are jewels or something like that?"

"Take 'em if you want."

"No, no. I meant, can you fence them for me?"

Mark cocked his head to one side and merely stared at Cliff for a minute. "Yeah, sure. Why not? I'm sure I can find a buyer somewhere for them."

"Great. Then I guess I've got everything I

need. Do you have any words of advice for me?"

"Yeah. Keep your ass down and don't get caught."

CHAPTER 16

312 OD—September 4—8:13 am

The twinkling stars did little to lighten the early morning. They faded into the brightening eastern sky. Cliff liked it this way. It made it more difficult for someone to see him as he crept along the side of the building facing the alley. People tended to see figures better in the dark of night and brightness of day. The time between dark and light is a thief's best weapon.

While Cliff leaned beside the wall, the cold bricks were refreshing against his arm, as was the somewhat cool breeze that wafted across his face. The straps of his backpack chafed somewhat, so he shifted the pack as much as he could to gain some slight measure of relief.

With his limited vision, it was hard for him to see more than fifty feet in the pre-dawn's light. What he did see at that distance were darker shadows that danced madly at times.

For the hundredth time he froze in place. His eyes searched the greyness for any sign of life.

"*C'mon Cliff*," he chided himself. "*If you're going to jump at every little thing, you'll drive yourself nuts.*"

Tearing his gaze away from the shadows wasn't easy. The darkness in the alley provided him with some hiding places from the occasional nocturnal passers-by. Even with that, he tried to look as innocent and inconspicuous as he could. His white cane and dark glasses had been left at home. They would have made him much too visible, even though people tended to look away from those with disabilities. In his normal "work" this was an advantage, but now it was a definite liability.

He moved as close to the front as the shadows would allow. There was a long break in the sporadic flow of pedestrians, so Cliff scurried to the front door and leaned against it. The doorway's shadow hid most of Cliff except for his waist and legs.

Closing his eyes, he tried to get a sense of the lock. He knew there was an alarm system, but the panel, according to the schematic he studied, was more than a yard from the door, too faraway to disable first. He would have to use his talent to unlock the door, and pretending to fuss with a key in the lock, he mentally moved the pins in the tumbler and was in.

The plans told him exactly where the alarm key pad was located. He shut the door silently and hurried down the hallway. In the half minute that he had before the alarm sounded, he held his breath while silently counting down the last seconds before he easily disabled it.

"Whew!" His sigh was almost deafening in the silence of the hallway. According to the schematic, there was a laser-eye beam grid starting a few feet from the alarm box. Cliff donned a pair of omnis and turned them on. The brilliant red beams shown by the glass-like omnis criss-crossed the hall like some sort of dishevelled spider-web. The time-delay switch for the grid was at the other end of the hall. It looked a million miles away. Taking a deep breath, Cliff started inching his way through the maze. At about the half-way point, he stopped. He couldn't go any further because the grid was becoming too small for him to pass through. Thankfully, he had something in his backpack that could get him around this, but there wasn't enough room for him to manoeuvre himself to reach it. Putting his hands out in front of himself, Cliff concentrated. The apparatus appeared in his hands.

The gizmo was a complicated series of mirrors that, once unfolded, formed a 40-inch wide arch. This arch slid effortlessly across the tile floor and diverted the red lasers up and around itself. His "doorway" was complete. He crawled and, once through, he slid the gizmo towards himself and collapsed it prior to putting it back into the pack. Then, he made his way quickly to the control panel that shut off the laser grid. He recognized the model so he knew where the relays were to turn it off.

It was a lot easier being a pick-pocket, and he readily admitted that he was basically lazy. He preferred to take the easy way, if at all possible. There was just too much stress and danger for his liking in being a cat burglar. Oh, the rewards were greater, but the work was harder.

Once the grid was off, Cliff re-pocketed his omnis. The schematic told him that this was the last of the electronic stuff he needed to worry about. It was smooth sailing from then on. A quick glance to the left showed him that he was next to the employee's lounge and change area. To the right were the stairs.

Taking his time, he walked slowly up the staircase to the second floor. The lock on the door to the reception area proved to be no challenge to his talent. Rather than just move the pins in the tumbler to unlock the door, he opted to 'port the pins into a neat pile next to the door. A "normal" would have to take the lock apart in order to do that. Cliff wanted them to wonder why he went to all this trouble. Hopefully, they would think that he was leaving them a message that their security was so easy that he had time to play around. The truth was too far out there for them to believe. And, besides he wanted to show off.

The door to Pharen's office was no harder to get into. This time, he 'ported the entire door handle off and left it in a single piece by the door. That would frustrate then drive them totally crazy. This was a tactic that Adam Valor might use to confound his enemies. Adam was a fictional pocket book hero. Cliff collected the entire Adam Valor series of holo-readers and often emulated his hero.

There was the safe—right next to the door. If he would have known that, he could have gotten to the stuff inside without even opening the door. Oh well, too late now.

As he was kneeling in front of the safe, he glanced out the floor-to-ceiling window. The early morning traffic was starting to build up. Cars of every model were wending their way through the streets. The only unusual vehicle was a large van pulling a trailer advertising some mentalist, Marani somebody, next to the building trying to make a right turn without mowing down any pedestrians. That wasn't something you saw everyday in this area. The slidewalks were filling up with throngs of pedestrians on their way to work. Cliff concentrated on the safe.

When he used his talent, Cliff couldn't really "see" what was in the safe. After all, it was pitch black in there. What he did get was an impression of objects, which he could then teleport out into the open and pick and choose what he wanted to take with him.

This time he decided to do something different. While staring at the combination lock, he focused all his strength. The lock should 'port off the door totally. Instead, there was a surge of energy through him, and the entire door vanished and reappeared twelve feet away, crashing into the opposite wall of the large room.

Startled, he staggered backwards. "What the hell?"

A warning bell went off in his mind. This wasn't typical. Normally, he could move the safe's door a couple of inches at the most, but there was just no way he should've been able to move the safe door the distance he did.

Wasting no more time, he pulled out the gym bag from his back pack, and began stuffing it with the empty backpack and contents of the safe. Cliff made sure that he took all of the paperwork in the safe for Mark. The rest of the gym bag was reserved for whatever he could take for himself. But money was bulky, and he spotted stuff that was more easily portable. Scooping up the contents of an oak jeweller's box into a velvet bag took time, but it was worthwhile. Mark would give him top dollar for the gems or he'd send him to someone who could. He would still have enough room in the bag to pack in about thirty or so bundles of cash. He tried to take those with the largest denominations first.

As he left, Cliff decided to have a little bit of fun. Once he was down by the laser grid box, he used his talent to turn it back on. Now, he had twenty seconds to make it to the front door before the laser grid came on-line. He turned the door alarm back on while he was walking out the door and locking it.

He wasn't worried about the people on the slidewalk. As far as they knew, he was a night guard on his way to exercise classes after work. They had no way of knowing that he had almost a million dollars in money, gems, and information in his gym bag.

"Hey, you!" A voice called out. "What are you doing?"

The hair on the nape of his neck stood up. Turning around, he saw three guys in suits rushing towards him. One of them, a mutie, was over six-feet tall and not pleasant looking at all. Cliff didn't know if it was him that they wanted, but he wasn't taking any chances. He bolted.

312 OD—September 5—9:15 am

The roving gang of Furries passed well ahead of Cliff. With what he was carrying, he didn't want to cross paths with them. The gym bag was clutched a little closer.

MallWorld was unusually crowded today. There seemed to be some sort of activity, slidewalk concert, or sales pitch at each intersection. He knew he was imagining being watched, but still…

Mark's pawn shop never seemed so far away. Cliff breathed a deep sigh of relief when he finally spotted the garish neon signs. He would be so glad to get rid of the stuff in the bag. He was also a bit excited to see what he had managed to garner for himself.

The sweat on his brow stopped flowing like a river when he finally stepped inside the pawn shop and the door closed behind him. Wearily, he slumped against the door.

"Never again!" he told himself. "This had better be worth it."

"I hope so, too," Mark exclaimed as he reached around Cliff to lock the door. "For privacy," he winked at him.

"Thanks."

"Let's go in back to see what you have," Mark said as he rubbed his hands together in eager anticipation.

"Sure," Cliff told him as he made his way around the tables in the shop. He always wondered why Mark had the tables arranged the way he did. "Why is your shop set up like this?"

"I organized it so that if I'm robbed, they don't have an easy escape route," he told Cliff.

"Makes sense, I guess."

He opened the door to his cage and motioned Cliff into his sanctum. "Did you have any problems getting in?"

"Nope," Cliff shook his head. "Someone spotted me, probably one of Pharen's people, but I don't think they got a good enough look to be able to ID me."

"You'd better hope so." He looked around and unconsciously lowered his voice. "Pharen may not be dangerous, but he knows people who are."

The hair at the back of Cliff's neck went up.

"How d'ya know that?"

"While you were gone, I've been doing some checking up on him. He's associated with William Simmonds."

"And that name's supposed to ring a bell with me?" Cliff asked.

"Simmonds is reputed to be in charge of a kill squad."

"Oops!"

"That's right, oops. If I'd known this, I wouldn't have sent you to Pharen's at all."

"If I'd known that, I wouldn't have gone either! I wish you would've done more research." Cliff stared at his friend. "Now I've got to find someplace to lie low."

"At least until the heat dies down," he added. "If ever." Cliff looked over his shoulder and out the front window of the shop. No one seemed to be giving it too much attention.

"Don't worry. Something will come along to take their minds off of you."

"I wish." A cold shiver went up his spine.

Mark decided to liven the mood. "Let's see what you managed to acquire."

Swinging the gym bag down onto the corner of a desk, Cliff opened it and started pulling out the booty. He was surprised. He had almost thirty bundles—three thousands, five five-hundreds, and twenty hundreds. Three quarters of a million dollars in cash alone! He wouldn't need to worry about the grand that Mark had advanced him any longer.

"If this is what Pharen had in only one of

his shops, how much has he got stashed through-out his operation?"

Mark didn't answer. His attention was riveted on the papers he was flipping through. He looked like a kid at Christmas surrounded by presents.

Cliff yelled, "Mark!"

Mark jumped with a start. "What?"

"There's over a million in cash and jewels! What the hell was Pharen bank rolling?"

"I don't know, but my contacts might. How about you go and hide for a while, somewhere he can't find you?"

Cliff held up his hands in wonder as he shrugged his shoulders. "Where the hell is that supposed to be? If Pharen's men did recognize me, then my place isn't safe."

"Yeah, you're right." Mark snapped his fingers. "I know this place. It's perfect. No one will know you're there."

"And exactly where is this place?"

"It's in the MallWorld Apartment Complex. I've got a key here somewhere." Mark began to rummage in his desk. "Here it is." He gave the key to Cliff.

"I sure hope this place is as safe as you say it is."

"Don't worry. You're a special person, and I want to keep you around."

312 OD—September 5—1:10 pm

Where can I hide all this money? Cliff thought to himself. "*I can't deposit it in the*

bank. The authorities will ask too many embar-
rassing questions about where I got it from. I
guess I could put it in a safety deposit box,
but I need it close by just in case."

He scratched his head as he looked around his austere apartment. Including the gems, he calculated he had almost two million dollars in his gym bag, less the grand he still owed Mark. He smiled with the knowledge that he now had more than enough to "retire comfortably."

The trip to his place to hide the money had been nerve-wracking, more so than the original trip from Pharen's warehouse to Mark's pawn shop. Then, he hadn't known exactly how much he was carrying around so nonchalantly.

Cliff had prepared for the eventuality of having enough to retire. He had built a wall safe, hidden in the entrance closet that backed into the laundry room. He constructed a fake wall in the laundry room to hide the safe, so that the only way someone could tell it was there would be to actually measure the floor space in all the rooms. He didn't think anyone searching his place would go to that extreme.

The safe wasn't very big, but it was large enough to easily hide his newly-acquired retirement fund.

After placing the money and jewels away, he was so pumped he couldn't sit still. He decided to go to Mark's safe house. His glasses and white cane stayed on the dining room table where he had, a lifetime ago it seemed, last placed them. In order to get to the safe house he had to return to his favourite haunt—MallWorld.

312 OD—September 5—1:55 pm

The Mall was alive with bustling crowds. Cliff sighed gratefully when he finally reached the security of their anonymity.

He decided to get something to eat in order to quell his rumbling stomach. Turning towards the Atrium East Food Court, he bumped into a pedestrian. He put out his hands to brace himself and before he knew it both his wrists were handcuffed together.

"What the hell?" he called out.

"Gotcha! Ya stinking pick-pocket!" a harsh voice barked into his ear.

"I haven't done anything," Cliff protested. "I... I was...I was just bracing myself to keep from falling."

"Yeah, yeah. I've heard that one before." The mall security cop grinned at Cliff. "Now you can tell it to the cops!"

"But, I didn't do anything," protested Cliff as he was roughly hauled out of the food court.

312 OD—September 5—2:10 pm

The bench in the MallWorld police station was extremely uncomfortable, made more so by the fact that Cliff was handcuffed to it. He had to sit sort of hunched over in order to find any hope of a comfortable position.

Cliff was fuming mad. It was one thing to get nailed while "working", but to get caught while off-duty by an over-zealous cop wannabe was infuriating.

To while away the time Cliff teleported small pieces of dirt into a pile. He was building a tiny pyramid in the corner of the waiting area out-of-sight of the desk sergeant.

The noise level suddenly increased as the doors to the mall opened up. A pretty brunette sauntered into the room. Their eyes met briefly and she looked a little familiar, so he smiled pleasantly at her. She broke eye contact and continued walking towards the desk sergeant. A rush of energy filled him, just like the last time, then one of his dirt chunks flew across the room—well past his normal limit. The only other time it did this was when he was in the vicinity of that blond mentalist and her assistant, but neither was around now. He wondered what could be causing the power increase.

The door to the left of the sergeant opened and some guy came out. He looked at Cliff as if he knew him, and was searching for a name to connect with the face. Cliff recognized him as the guy in the bar that he saved from getting knocked over the head with a bottle.

The desk sergeant reached for the can of pop on his desk. Cliff grinned and concentrated. He had meant to 'port the contents of the can to the wastebasket by the lockers. This was definitely past his normal range, but easily within his increased range.

A scream of anger from outside sounded just as the desk sergeant exclaimed, "What the hell?" The sergeant shook his pop can upside-down. "I just opened this!"

Seconds later, a very splattered and irate individual stormed into the station demanding to know why someone dumped a can of pop out the window.

Somehow Cliff had managed to teleport the contents of the can through the wall! That was something he'd never been able to do before, not even when his power increased the last time. There was something strange going on—he just wished that he knew what the hell it was. *Maybe the guy I saved from the bottle in the bar fight had something to do with these power spikes. He had been around a couple of times when this happened.*

The guy that had come out of the back office tossed his visitor's badge onto the sergeant's desk, then, while staring at the brunette, jammed his hand onto the mall doors.

"Dick," Cliff muttered under his breath, wondering if saving this guy's bacon at the bar was worth it after all.

The brunette walked into the back just as the mall cop walked out of the other door with a "real" cop in tow.

"I tell you, he's a pick-pocket," he was exclaiming.

"And I tell you, unless he has someone else's wallet in his possession, you can't arrest him."

"But… but…"

"No buts about it," the cop pointed a finger at Cliff. "Let him go, and you better hope he doesn't decide to press charges against you for false arrest."

Cliff couldn't hear the words that his arrester was muttering as he trudged angrily towards him while digging for a key in his pants pocket, but he could imagine what they were.

CHAPTER 17

312 OD—September 7—8:00 am

"You didn't catch him?" Frank thumped his fist against the wall in frustration.

"Sorry, Frank." Block spoke so fast that his words blurred together. "By-the-time-we-started-chasing-him-he'd-blended-into- the-crowd." He paused for a second to catch a breath. "You'd-be- surprised-at-how-many-people-carry-gym-bags-at-that-time-of-the- morning."

Frank looked down the street hoping to catch sight of the thief. He shook his head and muttered, "It couldn't be him. He was blind. This guy isn't."

"We should look… in the warehouse… and check it… out." Troll's speech pattern was the exact opposite of Block's—slow and methodical.

"Yeah," Frank agreed. "The boss ain't gonna be happy about this. Let's see what the damage is."

Frank opened the door and walked slowly in.

By the time he got to the laser alarm grid, the alarms went off.

"Damn it to hell!" He yelled as he punched in the abort code on the alarm panel. "The son-of-a-bitch reset the alarms!"

Frank grinned to himself when Troll and Block looked at each other. Both with disbelief etched on their faces. Their twin expressions were almost comical.

"If he had time to do this," Frank told them, "then how much time did he have to work in here?"

"I dunno…" Troll began to answer but stopped when Frank held up his hand.

"Better check upstairs," Frank exclaimed. "Let's hope he didn't hit the office."

He ran up the stairs two steps at a time. Block was right at his heels, but Troll followed at a much slower pace.

When Frank got to the reception door, the first thing he noticed was the neat row of pins from the door lock. He'd seen a locksmith at work once so he knew exactly what they were. He yanked the door open and rushed in, but stopped dead in his tracks when he saw the door knob to the boss's office laying beside the door.

He walked slowly over and picked it up—gingerly. He turned it over and over in his hands for a moment to examine it more closely. Except for some wearing of the knobs from many hands turning them over the years, it looked like a brand new lockset just out of the package from the store.

"Impossible," he murmured under his breath. He glanced at Troll and Block and said, "This guy had enough time to take this apart and put it back together. He wasted even more time on the reception room door. He took the pins out of that one."

"Let's see what he did in the office." Frank shuddered as a cold prickly feeling crept up his spine.

They slowly walked into the office. The first thing they noticed was the safe door lying near the far office wall.

"He-blew-the-safe!" Block blurted out as he hurried to the safe door.

Frank was more concerned with the contents. "Damn," he shouted. He cleaned it out!"

"Frank," Block had rushed back and was tugging at Frank's sleeve for attention. "You-gotta-see-this!"

"What!" Frank shouted impatiently.

"The-safe-wasn't-blown!" Block's fast speech seemed even faster than normal. "There's-no-blast-marks-on-the-door."

Troll spoke up. "Maybe...he opened... the safe... and took... the door... off... and moved it... by the wall."

"I don't see it," Frank broke in while he scratched a spot on his head. "Why would he go to all that trouble again? If the safe is opened, then the door would swing out of his way."

Troll pointed up to the far corner of the room and piped up with, "Well... at least... we got him... on video." The camera was aimed directly at the safe.

"Let's hope he didn't cut the feed to that, too."

312 OD—September 7—8:30 am

Kevin Pharen screamed. "He got away with everything?"

"Yeah," Frank replied apologetically.

"Who is this guy?" Pharen stood up and began pacing back and forth behind his desk.

"We only got a glimpse of him as he was leaving. It was weird though." Pharen could tell by Frank's tone that he was more than a little confused.

"Weird?" Pharen stopped pacing for a moment then continued.

"Well, remember when I told you I lost my comp-u-link at the mall?" Frank's bravery appeared to come back.

"Yeah, what about it?"

"This blind guy caught me as I fell." Frank paused, sure that what he was going to say would sound crazy.

"Go on," Pharen urged.

"This-thief-looked-a-lot-like-the-blind-guy," Frank stated Block-style.

Pharen stopped pacing once again, put his hands on the desk and leaned across it as he glared at Frank. "Did we get him on the security camera in my office?"

"Yep," Frank smiled for a second then frowned.

"Well, at least I hope so. Billy's going over the tape right now. He should have a picture for us pretty soon."

Pharen could see Frank's anxiety lessen when Billy, the resident chauffeur and IT guy, came rushing in with a handful of pictures.

"Here you go, Frank. The best one is on top." Billy passed the pile of pictures to R.J.

After examining them, Frank stated, "He definitely looks like the blind guy."

"Then your comp-u-link was stolen using the oldest trick in the book. He just pretended to be blind."

"But he *was* blind!" Frank protested. "I've seen plenty of blind people walk and he used his cane exactly like they do. He even held his head like a blind guy."

Pharen sat down heavily in his chair and leaned back until the front wheels threatened to lift off the floor. He stared at Frank for a full minute before he finally asked, "Held his head like a blind guy?"

"Yeah, not looking directly at you. Head cocked slightly to one side, you know, to hear what you're saying rather than seeing your lips move. Like that."

"And you're the only mook who knows how a blind guy acts? Dumbass!" Pharen leaned forward and put his elbows and arms on the desk. "Either way, his base of operations is probably the mall, so you gotta go there to try and find him again. He got over two million in cash and jewels that don't belong to me, and I want it back!"

312 OD—September 7—11:30 am

The stationary knot of men at the mall formed a solid barrier to the moving mass of humanity comprised of mall shoppers and the occasional tourist.

Frank gestured for the men to move closer. He handed them all copies of the best picture they had of the thief.

"This is the guy. Now, he may be pretending to be blind, so also look for someone with a white cane and dark glasses, the whole bit."

The group silently split up. Frank had only been able to round up four men from Pharen's operations, so he had to "borrow" the other six from Simmonds. He was a little leery of them. After all, they were members of a ghosting squad, and he didn't know if they'd be able to forego their training and bring in the blind guy alive.

"Remember guys, we need him breathing and able to talk—at least until we have our hands on what he took from us. Then you can use him as target practice."

312 OD—September 7—1:30 pm

After two hours of fruitless searching, Frank had almost given up on the hope of ever finding the blind thief. It felt like he'd talked to everyone in the entire mall. Just as he was about to call it quits, he spotted a couple of undercover cops he'd dealt with on numerous occasions. He'd fenced some "evidence" for them that had never made it into the police report. Pharen owned them.

"Hey guys!" he called out.

"Hi Frank," the shorter one greeted him with a hearty handshake. "How's it going?"

"Not bad. Is this your beat today?"

"Yeah, we've got this end of the mall. Why?"

"I'm looking for someone who…" he paused for a second in deliberation. He didn't want to tell them about the robbery. "… may know where my comp-u-link is. I lost it here four days ago when I bumped into a blind guy."

"A blind guy, huh?" the taller cop grinned to his partner. "We know a guy who pretends to be blind and works the mall."

"Works the mall?"

"Yeah," shorty answered. "He's a pickpocket. He tried telling us he'd lost more of his sight and had given up the business. We didn't believe him, but before we could arrest him, some high-priced lawyer stepped in and stopped us."

"You want to talk to this guy?" the taller cop piped up.

"Yeah," Frank smiled, knowing he was close to getting his hands on the thief. "What's his name?"

"The mook's Cliff Bowen. He lives just a little ways away from here at the Waterfront Apartments on twenty-fifth street and fifty-second avenue. We'll help you find him, if you want," the shorter one offered.

"No. It's okay." Frank didn't want any witnesses to his meeting with this Cliff character. "I just need to roust him a bit and find my comp-u-link. I think I can manage on my own." He didn't want to mention the ten men he had at his disposal to extract information from this Cliff.

"Thanks," he told them as he turned away.

312 OD—September 7—9:30 am

No sooner had Cliff gone than Mark ran to the front door. For the first time since he'd opened it, he closed his shop for the day. It felt odd locking the door and putting up the closed sign, but he had no choice.

What he needed to do had to be done in the strictest of privacy. He moved quickly to his office and pulled out a second, hidden uplink from within his cavernous desk. This up-link was not on the books.

He punched in a secure twenty-digit number and waited. There was no ring tone only silence. After about a minute he heard a series of clicks that sounded like relays being tripped.

A harsh voice barked out, "Speak."

"Mark here," was the equally terse response.

"Stand by for the Ops Chief."

Mark waited another minute before a bass voice came on and asked, "Maller?"

"Yep. I've got a bit of a problem."

"You don't say," the voice snickered. "If what you told us on your last call is true, we may have Pharen's ass."

"It's better than I first reported," Mark gulped, unsure of exactly how to start this. "My operative managed to get a lot more intel from the safe than I imagined. Pharen's a meticulous records-keeper. I've got enough here to blow not only Pharen but Simmonds and possibly even Paggett out of business."

A whistle of appreciation blasted over the up-link line.

"No kidding?" the deep voice asked.

"Chief, I kid you not. Cliff managed to stumble onto a goldmine." Mark couldn't keep the tone of pride out of his voice.

"Is the chain of evidence unbroken?" Mark's boss demanded.

"As far as I can tell, it isn't." Mark looked over at the pile of incriminating papers.

There was a half-minute of silence as the chief digested Mark's response.

"How about Bowen?"

"What about him?"

"Is he secure?"

Beads of sweat peppered Mark's brow. "No, why?"

"He's the key. We have to be able to show where we got the intel on these three."

"I sent him to a safe house of mine. He should be secure there."

"Not safe enough!" the bass voice boomed out.

"How so?"

"We need him in protective custody, but I

can't spare the men to baby-sit him."

"What can I do?" Mark asked, his voice stressing the "I". "I'm out here by myself."

"Get him picked up by the police," the chief demanded.

"The cops?" Mark was aghast. "They can't protect him as well as we can."

"They can if you tell the Chief of Police what's happening. He can arrange for Bowen to get lost in the system. No one will know where he is."

"But…"

"But nothing. We need Bowen alive and safe. Do it!"

There was an abrupt click as the chief disconnected.

"I'm sorry, Cliff," Mark muttered to himself as he put the illegal up-link away.

312 OD—September 7—2:20 pm

When he'd called the safe house an hour ago, Mark hadn't reached Cliff. He decided to go to the apartment because Cliff had no home comp-u-link. He needed to be put into protective custody as soon as possible.

Mark's car sped along towards Cliff's place.

"Bowen," he wondered aloud, "Where the hell are you?"

He pulled to a stop at Cliff's apartment and parked behind a large black sedan. As he was reaching for his door handle, out of the corner of his eye, he caught sight of someone he recognised.

"R.J.," he muttered under his breath.

Not only R.J., but also a large group of burly individuals trouping along with him like a flock of baby ducks following their mother.

A shiver went up his spine. Mark slunk down in his seat trying to make himself as small as humanly possible.

"Damn," he swore. "If R.J.'s here, then he already knows about Cliff."

Mark searched the group for any sign of Cliff.

"Good. They haven't gotten him—yet."

The group piled into the dark sedan as well as one ahead of it. Both vehicles accelerated away.

Mark waited for them to get out of sight before he dared to step onto the pavement, and look up towards the third storey of the walk-up building.

Taking them two steps at a time, Mark ran up the stairs. Though he'd never been to Cliff's apartment, he knew where it was because of all the pawn receipts he'd written up over the years. He rushed to the door and wasn't surprised to see it hanging askew. He didn't have to see the large footprint on the door to guess that one of R.J.'s men had applied his foot judiciously near the door knob.

The apartment was a shambles. No piece of furniture was left whole. Cushions were torn inside out. All the drawers had been opened and dumped into messy piles around the room.

The closet was empty, and the shelves taken down.

From their frowns, Mark deduced that they hadn't found what they were looking for. He also guessed that the rest of the apartment looked like the entrance-way and living room—a mess.

"I've gotta get Cliff," Mark promised himself. "Maybe he finally made it to the safe house.

312 OD—September 7—1:30 pm

"There's nothing in here Frank," yelled one of the members of the ghost squad.

"Yeah," a voice called out from the bedroom. "I got more money in my ashtray."

"Where else," Frank muttered to himself, "could he have hidden it?"

Ghost squad member, Jimmy, overheard Frank's muttering and butted in with, "Maybe he's still got it with him?"

"I doubt that very much," Frank told him. "There's no way he's gonna walk around with almost a mill in his pockets."

Jimmy gestured around at the men still open-ing drawers and spilling the contents into large piles in the centre of the room and ex-claimed, "Well, it sure as hell isn't here!"

"I know," Frank admitted, "and neither is this Cliff character."

"What are we gonna do now?" asked Jimmy as the last drawer was pulled out. The man tore it apart with his bare hands and let the pieces drift to the floor.

Frank looked around at the chaos left behind by the search and shrugged his shoulders. "We're gonna go back to the mall and continue searching for him."

As they started to leave, Jimmy stopped them and turned to R.J. to ask in a low voice, "Are we gonna leave someone here just in case he comes back?"

Frank shook his head. "No. We need every-one looking for him. We can't afford to leave anyone behind on the off chance that he comes back here."

As he was walking out, Frank stepped on a pair of dark glasses. By the time the last member of his team had left there was noth-ing left of the glasses but shards of black plastic.

Frank trudged angrily towards the black sedan. Angry at not finding anything from the safe, angry at not finding Cliff, and especially angry at not finding his comp-u-link. He was so blinded by his anger that he never noticed the car that had pulled over and parked a hundred feet down the road.

312 OD—September 7—3:00 pm

For being mid-afternoon, the MallWorld Apartment Complex was surprisingly quiet. Only a few people milled about in the lobby, each lost in their own world and not paying any at-tention to anyone else.

Mark walked quickly across the lobby and entered the elevator. He punched the button for the fifteenth floor and impatiently waited through the voyage.

"Bowen," he muttered to himself, "you had better be here, or else…"

The threat was left unuttered as the door opened.

Mark exited the elevator and walked quickly down the brightly-lit hall to the safe room. He pulled out a key and inserted it in the lock. He paused. Then he decided to knock first.

He heard some furtive movement from inside followed by a period of silence.

"Whew!" It looked like Cliff was here after all. Mark turned the key and opened the door.

He caught a glimpse of something out of the corner of his eye and ducked.

The lamp whistled by his ear—a clean miss.

"Cliff!" he yelled out. "It's me, dammit!"

"Sorry about that," Cliff peeked from around the door. "I wasn't sure who it was."

"That was a stupid thing to try. What if it had been Pharen's men? The rest of them would have beaten the crap out of you."

"Yeah," Cliff agreed. "But I would have gotten one of them anyway."

"Irregardless, don't do that again."

"Okay," Cliff consented. "What's happening? Have they discovered who I am?"

"Unfortunately, yes. I just left your place and there's not much left there for you except the cleaning up."

"What did they find?" The worry was evident in Cliff's tone.

"I didn't stop them to ask," Mark replied. "They didn't look happy when they left, so I assume they didn't find anything."

"Good," Cliff smiled. "Then that means they didn't find the safe."

"That's a relief for you anyway. What are you going to do now other than stay hidden here?"

"Wait them out, I guess," Cliff answered plunking himself down on the sofa.

Mark walked over towards the kitchenette. "I'm going to get something to drink. Want anything?"

"Nah! I'm good, unless you've got something for my nerves?" Cliff called back over his shoulder.

Mark paused when he got to the kitchenette and looked around. He reached into his pocket and pulled out some papers. The fridge was the obvious place. He grabbed a bottle of Grample's, stuffed the papers into the cheese bin then closed the fridge.

"Now that I know you're safe," he told Cliff, "I'm going to go back to the shop and take those files you took from Pharen's safe to my contact. The sooner I'm rid of them the better I'll feel."

"How long do I have to stay here?"

"Until the heat's off and he stops looking for you."

Cliff jumped to his feet and swore, "Damn! Pharen's got a long memory. I could be here forever!"

"Nah," Mark reassured him. "I think my contact has plans for Pharen's organization, and the files you got for me will give him enough ammunition to keep Pharen busy for a long, long time."

The last thing Mark heard as he left the apartment was Cliff plopping himself back down on the sofa.

312 OD—September 7—4:30 pm

Frank's voice trembled slightly as he explained, "No, we didn't find anything from the safe, sir."

Kevin Pharen didn't have the same explosive temper of Jonny Paggett or William Simmonds. His was more of a smouldering kind. He never exploded. The angrier he got the quieter he became.

His voice had now become so soft that Frank could barely make it out. "I want him found. I want my property found. Use as many men as you can. Blanket the mall. Make sure that no one…" he paused for a second, "…I repeat, no one lets him slip through their fingers. Have you got that?"

Before Frank could say more than "Yes, sir," and tell him that he had already called in reinforcements, the up-link clicked off. Frank had been straining his hearing so much to hear his boss' quiet tones that the click sounded almost deafening.

He looked around at the small group of men around him, then handed one of the pictures of Cliff to Jimmy.

"Take this to the nearest copy shop and get a hundred more printed as fast as you can. We've got lots of help on the way. We're going to find this character or our asses will be handed back to us."

As Jimmy sped off, Frank noted a group of about twenty men, pushing their way through the throng of people, heading directly towards him.

312 OD—September 7—5:00 pm

"Why do you want more men?" asked Simmonds.

Kevin Pharen's voice dropped to a whisper, "Because the son-of-a-bitch that broke into my warehouse got everything from the safe."

Simmonds knew that Pharen was livid with anger. He'd heard this tone before.

"I've got men combing the mall for him now," Pharen continued, "but it's a big place, and I need more manpower than I have at my disposal."

"No problem. I can lend you a hand, but it will cost you a future favour."

"I don't think so," Pharen told him.

Simmonds was aghast. "You know how it works—a favour for a favour."

"You have a vested interest in finding this guy too," Pharen explained. "When I said he got everything from the safe, I meant *everything*."

A blank stare forced Pharen to admit more.

"My ledgers have detailed records of all of our transactions." Pharen stressed the last part, "Every one of them."

"You keep track of everything?" Simmonds sounded outraged.

"Yep. It's in my nature to be precise, and I keep all the records from our meetings with the boss. If he ever needs them, I want them to be complete and precise."

William thought for a few seconds before relenting, "Okay. In that case, you can have all of my available men at your disposal. Should be around 60 or 70. I'll send word down the network and free them up for you."

312 OD—September 7—5:00pm

Cliff was tired from his experiences over the past few days. He had experimented with his powers and found out why or at least how they increased. For some reason whenever he was around that blond mentalist from the Centre Stage Club his powers jumped.

When he was picking pockets at the Centre Stage Club four days ago he'd found that he could pick someone's pockets from more than a three feet away—actually from more than fifteen away. He'd been so sure it was the mentalist or her assistant, that he'd followed them the next day and broken onto the property of where they had been doing their act. He'd watched the mentalist through the window when she broke into the safe and he'd moved a couple of boulders—only a couple of inches, but they had definitely moved. It was an exhilarating experience but also a tiring one.

His brief stay at the MallWorld Police Station tired him out even more, especially when he'd recognized her there. His power had unexpectedly advanced even more when he 'ported the pop can contents through a wall, then they returned to normal just before he was released from custody. After the mentalist left, he had tried to teleport one of the pop cans that had been lying next to the waste basket but had no success. It had moved less than a few feet. The only after-effects he retained from his brief power spurt were a nagging headache and an overall feeling of tiredness.

Even though it wasn't yet supper time, he decided to have a bit of a nap. Maybe this would help with the headache.

———·◆·———

It seemed that he had just hit the couch when a loud noise startled him awake.

A haze of interrupted sleep hung over his head. He tried to jump up off the sofa, but a pair of large, heavily gloved hands had pinned his torso to the dusty futon.

"What the…" he yelped out as one shadowy form after another passed in his field of vision. The only light in the room came from the high-powered lights attached to their helmets and railers. The glare assaulted his eyes, and he flinched as much as the hands on his shoulders would permit, each time one of their beams speared through his eyes into his brain.

Shoved onto his side, his arms were twisted behind his back, and his hands manacled. He tried concentrating enough to 'port the hand-cuffs off his wrists, but each time he thought he had sufficient focus another beam struck his face and his concentration lapsed.

"Found it!" a voice yelled from the kitchenette.

"Found what?" Cliff asked struggling to right himself.

"Shut up ass-wipe!" His guard pushed him back down into the couch. One of the lights came from the kitchenette, and he could see a sheaf of papers outlined in the light.

Cliff finally managed to focus enough to tele-port the handcuffs off his wrists. He twisted his body to free it from the iron grasp on his shoulders. The open door beckoned to him. He tried to jump up off the couch but was too off-balance. One of the shadowy figures stepped forward and punched him in the stomach.

As the wind left his body he folded in half, dropping unceremoniously back onto the sofa—gasping for breath.

"Don't…" a very menacing voice warned, "…ever do that again."

A voice from behind him began droning, "You are under arrest. You have the right to remain silent. You have the …"

Cliff tuned out the droning voice.

Cops, he thought. *Thank God they're cops and not Pharen's goons.*

With cops he had a chance—a slight chance—of getting out of this alive. Pharen's men would have killed him.

BOOK Four—The Confrontation

CHAPTER 18

312 OD—September 7—8:05am

One side of the long cement-walled hallway was lined with small narrow metal doors placed a yard or so apart. Paggett walked quickly to door number seven. He wanted to get this over with as soon as possible, because he didn't feel comfortable being in the Remand Centre to visit Lori.

He opened the designated entry and sat down on the small seat. He leaned his elbows on the narrow counter and picked up the telephone. Lori was waiting for him.

"Hi sis," he began. "How are things going?"

There was no one else on her side of the room.

"Fine, I guess." She motioned around her. "It would be better if I had company, but I'm being kept apart from the general population for my own safety."

"Why?"

"Some silly rumour got started that I was marked by deSalle's people."

"As long as you're safe, I don't care," Paggett reassured his sister. "I wanted to go over what happened at the warehouse again." He pitied her tired demeanour, her blonde hair haphazardly bunched into a ponytail.

"How come? I've told you everything already."

Paggett shrugged. "I know you did, but I have an important meeting with the boss today, and I want to be sure about everything you told me." She stared at his worried expression and sighed.

"The only thing I can add is that I'm sure this guy had eyes in the back of his head or something. He knew exactly where the boys were at all times and was able to elude them with ease. It was like the guys were calling out where they were. It was spooky."

"And you never got a good look at his face?" Paggett inquired hopefully.

"No. He was too far away. I could tell it was rounded and that he didn't have a beard or moustache, but that's it. If I saw him from that distance again I *might* be able to recognize him, but if he were standing next to you, I'd be hard pressed to tell you apart, other than by height."

"I wish there was something else I could bring to the meeting," Paggett sighed wistfully.

"If I knew more I'd tell you."

"Changing the subject," Paggett looked deeply

into his sister's eye. "Why on earth did you give yourself up to the cops, Lori? I could have protected you."

"It was just a matter of time before de-Salle's people found me. As it was, when I was caught, one of deSalle's people was nearby. If it weren't for being in protection mode here I'd probably be dead. DeSalle has a lot of workers in here, and they'd love nothing better than to get their hands on me."

"You just be careful," Paggett warned her. "I'm working on getting you sprung. Keep your head down. DeSalle's people are chasing shadows looking for their murderer."

"Make it quick, Jonny" Lori begged. "I'm starting to go loony being cooped up in here."

312 OD—September 7—10:10am

The house was palatial. It had twenty bedrooms and two fully functional kitchens. It was, in terms the young used, a trillion dollar crib.

The manor's owner, James MacDonald, was indeed a stock market trillionaire. That was his legitimate fortune. He had amassed another wealth, equal to his first, illegitimately, as over-lord of the city's major crime families.

MacDonald wasn't a striking individual—average looking for a nearly sixty-year old. His greying hair was close cropped and gave him the appearance of a patriarch of some rich, reputable city law firm. In reality, this was a role he enjoyed even though it was the furthest from the truth. He actually cultivated this "look", and he could blend into any downtown crowd with practised ease. After all, he was a business-man and a very successful one at that.

His money came from investing in market changes. He would buy shares say in a copper mill just before its board of directors decided to go public, and the shares he purchased would increase dramatically in value. Then it would be time to sell. Many other investors had made fortunes by "riding his coat-tails" and buying what he bought. They didn't make as much as he did because he spear-headed the frenzy of the moment.

He was also a substantial investor in MallWorld. This brought him respectability and a good monthly income—enough to keep him in expensive suits. His favourite office was the one in the Admin Building of MallWorld. He had a prestigious 12th floor suite of offices which he normally used for his regularly scheduled meetings with his underlings. Today's meeting was an unscheduled one. Being precise and living according to a schedule made it unpleasant.

This morning, he looked across the table at his three subordinates. He wasn't a happy man.

"Our bottom line is in the toilet," he yelled at them. "Tell me what's going on; why each of your operations is so shoddy that it's affecting the rest of the business?"

He paced up and down at the head of the con-
ference room table and stared at each of the
men fidgeting under his penetrating glare.

Jonny Paggett looked over at William Simmonds
and Kevin Pharen, and opted to go first.

"I had a minor setback," he began while brandishing his ever-present cigar like a dagger.
"A couple of my paid-off people got made and
are being watched by the cops. I can't operate
successfully without their protection. As well,
two of my call girl operations were busted
and…"

He paused and tapped the ash off his cigar
as his right hand reached up to his ear and
tapped his up-link.

"I told you that I had a meeting this morning and wasn't to be disturbed," he yelled into
thin air, then stopped to listen for a moment.
His face went white.

"What?" he blurted out.

Another pause.

He snarled, "Keep me informed." He tapped
the up-link again and stared at the cigar in
his hand.

Paggett grumbled and put out the cigar. Then
he looked up at his boss.

"What was that all about?" MacDonald asked
while glowering at his underlings.

"Make that three of my call-girl operations
shut down by the cops. I told you, I had no
protection," he moaned in lament.

"That alone shouldn't affect our bottom-line
to this extent," MacDonald shook his head.

"What is going on?"

"I don't know," Paggett shrugged. "It's like the cops know what I'm doing before I do it!"

"How? You got a rat, maybe?"

Paggett cowered as he leaned back in his chair.

"Has anything else happened recently?" McDonald grilled.

"Well… yeah…," Paggett's face lit up a little. "We had a burglary a few days ago."

"You were robbed?" both Pharen and Simmonds piped up at the same time.

"Yeah," Paggett told them before he looked back at MacDonald. "Maybe that had something to do with it?"

MacDonald sat down in his leather chair at the head of the table. "Tell me about it."

"Some guy broke into my warehouse and got away with a lot of sensitive papers right under the noses of my men."

"How?" Pharen asked.

"They had him cornered a few times, but he kept slipping away. My sister watched the whole thing from a balcony on the second floor. One of my men would be on the crook's right and another on his left. The thief would be heading directly towards the third man then he'd stop and turn around to keep from getting caught."

"He heard them," MacDonald offered.

"No," Paggett shook his head briskly. "My men and my sister all swear that they were quiet and actually weren't moving a couple of times that the thief did this double-back routine.

286

There was no way he could have heard them. He just seemed to know they were there."

"That's ridiculous," MacDonald said.

"Yeah," Paggett agreed. "She said it was the weirdest thing she'd ever seen in her life."

"Weird is right," MacDonald muttered.

Simmonds obviously heard this mutter and spoke up, "If you think that's weird, I've got one even better than that."

"Go on," MacDonald told him.

"Have you ever heard of the Great Marani?" Simmonds asked.

"Yeah. I caught her show the other night," MacDonald said. "She's good… damn good."

"Good… yeah and also a thief," Simmonds snarled.

MacDonald leaned forward in his chair and put his arms on the table, "What do you mean?"

"Yes. We caught her act for the first time four days ago," Simmonds said.

"First time?" MacDonald was curious as to why he'd go a second time.

"She came and did a private show at my place for my birthday."

"That's right," MacDonald leaned back in his chair. "Your birthday was a couple of days ago wasn't it?"

"Yeah, anyway, she showed up with her entire troupe, and they did their show." He looked directly at MacDonald and told him, "After I finished talking to you, I was heading back to my seat to finish watching the show. I heard a noise from my office. When I looked in, all that

I saw was a bird sitting on the window sill. For some reason I opened the safe, and before you ask, I have no idea why I opened it."

MacDonald nodded. He remembered the call. He had wanted Simmonds to get something on Judge Knoll and District Attorney Eduardo. He recalled that Simmonds called both of them saints and that he would find or make up something to implicate the two.

"The damn fool bird got spooked somehow and flew around my head," Simmonds explained. "I have no clue as to why it flew into the open safe, but it did. That set off the alarms."

"It actually flew _into_ your safe? No way!" Paggett's voice showed disbelief.

"I ain't no liar."

"So why's she a thief?" MacDonald asked.

"Well, after they left, I had one of my men follow them while I checked our security tapes. Damn, there I was walking into my office and I came face-to-face with her!"

"You said there was no one except the bird in your office," MacDonald leaned forward in his chair.

"There wasn't, except the tape showed her and I there. I swear, boss, I don't remember seeing her at all!" The tone of his voice desperately wanted them to believe him, even though he didn't believe it himself. "I can't explain why I didn't see her. The tape showed her reaching into the safe and pulling out some papers, and that's when the alarms went off."

"So it wasn't the bird then?" MacDonald spread

his hands out and shrugged.

"No, it was her. The tape shows her heading out the door. One of my lieutenants popped his head in to see what was happening, and he claims he didn't see her in the hallway or my office either."

"So now two of you didn't see her," MacDonald shook his head in bewilderment and gave a sarcastic sneer.

"The only reason I know she took the papers is because I had someone go through the safe with me and call out what they saw. Even then, I'd swear that nothing's missing from the safe. It's like I see it there, but it isn't there." Simmonds couldn't keep the tone of exasperation out of his voice.

"All the next day, I had my men following her and her people everywhere they went. Some of the guys even managed to frisk a couple of them but found no suspicious packages. They followed her to the MallWorld Police Station and think she passed on the folder to someone there. I guess that might be why a couple, uh three, of my operations have been compromised."

"If she passed on your ledger, then you're screwed, you idiot!" MacDonald scolded.

"One of my safes was compromised as well," Pharen grudgingly broke in.

"By her?" Simmonds glared.

"Not sure," Pharen shook his head. "It happened overnight."

"Which safe?" MacDonald stood up and began pacing as he asked the question.

"At my downtown warehouse." He wasn't as mad as he'd expected.

"You had tons of security on that safe." MacDonald stopped pacing and stared at Pharen. "You told me it was one of your more secure locations."

"I know," Pharen nodded in agreement. "Damn if I know how he was able to pick the front door lock and disable the alarm. Then he got past the laser security grid, and here's where it gets really weird."

"Not again!" MacDonald exclaimed.

"Yeah," Pharen continued. "He *took apart* the lock and *removed* the lock pins from the door to the reception area! Then he took the door knob right off of my office door! And he had the gall to put them back together and place them neatly on the floor beside the doors! It's all on tape."

"How long do you figure it would take them to do something like that?" MacDonald asked, resuming his pacing.

"I don't know, at least ten minutes, but that's not the weird part."

"Huh?"

"The crook took the door completely off the safe and put it on the other side of the room."

Paggett whistled in appreciation of the strength and time it would take to do something like that.

Pharen continued. "The crook cleaned out the safe and took everything including the notes of our last meeting."

"Our notes?" MacDonald gaped at Pharen.

"Yeah, but there's no way anyone's going to decipher them." He didn't like their stares. "I made sure to code them before I put the notes to paper. I'm more concerned with the information that wasn't coded—stuff like payment schedules for the protection end of the business, and loan information aren't coded."

"Why didn't you code that, too?" Paggett piped up.

"Because," Pharen snarled. "I didn't expect it to get boosted, that's why."

"Enough!" MacDonald barked out and the ensuing argument stopped.

"He took everything from the safe," Pharen shot a glance at Paggett then continued, "I figure he got away with almost two million in cash and jewels."

"Two million!" MacDonald sat down heavily in his chair. "Why so much?"

"He couldn't have hit us at a worse night. I normally don't keep that much there, but that day was busier than normal, and we couldn't get everything put away in time... and we weren't expectin' trouble."

"When did you find out you'd been robbed?" MacDonald sighed.

"My men spotted him as he left. The guy had the balls to re-arm the security system so that it went off when my men walked into the place. We've got a lead on him, boss, and my men are on it, don't worry."

He pitied their childish bravado.

"It looks like you've all had the same sort of problem," stating the obvious. "You should know better than to keep hard copy files in safes. From now on, you keep everything encrypted on your computer or I'll find replacements who can."

"What do we do about the creeps that robbed us?" Paggett asked while fussing with his cigar and trying to relight it.

"So far as we know, there are three different individuals." MacDonald paused while re-arranging himself in his leather chair. "The one that hit Paggett has some sort of sixth sense that warns him when he's in danger. The one that hit Simmonds has the ability to mess with your mind. Hmm. And the one that got to Pharen is a master locksmith and practical joker. The second one is the most dangerous one of the lot. Psychic talent like that can do a hell-of-a lot of damage."

He paused again and placed his elbows on the table. With steepled hands he sat in silence gathering his thoughts. Of the three thieves, he was most worried about the psychic.

His legitimate business was built on his stock market dealings. The one thing that no one knew, or could ever know, was his ability to influence the minds of others as well. He found that he couldn't affect individuals, only large groups of people, like the twenty million dollar windfall he made by "suggesting" to the Cooper Brothers Steel Mill board of directors that they should accept the merger proposal of their rivals, the Amalgamated Steel Works Company. He had made sure to purchase as many shares as he could of their company before the merger. Once it was announced, the price of his shares more than doubled.

"We have to neutralize these three inconveniences," he told his subordinates.

"How?" Paggett blurted out.

"Simmonds is in the ghosting business, so I suggest we use his men."

Simmonds sat forward in his chair. It was easy to see that he wasn't pleased with this idea. "My men know exactly who did this, and we're going to deal with *her* ourselves. Why should I use my people to help Paggett and Pharen? What's in it for me?"

MacDonald told him, "The satisfaction of knowing you've helped the community, should be enough."

Simmonds shook his head. "I don't think so!"

MacDonald leaned as far forward as he could to get closer to Simmonds and, with emphasis on certain words, told him, "Then I suggest the *knowledge* that you've helped *me* in this matter should be *more* than sufficient to *hire* your men."

No one in the room spoke. Paggett and Pharen were both staring at Simmonds who, in turn, was locked in a staring contest with MacDonald.

"I suggest," MacDonald began, "that we concentrate on capturing our three friends, and find out how much they know before we ghost them."

Simmonds was the first to break. He looked away from MacDonald in resignation.

CHAPTER 19

312 OD—September 7—4:50 pm

"Boss, I'm getting tired of these guys. Isn't there something you can do?"

"I'm not sure," Kathee replied to Beth's question with a definite *I doubt it* tone. "But I'll see what I can do."

Kathee sighed dejectedly when Beth left. She could do something—it just wouldn't be enough to fix the problem permanently.

If she could plant an idea into one of her shadower's minds, the guy would then wander off to do whatever Kathee had impressed on him. The only problem was that the other shadowers might notice her approach, and she wouldn't be able to get close enough to do her thing. But the even more dangerous problem was that of Simmonds sending out more men to replace the one that wandered back home.

"Maybe I'm going at this from the wrong direction," she muttered aloud while pacing her hotel room like a caged lioness.

"What if, instead of trying to control them one at a time, I somehow controlled them all at once? That would work, but how am I going to arrange that little illusion?"

Nothing came to mind immediately, but she continued her aimless pacing. Their lives had fallen into a dull routine. Other than staying in her suite most of the time, the only parts of "outside" that she saw were the hotel's hall and elevator, and a brief walk through the lobby to the back door of the club.

It wasn't much of a scenic tour, especially with burly "gentlemen" dotting her path. They tried to look inconspicuous but they failed miserably. How believable would it be for the same guy to be going for ice each time Kathee left her room?

"I need to get them all off my back at the same time, and forever." As far as she knew they didn't have "eyes" or "ears" in her suite. She'd had Bill Simpson run his spy-detecting tools over every wall, ceiling panel and floor board.

Remembering Bill's paranoia that the cops were always trying to listen in on him, led her to think of an alternative answer. "Maybe there is something I could do to get Simmonds' men off my back."

She could make the cops think they saw the goons molesting her. They'd arrest them, but then they'd soon be out doing the same thing. There had to be a more permanent solution—

there just had to be. She couldn't see Simmonds giving up on her even after the current show run was over. He'd have someone following her no matter where she went.

"Maybe if I find out who Mariyan gave the paper to, I'll be able to get a better handle on this."

Her usual "let it happen" attitude leading to a more "I'm not putting up with this any longer" demeanor made her pacing slow until she had stopped in front of the suite's door. A sudden *"Am I sure I know what I'm doing?"* emotion struck but was quickly squelched.

She yanked open the door and hastily stepped into the hallway, almost bowling over one of her burly shadowers. She didn't acknowledge him—walking resolutely towards the gleaming elevator doors, pretending not to see him madly tapping into his up-link. She might not be able to lose them, but they were going to have to work hard at keeping tabs on her from now on. They were going to earn their boss's money.

312 OD—September 7—5:30 pm

MallWorld was the same as usual—noisy, bustling, and crowded. Scientists had performed noise level tests throughout the mall, monitoring various locations at different times of the day and night. Surprisingly, the "ambient" noise level remained almost constant, although mall officials claimed that the noise decreased during the night. This was a fallacy. The level was the same—it was just a different kind of noise.

The transition period between "day" and "night" in the mall was especially chaotic. It seemed like the day was holding its breath for the explosion that would eventually come.

Kathee could feel this tenseness. The mall was purported to be just as safe during the day as in the evening, despite the roving gangs increasing their activities at night. Being able to "hear" voices, especially when the thinker was stressed, meant that no one could sneak up on her. She was safer than most as long as she kept an eye out for the gangs.

She walked purposefully towards the police station, and could hear occasional thoughts from her shadowers. Hopefully, they would not physically bar her from where she was going.

The station came closer and closer but so did the shadowers. She could feel their urgency. Kathee pushed through the crowd and finally reached the front doors.

Just as her hand touched the door handle, her mental murmuring died down, and she heard the shadowers' thoughts more clearly.

Why's she going into the cop shop?

Would the boss want us to stop her?

I wonder what we're supposed to do now?

Kathee didn't waste any time in trying to figure out what caused the clarity. She opened the door and walked in.

The first thing she saw was a police officer, in full tactical gear, filling out some papers.

He had a prisoner handcuffed to his left arm. Kathee recognized him as the guy who was handcuffed to one of the benches the last time she was here. She smiled to herself. *Career criminal.*

She walked up to the desk sergeant. "I need to speak to Mariyan. Can I get in to see her?"

While the desk sergeant fumbled for the log book, she heard him thinking.

Everybody wants to see Mariyan today. She should have her own secretary.

Kathee shook her head. *Why am I getting such clear thoughts? What's causing this? This is the second time that this has happened to me while I'm here. What's the common factor? The desk sergeant? No, different guy than the last time. That creep? Possibly. He's definitely the same guy. But he wasn't around the other times. Or was he?*

"I'm going to put this guy into one of the holding cells," the heavily armoured officer told the desk sergeant. "Thanks, Sarge."

"Yeah, sure," the sergeant replied mechanically as he handed a visitor's badge to Kathee. "Here you go, lady. You know where Mariyan's lab is, don't you?" He jabbed the buzzer to unlock the door to the interior of the police station and gestured for Kathee to go in.

She dutifully followed the officer and prisoner inside. She had a plan in mind, but she needed someplace relatively quiet and out-of-the-way to implement it. The interior of the station was perfect.

312 OD—September 7—5:30 pm

Mariyan is busy so I don't stay for very long. Just as I make my way down the hallway, a police officer comes through the doors. He's leading a prisoner in handcuffs. He's the same guy that I saw the last time I was here. What a loser! That's not what catches my attention, though. It's *who* follows them into the police station.

My mouth goes dry and my palms turn to liquid.

It's that pretty brunette that I noticed on my previous visit.

"Hey, Jack. How's it going?" the police officer calls out to me. He's so busy hustling his prisoner along that he doesn't wait for an answer. That's okay. I'm so dumbfounded by the brunette that I can't think of a reply fast enough. He's gone by me before I even get myself ready to say anything. By then the brunette is standing beside me.

I make a squeaking noise.

It must sound as if I was trying to talk to her. She looks at me with pretty brown eyes. She licks her lips then speaks.

"Hi Jack."

The words stun me, and I go weak in the knees.

I don't know why, but the guard and prisoner also stop. I turn to look at them.

The guard suddenly reaches for the handcuffs and places his thumb on the lock. A quick twist to the right and the cuffs silently pop open and drop into his waiting hands. He calmly puts them away and blankly turns his back on his prisoner. I don't know who's more surprised... him or me. It's definitely not police procedure to let a prisoner loose in the hallways.

The guard walks away and is soon gone around the corner.

When I concentrate on the brunette and the prisoner I get a clear image of the three of us sitting in a restaurant as cozy as can be. The clarity of the image is surprising. It's almost like I'm actually there.

The three of us are alone in the hall.

"We need to find someplace quiet where we can talk," the brunette tells us.

I don't move. Neither does the ex-prisoner.

"Come on, Jack. You too, 'Cliff,'" the brunette orders from her position at the exit doors.

Neither of us budges.

"Now!" she calls out harshly.

We both jump as if a bolt of electricity passes through us and slowly begin walking towards her.

No sooner do we get to the door, than she holds out a hand and makes us stop. She opens the exit door and peeks her head out then back in to us.

A thousand questions pop into my mind. Unfortunately, I don't have the wherewithal to voice them.

"There's someone talking to the desk sergeant. Hang on a minute," she says as she furrows her brow in concentration. It takes less than a minute.

"Okay, I know the way now." She turns us around and we head into the bowels of the station. We pass numerous police officers, but no one stops us. As a matter of fact no one even seems to see us. Pretty soon we're at another door.

"This is the back entrance," she tells us. "Simonds' men shouldn't be able to spot us here. I can't hear anyone, so I hope I'm right."

312 OD—September 7—5:40 pm

If I didn't recognize landmarks in MallWorld, I'd swear on a stack of bibles that we are lost. We've taken so many twists and turns in the past ten minutes that even I, with my vast knowledge of the various levels of the mall, would be hard-pressed to find my way back to the police station.

We have passed out of the "normal" sections of the mall and are now in the "mutant zone". Very few normals wander into these areas, just like very few mutants roam out of their comfort level. Only the mutant gangs travel all areas of the mall with relative impunity.

"Okay, we're here," the brunette says as we enter a small Thai restaurant and sit down at one of the booths in the back. We sit in total silence for a few minutes just staring at and sizing up one another.

"Okay, Sweetie. I guess we should start by

introducing ourselves," the ex-prisoner begins. "My name's Cliff Bowen and the pretty lady is Kathee Marani. Who are you?"

I notice that the brunette is mildly surprised that Cliff knows her name. "I'm Jack Valencz. Do you know what's going on around here?"

He shakes his head. "No, but I can make a couple of educated guesses." He reaches out for one of the menus on the next table, squints then searches his shirt pocket for a pair of thick-lensed glasses. "We each have or share a special ability that seems to get better when we're in close proximity with one another. Anyone else feel it?"

Kathee's jaw drops. No big surprise. Mine does too.

"How do you know that?" she asks him.

"I'll tell you, sexy. I noticed it when I was picking some pockets at the Centre Stage Club a few nights back. I didn't know why my ability increased, but I saw by the expression on your face while you were on-stage that you were sensing something, too."

A question pops out of my mouth without my even thinking about it. "What ability are you talking about?"

"I can teleport small objects about ten feet as well as telekinetically manipulate small objects like tumblers in safes and latches on windows," Cliff proudly states.

This confirms to me that he is definitely on the wrong side of the law.

"Well, I'm able to read minds," Kathee admits. She pauses for a second as if in deliberation then adds, "but I can only get some surface thoughts and even that is difficult. It's sort of like trying to tune in a faint radio station amidst a whole bunch of strong signals. I can also implant suggestions into someone's mind, but it takes a lot out of me. This is very hard." She looks at us for understanding nods, but I'm busy trying to make sense of these two, and what I should confess to them.

"I get visions of where things are as well as arrows showing me where to go." Realizing how lame this sounds, I continue. "When I'm on a case looking for someone or something, and I concentrate hard enough, I sometimes see faint arrows that seem to point to where the person is."

"When you're on a case?" Cliff asks, "What are you, dude? Some kind of private cop?"

"Yeah. I'm a private investigator with Finders Keepers."

"I've heard of that place," Kathee says.

My heart drops slightly. I hope she's only heard good things.

"Didn't the police call you in on a case recently?" she continues. "The chief wasn't too happy about it. There must be a bit of bad blood between him and your boss."

"Actually, the bad blood's between him and me. It's not hard to go over their work and find clues to match the visions I've already had about the case. It makes me look like a genius investigator. By the way, I'm the owner of Finders Keepers, not just one of the investigators."

Cliff breaks in. "Have either of you noticed your powers getting stronger or more focused whenever we're around one another?"

"What do you mean?" I ask warily. "Mine has increased, but I never noticed you guys around."

Cliff grins. "I know from practice that whenever I get close to Sexy over here, my power increases. I'm willing to bet that when your power "spiked", either Kathee or I were close to you at the time."

"So what are we besides freaks?" Kathee blurts out, "Some sort of lodestone or power batteries for each other?"

"Something like that, Sweetie." Cliff tosses the menu aside. "It's like in the police station the other day. For fun I teleported the contents of the desk sergeant's pop can through a wall which was easily thirty-five feet away. I've never been able to do that before. And I'm willing to bet that I was able to do that only because the three of us were in the same room together."

"I remember that," Kathee laughs while running a hand through her short dark hair. "I got more than a thought out of you, Jack. I got an actual vision of you talking to Mariyan. Normally, I just hear what a person is thinking. I've never gotten that much clarity before." She looks at me, "How about you, Jack? Have you any unexplainable power moments, too?"

Nodding, I disclose, "Well, I have gotten a few vibrant flashes lately." I decide not to tell Kathee that one image was of her in a wedding gown. "They're normally fuzzy, like looking through fogged-up glasses. But these have been real bright and sharp, so maybe you two are doing something to me."

Cliff snaps his fingers and an expression of realization fills his face. "I just remembered where I saw you before, Jack - when I was in the alley by Mexicali Rosa's. I saved your ass when you were fighting that mob in the bar."

"You did? I remember getting beat up." I try and recollect as much of the fight as I can. Cliff is nowhere in my memory.

"I was watching you from outside the window. You were about to be attacked by some goon with a bottle. I teleported the bottle and startled him enough for you to get the drop on him and frighten him away."

Casting my memory back, I remember that dumbfounded opponent staring at his empty hands.

Cliff is on a roll so he continues. "I practiced my ability at some dude's estate while Sweetie over here was breaking into a safe."

I quickly glance at Kathee to see if this is true. Her face tells me it is.

"I moved some boulders around. I wasn't able to move them much, but it was enough to move them out of place. Again, they were much bigger than I've ever been able to move before. I bet that if we were together, I'd be able to move them much more easily."

Kathee smiles and looks from Cliff to me, "Together, we have almost god-like powers."

"Well, maybe not quite god-like," I tell her, "but definitely super-powered. I wonder if anyone else gets a boost when they're around us? And why do we have powers that increase when we're together?"

We sit in awkward silence for a few minutes, trying to make sense of our answers to our new discoveries.

"Ahem," Kathee clears her throat. "I may not have all the answers, but maybe we got our powers because of the on-going depletion of the ozone allowing more cosmic rays to hit the earth. There's certainly been a large increase in the number of visible mutations in the past few years. Maybe we have invisible mutations?"

"That's possible," I admit. "Look at the number of mutations in MallWorld. It's getting to the point where the mutant levels will soon out-number the non-mutant levels. I deal with quite a few of them in my business. Now I know why I'm so comfortable around them."

"I move in and out of the mutant community all the time," Cliff adds. "Quite a few of my friends are visible mutants."

"They tend not to come to my shows," Kathee states. "But that's probably because all my bookings are in non-mutant clubs."

Cliff moves close to Kathee and nonchalantly puts an arm around her shoulder. "Hey, don't worry about it. Now that you're a mutant, maybe you'll get a whole new audience, Sweetheart."

Kathee shrugs her way out from under the un-wanted embrace and tosses a quick glare at Cliff. It doesn't take a mind-reader to know that she didn't appreciate Cliff's attempt at a smooth move.

I get a curious feeling in the pit of my stomach watching them. For some reason, I don't appreciate Cliff's actions either. Something is just wrong about Cliff and Kathee being together.

"Hey no problem, Sweetie." Cliff seems totally unaware of Kathee's glare and continues as if nothing has happened. "Did either of you notice getting weaker when we part company?"

"I notice that I get momentarily weaker after my power spikes," I tell him. "It doesn't last long, though."

"Yeah," Kathee agrees. "Only a minute or two. The more we're together though, it seems as if the weakness is less and less."

"You're right, Doll-face," Cliff leans towards Kathee once again.

I block Cliff's move by opening my arms wide to embrace them both.

"So we're like the Three Musketeers—together we're better than when were apart."

Cliff moves away from my arm. Kathee moves away as well, but not as fast as she did from Cliff's advances.

CHAPTER 20

312 OD—September 7—7:00 pm

"What do you mean, you lost her?" William Simmonds screamed at the cowering man. "You had seventeen men watching her!"

"Sorry boss," Jimmy's voice broke slightly, "she walked right into the police station. There was nothing we could do to stop her."

"You couldn't get a man into the station to follow her? None of you were brave enough to just go in there and ask to see someone on some trumped-up excuse? None of you thought to go in and report a robbery? Or an accident? You could have made something up!"

Simmonds brought in a deep lungful of air to continue his tirade, but then stopped. The air was slowly released and replaced by a more re-laxed breathing pattern. He looked at his man for a moment while the silence built up in the room.

"I want you to find her. I don't care what it takes.

I want her found." He paused for a short moment. "I want her found, and I want her ghosted."

His underling snapped to attention.

"I want her ghosted, and I don't care if it looks like an accident or not. Just ghost her. She's stolen from me. She's made me look like a fool. She's manipulated and controlled me without my knowing about it. I want her ghosted..." he paused for exactly one second then forcefully added, "...now!"

"Okay, boss," his subordinate acknowledged with a sketchy salute.

"And when you get it done, I want you to come back and tell me exactly how you did it. I want all the details. I want her to suffer for all the humiliation she's caused me."

312 OD—September 7—7:30 pm

It's been only a few minutes since we left MallWorld. I'm bringing Cliff and Kathee to my office at Finder's Keepers to discuss our next move. This part of the parking garage beneath the busy mall is no different than any parking garage, other than it caters to larger vehicles like limos and buses that ferry people to the hotel.

As we're walking along, I get a sudden flash of a large stop sign riddled with bullet holes.

"Hey guys," I begin to warn my companions, when Kathee speaks up.

"We're not alone. I'm tuning in on some murderous thoughts. They're getting stronger," she turns to me, which means they're getting closer, Jack."

The screeching of tires accompanies her last words.

"Over there," I point to the far side of the parking level. Two seconds later a large black sedan comes into view. It pauses for a second or two then accelerates towards us

Something brushes by me. My jaw drops when I see a shiny silver limo float by and settle between us and the on-coming sedan.

I turn and see Cliff. He looks like he's passing a kidney stone or something, and I suddenly remember where I've seen that look before. It's the same look the weight lifter had on his face when he tried to lift those enormous barbells on the TV show last night. It's the look of exertion.

The car quivers slightly then topples over on its side providing us with a barrier.

"Get down," Cliff yells tiredly.

I yank Kathee's arm with my right hand and Cliff's with my left and pull them down behind the engine just as the first steel balls strike the car.

Projectiles pass through the roof and floor-boards with ease. Thankfully the engine pro-vides us with a denser barricade. Soon the car is riddled with holes, while the sedan powers away from us.

312 OD—September 7—8:00 pm

"What do you mean, you can't be sure?" Simmonds screeches at his underling. "You executed a classic drive-by and you don't know if you got her!"

"I can't explain it boss. One minute they're out in the open, and the next there's this car lying down on its side between us and them. We fired four full clips from our railers into the thing. It looked like Swiss cheese when we got through with it. A nervous smile quickly disappeared. We couldn't see any bodies, but boss there's no way they could have survived that!"

"You idiot. I want confirmation of a kill." Simmonds' voice got slow and methodical. "I want an eye-witness-account-of-her-death!"

312 OD—September 7—10:12 pm

"Hey, Jack," Cliff's voice is full of sarcasm. "Nice digs. Who do you have to kill to get a room here?"

"Actually," I reply, "that would be me. I own the building. I cracked a high profile case a few years back and netted enough to buy the whole building outright and set up my own shop here. I have the entire top floor all to myself, and I like it that way."

Proudly I survey my sparse but tasteful furnishings: couch and chair combo along with Rosie, my electronic secretary. I wonder what his home looks like.

"We were lucky," Kathee's voice chimes in as she smoothes out a small afghan on the couch and settles into it. She looks exhausted.

"Yeah," Cliff agrees. "If I hadn't been able

to get a barricade up in time, we'd be nothing but cadavers right now." He taps Rosie's flesh-coloured metal cheek.

"That may be true," I nod in agreement. "I spotted them, Kathee heard them, and you blocked them. We make a good team."

"I don't think so," Cliff objects, turning to face me. "I've never been a target before, and I don't want to be one again. This kid's managed to stay below the radar all his life and…"

"Yeah, right!" I break in. "Is that why both times that I've seen you, you've been in handcuffs?"

"That doesn't count," Cliff tries to defend himself. "Getting caught is part of the game. But I've never stayed caught, buddy boy, and I've beaten any charges against me. The last time, well, I was ratted out. I was in a safe room and the cops barged in and caught me anyway.

Kathee interrupts. "Jack, how long have you known about your abilities?"

Looking down into her tired brown eyes and squarish face, I begin my story. "I've been getting my hunches and fuzzy visions ever since I was a teenager. They came so often that I thought everyone was like me. I found out differently when I talked about my abilities to a cousin. He told me he didn't get visions, so I pretended I was talking about daydreams."

"My talent started when I was a teenager, also," Cliff volunteered. "I was too cagey to tell anyone about it though. Not even Fingers, my coach, but he found out about it when I began to boost wallets. Fingers just thought I was "outstanding" in my field."

"When did you guys start noticing your talents getting stronger?" I ask.

Kathee shrugs. "Oh, I don't know. I guess it got better a few days ago when I was doing my act. I normally just hear murmuring with occasional words coming through clearly."

"That's interesting, because I noticed I got kind of a boost at the same time," Cliff adds. "That's when I was able to lift a wallet from more than three feet away."

I'm more and more amazed at my new friends and our similar gifts.

"It's been about that long since I noticed some spiking in my talent, too. I was a little worried about the bursts, so I consulted a clairvoyant and teacup reader friend of mine to see what she thought was going on. She's a good judge of people, and I think she's also a closet mind-reader, but she won't admit to it, especially after she was reported to the police as a psychic by some normals. Sheesh. No wonder she only works the mutie population now. They're a lot safer to deal with."

"So, what did she tell you about the spikes in your talent?" Kathee asked me.

"I didn't talk about my talent. I asked her if her own abilities had increased. She told me she didn't know what I was talking about, but if she had some mind reading ability, then it

314

hadn't spiked in power."

"Oh, no! What time is it?" Kathee jumps up from her seat.

"It's about 10:45, Why? What's wrong?"

"I should have been back at the hotel by now. Beth must be getting frantic with worry. I've got to get back there."

"Yeah, it is getting late." I get up from my chair. "Let's continue this tomorrow. How does noon sound?"

"As long as it's a lunch meeting, and we get something to eat, I don't mind." Cliff stretches his arms over his head as if relieving a cramp.

I rush around the desk to open the door for Kathee. Cliff manipulates the lock and the exit springs open magically. *Show-off*, Kathee smiles—she "heard" my thought.

Once I've led Kathee to the elevator, I return to my office. Cliff is still sitting with his legs outstretched except now his feet are perched on my desk. He's certainly made himself at home.

I sit in my chair and lean back slightly.

Before I can say anything, he says, "Now that the skirt is gone, let's get down to business."

"What d'ya have in mind?" I'm a little leery of our new alliance.

"We need to get some evidence from the attack."

"The car that's riddled with holes? The shot-up building behind it?"

"I don't know," he shrugs. "How about the bullets?"

"Yeah," I agree with him, as I lean forward to rest an elbow on the desk. "I guess we could go back and pick up any bearings we can find and bring them to my police contact."

"I'd rather not go anywhere near the police station while I'm on the lam, thank you. But…"

THUD. His feet hit the floor. I feel the vibrations all the way up my arm.

"… let's go," he calls out as he's almost out the door.

I have a bad feeling about this in the pit of my stomach, but I hesitate to interrupt his strange confidence and go anyway.

312 OD—September 7—11:22 pm

It looks like a war zone. The upturned car is riddled with holes and the building behind it is pock-marked where the bearings missed our "barricade".

Cliff and I search for any steel balls that might be lying about. Most have shattered upon impact. A few passed through softer material such as car seats and slowed their velocity enough, so that when they did hit the building they didn't shatter. They merely bounced onto the slidewalk. These are the ones that we gingerly collect.

We had driven here in my Sol-Ray 7.2. This vehicle is my pride and joy. I built it from the ground up. Sure, it isn't the newest model around, but it gets the job done without too much fuss.

"This car is a heap of junk," Cliff sneers. "Why don't you get one of the new compact versions?"

"The compacts don't have the leg room that my Sol-Ray does," I proudly tell him. "Besides, look at all those dents and scars. They just scream character."

"Character, schmarecter," he jeered. "It screams that you're just too cheap to buy a new car."

I didn't want to argue with him. My bank account is quite flush, and I could easily buy any car on the market without making a dent in it. Money wasn't the limiting factor. My Sol-Ray has a great engine even though the body is banged up a little. In the neighbourhoods that I frequent a nice shiny new car would be a target. My car blends right in.

"Here's another one," I change the subject as I pick up a steel bearing that's intact.

"That makes ten in all," Cliff states. "Do you think that's enough for your cop friend?"

"It should be," I reply. "I really don't see any more. How about you?"

"Nah. We've scoured the area. Everything else is just useless wads of metal. If they want them, they can come and collect the rest for themselves."

We head for my car. Cliff moans dramatically.

"We *have* to get different wheels," he states. "Something with some class."

"Now here's a car for you," Cliff gestures to a car parked in his garage.

I must admit it is pretty. It's a sleek, new, candy-apple red Jungle-Cat with the hard top convertible feature and racing tires.

"You must make quite an impression when you drive around in this thing," I tell Cliff as I look from my faded blue Sol-Ray to his J-Cat.

"Heads do turn for sure," Cliff brags, and his chest puffs out with pride.

"Now that we've seen your car, how about we continue on to the police station?"

"In that heap of junk? No way. We're going in style. Let's dump your ride and take mine."

"We're going for anonymity here, remember," I remind Cliff. "Showing up in a flashy new sports car like the J-Cat is not the way to do this."

"Yeah, but your car is damaging my image," Cliff moans. "I can't afford to be seen in that heap."

"That's right. You can't afford to be seen… period."

Cliff looks longingly at his sleek red baby then over at my dull bluish sedan, then back at his car. His shoulders droop as he resignedly closes the large over-head door to the garage. His steps are leaden as he trudges towards my car almost like a doomed man to his execution.

"Before we go to the cop shop," Cliff asks, "why don't we go see if we can find out something about these bearings?"

It's easy to tell that Cliff doesn't want to go to the police station at all. His search for excuses makes it look like he's being brave and civic-minded, a couple of traits that he lacks.

312 OD—September 7—12:04 am

Driving my Sol-Ray around the back of the corrugated metal building, I turn off the nearly-noiseless engine. Thankfully, there is no reaction to the sudden ceasing of the engine hum from any of the buildings surrounding us.

"When I was holding one of the bearings," I tell Cliff, "I got a mental image of Paggett's warehouse."

"I thought your flashes weren't that specific. How do you know it's that exact building?"

"I've had this image before, and it led me here. Odds are that it means the same thing."

Cliff silently opens his door and steps out, all the while heaving a sigh of relief at getting out of the car.

Closing my door without a sound, I motion for him to do the same. "No noise," I whisper. "We don't want to wake up the neighbours."

"No shit! Like I've never broken into a building before," Cliff harshly whispers back to me. "I know the drill. I've done this before."

"Yeah," I tell him, "I know, but, I've broken into this building a couple of times already, so I know exactly what I'm doing."

"Oh, goodie. An expert. Pray tell me… how do we get in?"

Letting his sarcasm slide away, I give him the details of how I've broken in before by using the exhaust fan at the back of the building as an entrance.

"No way!" he exclaims. "I'm not getting myself dirty for anyone. There's always more than one way to break into a building. Let's examine what we have to work with. Stay here. I'll be right back."

With that, Cliff jogs silently around the building examining the various doors and windows.

"I think I've found a couple of entrances other than the exhaust fan," he reports back to me. "Let's go in through two different ways and meet up on the inside."

"Why?"

"With my talent, I can lift you to the second floor, and you can get in through the partly opened window up there."

"Why can't we both go in that way?"

"I can boost you up there, but as soon as you get away from me my increased power will drop off and I'll only be able to lift small objects. There's no way I can boost myself up then lift you or vice versa. I can lift only one of us to the roof."

"That second storey window leads to Paggett's office," I advise Cliff. "That's where we've got to meet."

The second storey has never looked so high

before. And it is very disconcerting to feel myself being raised by an invisible hand to the second floor. I barely reach it when Cliff's control starts failing. I have to scramble at the very last to grab onto the side of the window frame and drag myself up the few feet to the safety of the second floor.

"How are you going to get in?" I whisper down to him.

"I'll work the lock on the back door," he replies. "Then, I'll disable the alarm the same way."

A sudden thought goes through my mind, *Why didn't we both go in that way?*

Before I can ask Cliff, I see him pause for a second or two at the door then yank it open and walk nonchalantly inside, while I struggle with getting myself through a small window.

Once inside the office, I focus my talent to see if there's anyone else in the building. I get only one indication, and I know that's Cliff. I hope he got the alarm turned off. He seems to be sure enough of himself to do so. Pretty soon, I hear his footsteps in the outer office. I go to the door to let him in when I hear the latch click, and it opens.

He's good. I've got to give him that.

"Why didn't we both come in through the door," I ask Cliff.

"It never occurred to me," he replies. "Once I saw two entrances, I assumed we'd each go in through each one."

"Next time," my voice drops down in volume

to a harsh whisper, "tell me what you're planning before you do it. I don't relish floating up to second-floor windows."

"Okay, sheesh," he whispers back, "some people are just too touchy."

I ignore his comments and point to the credenza behind Jonny's desk. "The safe is in there." Putting both hands together, I crack my knuckles. "Hopefully, Jonny hasn't changed the combination since the last time I was here."

Swiftly, I spin the knob. I'm rewarded by a satisfying THUNK and the safe pops open.

"Grab the sack and hold it open," I order Cliff.

He takes the bag that he brought and holds it as I empty the contents of Jonny's safe into it. Money, papers, books and ledgers soon fill up the bag.

"That's it. Let's get out of here," I declare once I've finished.

"I hope we've got something that we can use against Paggett in all this mess," Cliff states.

"If not, then we'll break into Simmonds' or Pharen's places until we get something the cops can use against them," I assure him. "We're going to take as many of them down as we can."

"Sounds like a mighty tall order, pardner," Cliff drawls out as we make our way out the back door. "You sure we're up to this?" He re-latches the door and re-sets the alarm with ease.

"Why'd you re-set the alarm?" I ask.

"That's my signature," he says. "I do this all the time to make the marks wonder how I got in and out. It drives them nuts."

There's nothing I can do except stare at Cliff for a moment. *Is he that good, or that pompous?*

"Let's get back together with Kathee," I suggest.

"Hey, no problem," Cliff states as he dumps the bag in the back of my Sol-Ray. "It feels kind of nice when we're cozying up together."

A sudden rush of anger fills me at his words. Without thinking, I tell him, "You know, I don't *see* you being with her in the future."

"Hey, you never know." He leers broadly. "I sure wouldn't kick her out of bed for eating crackers."

My chest tightens and my breathing shallows. I don't know why I'm feeling this. Maybe, I just don't like the idea of him taking advantage of her. I open my mouth to blast him with a scathing remark but nothing comes out. I gulp a few times until the tightness lessens.

"Hey," I finally manage to get out. "You shouldn't talk about her like that."

"Why not?" He flops down into the seat. "She's just a dame."

"She's more than that," I retort as I get behind the wheel. "She's a lady and should be treated like one."

"Don't tell me you're interested in her?" he exclaims as he stares at me in disbelief.

"No," I lie as I start the engine. "I just believe in treating women like ladies not like tramps."

"Yeah, right."

CHAPTER 21

312 OD—September 8—9:10 am

I push open the ornate wooden doors to the MallWorld Police station. It's relatively quiet this early in the morning. The mall itself, however, is bustling with activity.

The quiet of the station is a blessing to my ears, a sanctuary from the noise of the mall.

"Hi," I tell the desk sergeant. "My name is Jack Valencz, and I'd like to see Mariyan."

"What for?" the sergeant barks.

"It's a private matter."

"She's busy. Are you sure you have to disturb her?"

Normally I don't have this much trouble getting in to see Mariyan. For some reason the sergeant is busting my chops.

"She's never too busy to see me." I glare at the sergeant for a moment. "You gotta problem, Sarge?"

"Yeah," the sergeant snarls. "Every time you

show your face something weird happens. Just the other day the pop vanished out of my can when you walked by. Can you explain that one?"

"You think I took your stupid pop?" I smile. "I've got no beef with you. Why would I do something like that?"

"I don't know, but your ugly face always seems to be around when these things happen."

Shrugging my shoulders, I continue, "Be that as it may, I've done nothing. All I want is to see Mariyan. So how about letting me in?"

The sergeant snarls again. "Look PI, you can't just waltz in here whenever you feel like it. Consider yourself lucky I let you in at all."

He reaches over and grabs the sign-in register. He grudgingly tosses it across the desk to me. "Here," he orders.

I don't say anything. I don't want to get any further on the wrong side of this guy. He could make life miserable for me.

A plastic-coated visitor's badge goes skittering across the desk. "Put this on."

"Yes, sir," I mumble.

The desk sergeant glares at me.

I quickly grab the badge and clip it on my shirt. "Thanks."

He jabs the button on the desk and an audible click comes from the door beside him.

"Thank you," I say and nod. I don't like sucking up to people, but this guy's definitely on a power-trip today.

Grabbing the door, I pull it open and walk

into the labyrinth of the police station. Mariyan's office is just at the end of the hallway so I don't have to go too far.

I see through the glass walls of the lab that she's busy mixing some chemicals and putting a few drops of a solution in front of her into small glass vials lined up in a metal rack.

Knocking on the door, I don't wait for an answer before I walk in. I know that I'm not really disturbing her. Mariyan never gets upset when she's interrupted. That's why she's so well liked by everyone.

"Hi Jack," she greets me, "How's it going? Haven't seen you in a while."

"Hi, Mariyan." I walk over and give her a friendly hug. "Things are going okay, I guess. How about you?"

"Fine, fine." She also doesn't believe in small talk. "What can I do for you today?"

"I've got a bit of a problem. Yesterday, a couple of friends and I were at the wrong end of a drive-by shooting. We managed to duck behind a car, so we weren't hurt." I decide not to tell her about how Cliff provided us with the barricade.

Her motherly instincts kick in. "Are you sure you're all right?"

"Not even a scratch," I tell her. "But the car that provided us with protection is Swiss cheese now."

"So who attacked you? What were they using?"

"I don't know who," I scratch my head. I hadn't thought about that until now. "They must have had fully-automatic railers because of the speed of the shots. There were probably a couple of them, because of the sheer number of holes in the car."

"Who'd you piss off that wanted to take you out with that much firepower?"

"I don't have any enemies…" I lie, "…except for the ones in ten-foot cells or six-foot deep holes. And I'm not working on any high-profile or volatile cases right now." More lies.

Mariyan crosses her arms and stares intently at me for a moment. "Could they have been after your *friends*?"

"That's possible." Wondering about who could be after Cliff or Kathee, I tell her, "I don't think so, but you never know." I'm confused. "I picked up these railer slugs. I guess they flattened when they hit the car seats. Can you find out who has a hate-on for me or my friends?"

Taking the bag, she glances inside then places it on the workbench behind her. "I'll get them to ballistics. Maybe they can recover some information from them. Anything else?"

Shaking my head, I head for the door. "Nope. I'll try to find out stuff from my end. Thanks, Mariyan."

"I'll keep my ears open for anything," she assures me. "You be careful out there, okay?"

It's my turn to reassure her. "Yes, *mother*."

312 OD—September 8—9:20 am

The office was quiet, at least as quiet as it

can be with two people exploring it.

"It looks like Mr. Goody Two Shoes really enjoys his Gramples," Cliff said, investigating the mini-fridge beside Jack's desk. "I wonder what other vices our new friend has?"

"We shouldn't be snooping around," Kathee admonished him.

"You should talk," Cliff retorted. "You're the one who's studying the diplomas hanging above the file cabinets."

Kathee felt a wave of crimson rise up her cheeks.

"It's not the same thing." She pulled her attention away from the display. "They're out in the open. I'm not the one mucking about in his fridge."

"Just checking out what tastes our friend ascribes to. You never know when it could come in handy."

"Is this what you do when you break in to a place? Or maybe you just rifle through their drawers looking for little trinkets to steal?"

Cliff slammed the door of the mini-fridge. He sat back on the chair and plopped his feet on the desk. His hands were clasped together at the back of his neck, and he slouched down into its soft leather folds.

"Well, Goody-Two Shoes…"

"I wish you'd stop calling him that," Kathee protested irritably.

"Well Gum-Shoes has gone to the police station to get the railer slugs checked out. Maybe we'll find out who hired someone to attack us."

"Uh…" Kathee wasn't quite sure how to begin. "Uh… I think you may be the cause of who's attacking us." She put a hand up to her head and massaged her right temple as a thought entered her mind. "Something about a comp-u-link?"

Cliff's feet hit the floor and he jerked forward in the chair. "How do you know about the comp-u-link?" he asked in a worried tone.

"What comp-u-link?"

"Uh…" Now it was Cliff's turn to hesitate.

"What comp-u-link?" Kathee repeated.

"The one that I lifted from a guy in the mall food court. The one with all the mob information on it. The one that I fenced in a pawn shop. That comp-u-link."

"I didn't know anything about a comp-u-link," Kathee said.

"Then *what* are you talking about?"

"I sort of borrowed some papers from William Simmonds. They had lots of references to ghost squads and their targets. Some of the targets were pretty prominent people who've been found dead in the past few months."

"Hey," Cliff interrupted. "What do you mean by 'sort of borrowed'?"

"Okay. I broke into his safe. What about it?"

Kathee stood in front of Cliff, her feet slightly apart and hands on her hips in defiance.

"I just want to make sure that you're not condemning me because I'm a pick-pocket and a burglar when you go around and break into safes, just like I do. That's all."

330

"I only do it to take down drug dealers and criminals," Kathee spat out defiantly in her defence.

"Hey, and I only break into safes in order to survive. Who's the worse criminal here? I know that the people I steal from can afford it and that they're criminals. You're just guessing they're bad and looking for information to use against them."

Cliff stood up and confronted Kathee across the desk. They were face-to-face for about a minute, just staring into each other's eyes. Suddenly, Kathee pulled her attention away.

"Hah," Cliff gloated.

"I hear something!" Kathee put up a hand to Cliff in a shushing gesture.

"I don't hear anything," Cliff whispered back while looking around to see if anyone was coming.

"Not with my ears, you idiot," she explained. I hear them in my mind. Thoughts of murder."

Cliff moved to the window to see what he could see.

"There," he cried out. "There's a group of muscle-men getting out of a black sedan. Do you think it could be their thoughts?"

"What are we going to do?" Kathee exclaimed. "We're cornered."

"Yeah, I noticed that. And I bet Goody-Two… uh, Gum-Shoes doesn't have any guns here, either."

The sound of the rising elevator slowly filled the room, becoming louder and louder. The elevator doors opened, and the sound of numerous heavy footfalls could be heard approaching the doors to the office.

"It looks like this could be the end, Angel-eyes," Cliff whispered as he moved closer to Kathee.

"If I'm going to die, then I don't want the last thing I hear to be you calling me 'Angel-eyes'." Kathee couldn't keep the sound of anger out of her lowered voice as she pointed a finger at him in admonishment.

The door to the outer office rattled but remained locked. Jack's CompSec chimed out, "I'm sorry, but the offices of Finders Keepers Detective Agency are now closed. Please come again during business hours."

A heavy THUD could be heard followed immediately by the crashing of a door being kicked open. The CompSec responded, "Warning! That is an illegal entry. The police are being notif…" Its voice was silenced by a hail of gunfire.

Cliff moved closer to the window. "What? No fire escape out this window? We're trapped, Sweetie."

The door knob separating the two offices began to rotate slowly. The door moved inwards.

"Freeze," Kathee yelled with all the power she could muster with both her voice and mind.

It looked like a picture. Cliff and Kathee standing side-by-side in front of Jack's desk. Eleven gunmen filled the office. No one moved. Only the sound of crackling electricity from the ruined CompSec could be heard.

"Enemies," Kathee screamed out.

The group split apart. Four of them turned their weapons on each other and began firing. It was fortunate for them that while under Kathee's power their sense of aiming deteriorated. Only two of them went down immediately.

"Enemies, enemies, enemies!" Kathee kept crying out and straining her mind to repeat the words.

Four of the men rushed each other and began flailing with their fists—guns forgotten.

The other two gunmen weren't doing much better. They vanished as soon as they ran forward. They didn't disappear for long, though, re-appearing and crashing into one another. No sooner had they collided then they disappeared then re-appeared—falling into one another again.

Cliff pointed at one of them and yelled "Go!"

The gunman vanished and re-appeared just outside the 4th floor window. He seemed to float there for a second until he realized that he no longer had a floor underneath his feet, and then he dropped like a stone—screaming.

"Go!" Cliff yelled again.

The sixth gunman vanished.

Instantaneously, he appeared outside the window and followed his mate to the ground.

"I don't know how long they're going to keep this up," Kathee yelled to Cliff.

"Let's get out of here!" Cliff grabbed Kathee's hand and pulled her past the four remaining gunmen still struggling on the floor.

They made their way out the doors and down the hallway.

"The stairs are over here," Kathee said, pulling Cliff away from the elevators. "We can't risk getting stuck in there, 'cause I don't know how long they'll be under my compulsion. I've never tried to control so many people like that at once. One has always been my limit."

They rushed down the stairs.

"Neat trick you did back there," Cliff called to her as he rounded the second floor landing.

"Yeah, it normally works for about five minutes. I don't know how long it will last with four of them, though."

Just as they reached the bottom floor, they heard the upper door bang open and heavy footfalls on the top of the stairs.

"This way," Cliff called as he pulled Kathee towards the sedan.

They jumped over the misshapen bodies of two gunmen, and without any hesitation, hopped into the crooks' sedan with the keys still in the ignition.

Cliff yanked the black luxury car into gear and they peeled away from the curb.

"Well, I guess that proves that they were after Jack," Cliff said.

"How can you tell?" Kathee managed between rushed breaths.

"They attacked us in Jack's office, didn't they?"

"They could have followed… either one of

us… for all we know." Her heart lessened its pounding.

"Yeah," Cliff acknowledged with a nod. "You're right."

"Hey," Kathee cried out, "how'd you do that teleporting thing up there? I thought you said you could only move small things, not people."

The more distance they put between Jack's office and themselves the more relaxed they became.

"I know. Wasn't it cool? I was actually teleporting them one at a time, but it was so fast it almost seemed like both at once. It was easier doing it than explaining it."

"You know, my power spiked once before while I was driving by Jack's building," Kathee said. "I wonder if Jack was boosting my power?"

"Was it the time you slammed on the brakes on your way to that estate a few days back?"

"Yeah," Kathee reluctantly confirmed.

"I was following you that day," Cliff admitted. "It might have been me that you were reacting to."

"I see," Kathee glowered at him. "And how many other times were you stalking me?"

"I never stalked you!" Cliff spun the wheel and the sedan slewed around a corner.

"Where are we going?" Kathee asked, grabbing for the handrail above her head.

"Somewhere safe, I hope," Cliff assured her.

CHAPTER 22

312 OD—September 8—11:35 am

"Hi, Boss." Paul Dunne nodded his hello. "I found something you might be interested in."

He handed Kevin Pharen a comp-u-link with a red lightning bolt painted on the cover.

"Where did you find this?" Pharen snarled angrily. He sat down behind his desk and placed the comp-u-link in front of him.

"One of the guys picked it up this morning in MallWorld at Mark Maller's Pawn Shop."

"Did this Maller tell you who brought it in?" The tone of anger didn't diminish.

"He said he didn't know who gave it to him, but I don't believe him. He has to know."

Pharen turned on the comp-u-link. After a few seconds a blank screen appeared. "Somebody wiped it," he growled. "I wonder if they read it before they destroyed it?"

"They must have," Paul told him as he stood at ease in front of the desk.

"That's what I'm afraid of," Pharen said, his green eyes narrowed in concentration. He turned the unit over in his hands. "I want you to bring this to the lab guys and see if they can confirm that a copy was made before it was wiped. Then I want you to go and lean on Maller to find out who gave this to him. Got it?"

"I got it, but listen. In order to protect ourselves, why don't we find out how this guy did what he did? Let's set a trap for him instead of just killing him?"

"What do you mean?"

"We know that Maller got this from some pickpocket. Suppose this pickpocket is the same guy who burglarized your warehouse. Why don't we tell Maller about a house where, say, the owners are going away to a fundraising luncheon. We'll let him think the house is filled with money and jewels. I bet he'll tell his thief friend about it, and we'll be waiting."

"All nice and neat," smiled Pharen. "Let's do it."

312 OD—September 8—12:15 pm

After dropping Kathee back at the mall, ditching the sedan and sneaking into his own ride, he decided to check on his booty. Cliff wasn't sure, but he couldn't take the chance. This was the third time he'd been by his apartment building. Each time the same car was parked across the street, and the same two burly individuals were still sitting in the front. They had to be Pharen's men on the watch for him.

All the money he had stolen was stashed in the safe in his apartment, and it was basically lost to him unless he managed to get these guys out of here. There had to be some way to get them to move.

Cliff mulled it over in his mind. None of the plans he had thought of so far would work.

"What am I going to do?" he muttered while he sat in his J-Cat and watched them with his omniculars. He relied on these to see anything at over 100 feet.

He took off the omnis, and slouched back.

"All that money hidden in my apartment, and I can't get to it. That sucks!" He slammed the heel of his hand onto the steering wheel. Each blow was punctuated with a "Damn!"

A buzzing in his ear distracted him. He tapped his up-link and snarled, "Yeah. What is it?"

"I'm sorry," Mark Maller's voice replied. "Did I catch you at a bad time? Want me to call back?"

Realizing that Mark was not the root cause of his anger, he quickly managed to bring himself under control. "Sorry, Mark. I'm just trying to get to my place, but I can't. Pharen's guards are watching it."

"I'm sorry to hear that, but have I got something for you. I just heard about this place over in Terraced Heights. There's supposed to be a couple of safes in there with a million in cash and diamonds. Are you interested? Sounds like easy pickings."

Realizing that the two million in cash and jewels may be lost to him unless Pharen was inclined to remove his men from their guard duties, Cliff decided that he'd better come out of retirement.

"Yeah. Give me the information."

312 OD—September 8—2:15 pm

"Have you got a clear line of sight yet?" Paul Dunne asked for the third time as he watched the front door through a pair of Omnis.

"Yeah," replied Jason the sharpshooter, with a hint of exasperation in his voice. He gently caressed the stock of his modified railer. "I've got the front door targeted. Whoever walks through it will get taken down."

"This isn't going to kill him, is it?" Paul asked. He took off his omnis for a moment and looked carefully at the shooter.

"Nah. These tranquilizer darts will make him sleep like a baby. I can't miss."

"What if he moves faster to get inside." Paul was undecided about this new shooter. He'd never worked with him before, even though he had a good reputation.

"I've done this many times before," Jason reassured him. "I sense which direction someone is going to go, then I fire at that spot so that he moves into the shot. I fire where he's going to be, not where he is."

"And you never miss?" Paul asked in

amazement.

Jason chuckled and continued caressing the stock of his railer.

"I never miss," he bragged. "Never.

"Well, you'd better be as good as you say you are," Paul warned. "We want this guy taken down and questioned. We don't want him getting away.

312 OD—September 8—2:15 pm

The day was sunny with a crystal-clear, cloudless, blue sky.

Cliff cautiously drove his J-Cat past the spacious house a second time. He hated breaking into a place during the day. You just never knew who was home watching out their window.

"Damn," Cliff muttered again. "It looks peaceful enough. I just wish I could be a hundred percent sure."

Mark's contact had painted a good picture of this heist. He said that there were two safes and where each was located. The main safe was in the family living room behind the picture above the fireplace. The second was in the master bedroom behind a painting between two dressers.

Cliff was sure that he could crack both of the safes and be out of the house within 10 minutes. He'd done it many times before.

The only problem Cliff was having was that, as he drove past the house, a little alarm bell was going off in his head. He knew something was not right, he just didn't know what it was.

There were no other cars on the street. No one was loitering in doorways. Nothing looked out of the ordinary. This was just a normal suburban high-end neighbourhood.

Cliff pulled the red J-Cat to a stop in front of the house. He'd decided to go with the brazen approach. He parked the car as if he belonged here and was just returning to pick up some forgotten item.

He walked nonchalantly up the walkway past the flowering shrubs to the front door. He pulled out a set of keys and pretended to put one of them in the lock. He mentally manipulated the locking mechanism until he heard a distinctive click. He put the keys back in his pocket. So far he had performed flawlessly. Anyone watching would not have guessed that he didn't belong there.

A tiny prickling sensation crept up the back of Cliff's neck. Something was wrong.

The second he opened the door, he stepped quickly to the right, just far enough so that if anyone was taking a shot at him from inside, the bearing would go where he had been, not where he was.

The next instant he felt a sharp jabbing sensation slam between his shoulder blades. It knocked him forward into the doorjamb. A soothing warmth crept through his body turning his limbs rubbery and weak. He slouched down against the wall and slowly crumpled to the ground.

The warmth felt like he was sinking deeper and deeper into a soothing hot tub. His eyes closed as he succumbed to a gentle darkness.

312 OD—September 8—1:45 pm

The back seat of the sedan was roomy, but the two individuals sat close together, their words mere whispers to each other.

"Okay, Jimmy," Thomas glanced warily to the front seat then back to his partner. "So what's the plan?"

"The plan," Jimmy informed him in a voice slightly louder than a breath, "is to surround this dame and tranquilize her. Sweet and simple."

"Doesn't sound like it," Thomas murmured. "It would have been easier to tranquilize her from a distance, wouldn't it?"

"She's supposed to be some sort of mind controller or something. She can make you think you're doing one thing while you're really doing something totally different. Almost like you."

"Not like me," Thomas muttered a little too loudly.

The passenger in the front seat turned his head, glancing momentarily at the two friends.

"Well, similar to you then," Jimmy said while staring at the heads in the front seat for any clue that they were listening in on this private conversation.

"I can't help it if I can think of doing one

thing and do something completely different. Most people can do that."

"Not as well as you can," Jimmy stated. "No one can make up a complicated attack plan in their head and think that they're doing it while actually doing something else, like you can. There's a difference."

A thug in the front seat turned. "We're pulling up to the mall. Get ready."

312 OD—September 8—1:45 pm

"Hey, Kathee," Beth called out to her friend from the door, "are you almost ready to go to the club? Ann's going on in fifteen minutes. That doesn't leave us much time to get set up."

Kathee looked out the window of the suite into the bustling upper levels of MallWorld. "You go ahead," she told her friend. "I'll be right along."

Beth closed the door to the suite.

Kathee quickly finished the newspaper article she was reading. There was still no word about Simmonds' operations being shut down as far as she could tell. She'd been searching the newspapers for the past day vainly trying to find any news of police raids on drug lords.

Looking at her watch, she saw that she still had a good hour before Ann, and then the Juggernauts, finished their acts and it was her turn to go on stage. She had lots of time to spare.

Closing the door behind her, she walked to the nearest elevators at the end of the hallway. She was alone in the elevator as it sped down to the ground floor.

The doors opened and she stepped out into the bustling lobby of the hotel.

...trap... came in loud and clear in her mind. The rest of the sentence was lost in the dull roar of general conversation that was the norm in her mind. She looked around to see if someone had possibly whispered it to her.

...walk past...nonchalantly... A different voice echoed within her.

A cold shudder shot down her spine. Something was not right.

A burly man with a black Van Dyke beard started to walk past her, but stopped and reached for her. She lunged away and eluded his grasp.

Another man, that she hadn't seen, grabbed her arms from behind and pinned her.

She looked over her shoulder and screamed in her mind *Release me!*

Nothing happened. His pale-blue eyes bored into her face and his grip tightened.

She turned her gaze to the one with the Van Dyke and screamed *Attack him! Defend me!*

Van Dyke took a swing at her captor's head. A solid fist connected with his skull. He let go of her arms. She was free again. She moved quickly to the right.

Before she realized it, a throng of burly men had encompassed her. She tried to elbow

344

her way out of the mass of humanity. She felt a sharp pin-prick on her upper arm. She stared down and saw a bio-injector being removed from her arm.

A feeling of warmth crept from the site and suffused her body. The warmer she got, the more tired she felt. Soon her eyes closed and she surrendered herself to its embrace.

312 OD—September 8—11:00 am

The meeting room was dimly-lit. Only a couple of dusty small goose-necked table lamps provided illumination for the two men.

"So this guy's is supposed to be some sort of psychic," Jonny Paggett reported to his boss while puffing angrily on his ever-present cigar. "According to my sister, he can tell where somebody is without seeing or hearing them."

James MacDonald muttered to himself, "Almost like he's got a location sixth sense?" He looked down at Paggett and asked, "He's going to be hard to capture, isn't he?"

"Not really. I've got an idea."

312 OD—September 8—12:05 pm

"Jack" is barely visible in the broken glass of my door frame. I stop cleaning up for the fourth time since the gun battle this morning in my office. I'm worried about Cliff and Kathee. I've just about finished mopping up the mess, but I've decided to try to contact them again, so I reach for the uplink and punch in their numbers. Still no answer. I'm starting to get a little worried. The remnants of Rosie, my CompSec, have been removed, and my front office is starting to look respectable. That is, if you ignore the holes in the wall surrounding the CompSec.

Just because I volunteered to go to the police station and hand in those railer bearings. I would have been here. I could have shown them the secret entrance to the next office. I glance at the space beside the file cabinets and the wall where the hidden door resides. *They would have gotten away scott-free, and my office would still be….in one piece.*

My desk up-link rings and breaks me out of my regrets. Kathee and Cliff!

"Hello? Where are you guys?"

A harried and confused voice answers me. "Hello? Uh, my name is Margrit Mahoney. You have to help me! My baby boy's been taken! He was playing in the yard this morning, and now he's gone! Please, you have to find him!"

"Slow down, lady," I sigh, but I proceed to get the details from her. Funny, I feel compelled to hear her out.

While she's talking, I see a little boy all alone on small boat in a warehouse playing with pieces of ceramic tile.

"Do you live near the marina, Mrs. Mahoney?" I ask the distraught mother, trying to narrow down where the boy might be located.

"No," she sobs.

346

"Well, don't worry, Mrs. Mahoney." I don't know why I do it, but I tell the mother, "I'm able to see images, and I can see your little boy in my mind safe and sound. He's going to be fine. I'll get right on it."

I know. I know. I've just broken commandment number seven in the Jack Valencz's Rule Book—*be careful about what you do or say—it will return to haunt you.*

312 OD—September 8—2:15 pm

"Well, at least this'll get me out of the office so I won't have to fill those stupid railer holes in the walls."

I pull up to the warehouse district nestled next to Mrs. Mahoney's housing sub-division.

"At least the kid didn't stray too far from home. He should be right around here from what I saw in the image."

I park my battered Sol-Ray in the general manager's slot nearest the front door. This being a Sunday, the parking lot is empty.

The lock is easy to crack, and fortunately, there's no alarm in place.

I could have handed this one off to the police, but I needed to get out of the office. The last couple of days have been a bitch. My quiet, predictable life -- all gone. I'm now psychically connected to some low-brow pick-pocket and a crazy, though I must admit al-luring, mind reader. Now they're missing, my office is in shambles, and heavyweights are on my tail. Can my life get any crappier? I need to find this lost kid.

"Let's see, according to the image he should be in the basement playing with some sort of ceramic mah-jong tiles."

No sooner have I taken two steps into the building when a mental STOP sign appears in front of me. I freeze and feel a stinging sensation in my chest, obviously from the small metal dart now sticking in my jacket.

Looking up to the second storey I see the shooter. It wasn't hard to recognize Slim Jim, one of Jonny Pagget's men holding a railer and staring at me.

A warm sensation creeps through my chest and down into my arms and legs. My legs buckle and I slide to the ground. The last thing I see before darkness overtakes me is Slim Jim walking down the stairs.

CHAPTER 23

312 OD—September 8—5:05 pm

The darkness turned to grey accompanied by a throbbing headache. Kathee was used to migraines, preferring mind-control over chemicals to treat the pain. She would normally lay in bed, unmoving, for a few minutes every morning.

But this bed was much too hard and uncomfortable. It wasn't her normal fare. She'd never stayed at a hotel that had beds this hard.

Her eyes fluttered open, then closed again. The light caused a searing pain in her head. She moaned lightly.

Memories flooded back. Memories of being surrounded by burly men. Of her being injected in the arm. Of her slumping to the ground as darkness set in.

Something was wrong. She gasped and bolted upright. Cliff?

She was alone in a small room adorned with a

single cot and nothing else. Where was she?

Soft voices filtered in from another room.

"She should be coming out of it pretty soon now," one voice mumbled.

"I'll go give her another shot," a second responded.

Both voices sounded harshly familiar.

The door handle began to move.

Kathee dropped back down to her cot and closed her eye, waiting while the sound of footsteps got closer and closer. She felt a hand grab her arm.

Opening her eyes, she stared up into an unshaven startled face with a gaping mouth.

Wordlessly, she called out *Stop!*

The face froze in place.

You've given me the shot. I moaned when you did it. I'm sleeping soundly. You leave and go outside. Make an excuse and leave your partner alone. Come back in 10 minutes and take up your position.

A glazed expression appeared on his face as he walked out of the room.

"She's asleep. I'm going to go get a coffee. Want something?"

"Nah. I'm good," the other voice responded.

Kathee waited for half a moment before sliding off her cot and creeping catlike to the door. Silently, she cranked the grimy handle.

She could see the edge of a hefty form overflowing a small chair. Inching silently through the barely-opened door, she crept over and touched the man's arm.

He jumped up and spun around with his gun half-unholstered and stared at her, open-mouthed.

Freeze!

Her kidnapper struck a rigid pose.

You never saw me leave. When your friend comes back, tell him everything's quiet and normal.

"Do you know if they've got my friend Cliff?"

The guard nodded.

"Where is he?"

"One of them," he chanted in a dream-like voice, "is at Jim's Autos."

They got Jack, too! "Where's Jack? Where's the other one?"

"I don't know where he is," he droned.

"Then where's the way out, asshole?" she demanded.

The guard's fat arm raised. "Down the hall, turn left at the end of the hallway."

"Thanks," she told him. *You never showed me the way out.*

As silently and carefully as possible, she moved down the hallway towards the indicated exit.

312 OD—September 8—5:30 pm

Jim's Autos wasn't very big, just large enough to house a 3-bay car repair shop. Slightly larger than a back-yard garage mechanic's place would have been.

Kathee wasn't sure who she'd find here, but she was determined to find both and release them. Whoever had targeted them had targeted the wrong people.

She marched up to the front door and entered the office. Fortunately, there was only one guard.

"Freeze," she called out.

The guard went stiff.

"Where's the prisoner?" she asked.

The guard pointed to the back and said, "He's on the cot in the back room."

"He? Not they?" She was a little disappointed that only one of them was here.

"Stay here," she ordered him. "You never saw me come in or leave."

Moving quickly to the back, she found Cliff snoring gently on the cot.

"Cliff?" She shook him. "Wake up!"

It took almost a minute to free his hands and feet and get him to open his eyes.

"Hi, Sexy. What are you doing in my dreams?"

"You're not dreaming," she snorted in disdain. "Get up. We've got to get out of here before anyone else comes in."

"What about Jack," Cliff asked. "Do you know where he is?"

"No," Kathee admitted bitterly. "But I have an idea that this guy might know. Let's 'ask' him."

A little bit of prodding with her mind, and Kathee soon found her answer.

"Let's go get him, pardner," Cliff told her, "before they do something we'll soon regret."

312 OD—September 8—6:05 pm

James MacDonald and his three underlings occupied four chairs in the brightly lit but crowded office. The only difference between this office and any other in the city was the view--the windows overlooked the upper levels of MallWorld.

"Well, I suppose you're all happy now," began MacDonald while staring at his three minions across the spacious expanse of mahogany desk. "The three thorns in your sides have been removed. You each have them at your mercy and can do with them as you want."

"All I want," said Pharen, "is to find out where that son-of-a-bitch Bowen hid my money and jewels!"

"And I want," growled Simmonds as he glared at MacDonald, "that bitch Maran to suffer for passing on that information to the cops. She helped them put a major crimp in my businesses."

"Yeah, tell me about it," said Paggett, puffing angrily on his cigar. "That stupid sister of mine handed over some very sensitive files to that private dick-- what's his name? Valencz?-- and he's also got them to the cops. Six of my eight brothels could wind up being shut down because of it."

"Gentlemen, gentlemen. I agree that all of your establishments have been affected by these individuals," commiserated MacDonald. "But remember, *my* cut of your businesses is going to be affected by them as well."

Simmonds slammed his hand onto the desk with a meaty whack. "Damn your cut!" he shouted angrily. "The cops might have suspected us before this, but now they *know* what our operations are and how to shut us down! Then where's *your* cut?"

Paggett yanked his cigar out of his mouth and pointed it at MacDonald. "Yeah. You were supposed to protect us with all your high-ranking friends and contacts. Now what have we got?" He paused a moment, looked over at Simmonds, and then answered his own question. "Nothing!"

"Don't worry, my friends," MacDonald assured them. "Your businesses may be affected and your reputations reportedly sullied, but I assure you that none of you will wind up in jail. My contacts will see to that."

"Damn straight they'd better," muttered Pharen.

312 OD—September 8—6:05 pm

The large cube van hit a break in the pavement and wobbled precariously from side to side. The occupants in the back grabbed onto whatever they could to keep their balance in the cargo area.

"What are we supposed to do with this guy?" shouted Slim Jim once he stopped bouncing, and his feet stayed firmly on the smooth wooden floor.

Jack was still unconscious, lying crumpled in a corner of the noisy truck.

"We're supposed to bring him to the warehouse on the docks. They'll dispose of him there, I guess," replied the other guard.

"If they're going to take him out there, why couldn't we have done him in ourselves rather than tranquilize him?"

"I don't know. I just follow orders. Maybe they want information first," he shot back.

Slim Jim mumbled his disappointment just as the truck bounced shakily over another pothole.

A car engine roared by them, followed by the sound of screeching brakes.

The van's driver skidded to a stop, sending Jack and his guards slamming into the back wall.

Automatic gunfire sputtered out a few shots then went silent. Screams of terror could be heard in the distance, then all was quiet.

"What's going on?" the other guard yelled, rolling Jack off of his legs and scrambling to his feet.

"I dunno…" began Slim Jim, but he broke off the rest of his comment when both back doors of the van suddenly vanished and late afternoon sunlight streamed into their compartment. They were on a bridge over-looking a river.

A man and a woman stood outside staring at them. Cliff pointed at the guard quaking in terror beside Slim Jim and said, "Go."

The guard vanished then re-appeared on the other side of the bridge railing. Flailing his arms & legs in terror, he screamed and dropped like a stone. The sound of splashing water muffled his pleas.

"You're going to tell us everything we want to know," Kathee told a frozen Slim Jim.

"I don't know nothin'," protested Slim Jim.

"Oh, but you do," said the brunette. "You do."

312 OD—September 8—6:45 pm

The darkness brightens into a grey haze as I slowly regain consciousness. I'm laying precariously on the floor in the back of a large truck. Kathee and Cliff's beaming faces are the first thing I see as I awake.

"Wha-- What happened?" I ask groggily, struggling to my feet.

"Hey, pardner," Cliff replies merrily. "The posse came to the rescue, is what happened. We just saved your sorry ass, is what happened. We just..."

"He gets the idea, Cliff," Kathee interrupts. "Why don't you go move your car. I'll brief Jack on what's been going on."

"Okay, Toots. Your command is my wish." He moves out of my line of sight and around the side of the truck.

"Are you okay, Jack?" Kathee wipes grains of dirt from my cheek.

"I'm just glad you're safe," I reply with a

sigh.

"Cliff and I have been using our powers to get some information," she continues. "Once I located him, our increased powers made it easy to find out where they were taking you. They tried shooting at us, but amazingly, Cliff was able to teleport the bullets out of the gunmen's railers. He then "floated" the gunmen and one of your guards over the railing into the river. Slim Jim over there gave us a lot of information about his boss and his boss's boss."

"You guys have been busy."

"We make a good team," she comments with a nod, looking out the back of the truck.

"You know," I look down at my feet, "I've never been much of a team player because of the way I am."

I nervously try brushing the muddy marks off my now-torn favorite slacks. "In order to keep my talent a secret, I've had to push away anyone who tried to come close to me."

"Hey, no problem, Jack. I do the same thing. I can't have anyone around me either, because I can't tell if they're talking out loud to me or maybe projecting their thoughts into my mind. Sometimes I've even pretended to be deafer than I am in order to fool people. I've had to become strong and independent in order to protect my power, and probably because of my power."

"Looks like we're two of a kind," I tell her beautiful hazel eyes. A strange feeling wells up in my chest while I stare at her. I'm not sure what it is.

She sits down on a box beside me and pulls out a piece of paper. "Slim Jim over there had this in his pocket."

Ignoring the occasional annoyed driver's blaring horn, we both look over the document. Kathee tenderly lays her head on my shoulder. I turn my head and uncharacteristically plant a quick kiss on the top of her head.

Kathee murmurs, "I don't believe I'm doing this."

I think, *What the hell am I doing?*

"I don't know; 'what the hell are you doing?'," says Kathee with a slight smile.

"Oh, that's right," I chuckle. "You're a mind-reader."

"That's right," Kathee reminds me.

"I suppose if I start hangin' around, I won't have many private thoughts, will I?"

Kathee smiles mischievously up at me. "That's right."

"This'll be interesting," I murmur and lean down to give her a kiss where it counts.

"Hey, you guys," Cliff interrupts, as he comes around the side of the van. We break apart guiltily, pretending to get ready to go. Obviously not having seen us, Cliff continues, "How about we get out of here and take down some bad guys?"

A vision of an old mansion covered with spider webs comes to mind while we're driving to the warehouse on Slim's note. I wonder what it has to do with what we're hoping to find, and if Kathee's picking up my sensations, too.

But my question goes unanswered as we pull up in front of the non-descript warehouse. I clumsily climb out of the cramped back seat of the J-Cat after Cliff and Kathee have exited easily from the spacious front.

"This is where we're supposed to find information on Mr. Super-Boss?" Kathee remarks. "It's pretty understated if you ask me."

"Let's search the place," Cliff proposes.

"How are we going to get in?" whispers Kathee.

Cliff walks casually up to the front door. "Like this." He stares intently at the lock and the door pops open. He's good. Strolling in a few feet, he stands in front of an alarm box. Kathee and I are right behind him.

"Let's split up," I suggest, to move this search along.

"Sure," Kathee nods in agreement. "Why don't you take the main floor, while Cliff and I will check the second floor. If you see something, give us a signal."

I find my way to the other side of the warehouse searching for some sign of a safe. I wouldn't normally do this, but my talent has shown me that there's a safe somewhere on this floor. I didn't tell the others because I want a little time alone to digest what's happening between Kathee and me. She's quite the puzzle.

While we were together, I was able to sense that the safe was over here in the corner, but now I'm finding it hard to remember the combination that it told me would open it. I keep getting visions of Kathee.

My feet suddenly freeze in place. There's the safe all right, but it's covered with spider webs. Damn spider webs!

My arachnophobia back-pedals me away until I can breathe again. I know most spiders can't hurt me, but all the same…

Looking around, I find a broomstick that I can use to destroy their "barricade". I consider yelling for Kathee and Cliff to come down and rescue me, but I decide against it—not wanting to look like a coward.

I steel my nerves and edge bravely towards the spider web-covered safe. It takes me three tries before I'm close enough to take the enemy down. A feeling of victory comes over me when I finally clear the tumbler.

"Hey guys," I quietly yell up to Cliff and Kathee over the railing, "I found it!"

Pulling the papers out of the safe, I spread them out on a nearby table and start looking for important info. I hope I can spot it without having to read through them all.

Cliff and Kathee's footsteps soon break my engrossed attention. I feel my talent kick into high gear as they near. One of the pages in my hand seems to glow, so I scan its contents first.

"This talks about a James MacDonald. It seems he's involved in some way with Paggett, Simmonds and Pharen. They're paying him for something."

Kathee's at my shoulder reading the paper as well. Cliff's scanning some of the other files.

"Maybe this MacDonald is Paggett's upline?" Kathee surmises while rubbing her arm surreptitiously against mine.

"And it tells us where his office is, too." I don't move my arm as I continue. "Let's go pay him a little visit."

I feel bad when Kathee leaves my side and heads for the door.

312 OD—September 8—10:10 pm

The closed-circuit camera swivels towards us as we approach the door to the office tower. Cliff manipulates the lock as usual and the door opens silently for us, but on second thought, he should have worked on the camera. Walking down the corridor, more cameras scan our moves. This is too easy.

Just as we round a corner, I get the urge to stick out my arm and block Kathee and Cliff's way. A hail of railer bearings blasts into the marble façade near the elevator beside us.

"I bet they're not the welcoming committee."

"That was too close," Kathee whispers. "Did you see how many there were?" She's panting, trying to catch her breath.

I hold up three shaky fingers.

"I saw the same thing," adds Cliff. "I'll handle them."

He drops to the floor and slowly sticks his head into the hallway. The railers start to fire but then go silent. The silence is replaced with three thuds. There's some yelling, then more thuds and groans alternated over and over again. Ten seconds later, silence.

"What did you do?" I ask Cliff with a smile.

"I teleported their railers into that office over there," he grins. "Then I made the three of them hit the ceiling and drop to the floor a few times. They should be unconscious by now."

Sure enough, when we round the corner, three suits lay crumpled unconscious.

"I sense he's on the twentieth floor," I tell my friends. "He's in the office at the far corner."

"Stairs or elevator?" Kathee asks.

Cliff and I both say "Elevator".

The 20th floor hallway is spacious yet unguarded.

"Over there." I point to the door behind which our quarry is waiting, but I don't sense that he's hiding.

Cliff does his deadbolt thing and we are soon stepping into a well-appointed office. There are three chairs placed in front of a mahogany desk. The large leather chair behind it holds a single well-manicured occupant. He has black hair with traces of grey in it. His blue eyes are partly hidden behind his wire-rimmed glasses. They stare unflinchingly at us.

"How do you do?" he asks us in a clipped British accent. "It's a little late to be calling, isn't it?"

"Not considering you tried to have us killed, it isn't," I tell him. A quick glance around the room shows we're alone with him.

"I did no such thing," he mildly protests, as he stands and waves us to the chairs.

"You had your puppets Paggett, Simmonds and Pharen do your dirty work," Kathee disagrees.

"No, I did not!" he replies with a smirk.

"But you knew what they were planning on doing, didn't you" Kathee admonishes him.

"How did you know…? " he asks in amazement. "Ah, yes, mind-reader as well as mind-manipulation."

Kathee stares at him open-mouthed. She obviously hadn't expected him to know about her talent.

"Oh yes, my dear," he continues. "I know all about what you did to poor Simmonds. I can also guess that your friend over there," he points to Cliff, "can teleport people and things by what I saw on the monitors a few minutes ago."

He gestures at me. "And you, I guess your power is to find things, from what you said in the hallway on the main floor. Yes, my cameras also transmit audio. I've watched you three from the moment you walked into the building."

"Speaking of abilities," Kathee broke in, "what about *your* 'talent', Mr. McDonald? It's similar to mine, isn't it?"

Now my jaw drops in amazement.

He stares at her burning eyes and smiles.

"Yes, I find that I'm able to control groups of people." He casually begins to pace behind his desk."

"I can shift the economy whatever way best suits my purposes. If I want one company to merge with another, I concentrate and the board of directors thinks it's a good idea." He runs a ring-bejewelled finger along the top edge of a row of books on a wall shelf.

"You manipulate individual minds; I control group minds."

"That includes the criminals, I suppose."

"Why, yes, actually," he smiles at me. "They're actually easier to control since they have no morals for me to overcome."

"Well," Cliff bursts in, "We're here to shut you down."

MacDonald doesn't seem surprised. "And how exactly do you propose to do that? Arrest me?"

"A citizen's arrest is as good as a cop arrest," Kathee tells him.

"You can't and won't arrest me," MacDonald laughs.

"Why not?" Kathee asks the question we're each thinking.

"Because if you arrest me, then I'll have no choice but to tell the world about the three of you and your mutant talents, and that will be the end of you."

"And also of you," Kathee snaps back.

"Be that as it may," he sneers. "I don't think you're going to risk being exposed just to silence me."

Our eyes meet and we huddle. "What are we going to do?" I mumble to Kathee.

"I have an idea," she says.

But in the blink of an eye, MacDonald suddenly points at us and yells, "Fight!"

Cliff immediately turns on me and connects a vicious right to my jaw. Stars appear. I swing back wildly, but he ducks and delivers a left jab to my waist.

I can't seem to stop our puppet fight that McDonald must be conducting.

Out of the corner of my eye, I see that it's Kathee who's concentrating on us. *She's* making us fight. MacDonald must have done something to her.

I try to break out of the compulsion to fight but can't. We're both yelling apologies as we trade blows for the better part of five minutes. All my normal fighting skills are gone. I'm reacting on pure animal instinct.

Suddenly, I find that I can stop. Cliff is panting and slouched over with his hands on his knees. We're both bleeding badly, but unbroken. Kathee is looking around, and I join her scan of the office. MacDonald is gone. His spell must have worn off when he got far enough away from us.

EPILOGUE

312 OD—September 9—9:01 am

I lower myself gingerly into my chair, groaning from my new bruising, and eventually manage to get my feet up onto my desk. It feels good to be back at work. Kathee and Cliff rest in the chairs in front of my desk. Cliff has his feet up on my small bar fridge. He's got more bandages than me, but was spared my full fighting abilities.

"You know, I was going to be a bartender before I opened up my agency." I poke gently at my fat lower lip to see if it's still bleeding. "I have a good memory for faces and that's a good skill in bartending. But, I decided I didn't like it because the staff always tend to get friendly, and I couldn't afford to have anyone that close to me, you know, because of my talent. Fortunately, I stumbled into a job where remembering faces was useful, and I could stay at a distance from people."

"Hey," Cliff remarks, "whatever turns your crank."

"What turns my crank," Kathy breaks in, "is disrupting Pharen's, Paggett's and Simmonds' little empires." She looks at me for understanding. I nod and smile.

"And that McDonald creep! I owe him a good whompin'," Cliff announces.

We look at each other in our sorry conditions and break out in belly laughs at our bravado.

"Well, at least I don't *have* to work, ever since I solved a diamond case five years ago and was able to buy this building."

I look over at Cliff to make sure I have his attention. "I recovered $12.5 million in jewels, and got a flat rate of twenty percent for the job." Cliff whistles appreciatively.

"I bought this over time, and invested the rest of the money in the business and in mutual funds." Leaning back in my chair, I survey my "holey" walls. "I could retire, I guess, but I enjoy working too much, especially as a PI."

"Yeah, I know what it's like to be able to retire," Cliff joins in. "I've saved enough cash and jewels to take it pretty easy right now."

"Your nest egg came from stealing," Kathee sneers.

"Stealing maybe, but it's stealing from scum. Big difference!" Cliff begins to thumbs through a recent issue of PI Monthly.

"I have a proposition for you guys," I inform them. "We did a damn good job messing with one of the biggest crime groups in the city.

I would like to see Finders Keepers become a bigger, better agency—one that could use all of our special "abilities" to solve cases and stop any other mental mutants such as MacDonald from taking control once again."

"Sounds like an intriguing proposition," Kathee admits. "But what about my troupe of performers?"

"I guess we can always find ways to use them in the business. I still have a little in reserve from my diamond case. I can use it to refurbish the offices on this floor for you two." I search for any interest in their faces.

"Having a stable base of operations would be a good thing, I guess," Kathee admits, as she stands up and moves over to sit on the edge of my desk. She leans over and kisses me.

I kiss her back.

"You know," I smile, "It's going to be almost impossible to shop for, let alone keep secrets from, someone who can get in my head."

"You're right, and that's exactly where I want to spend the rest of my life. What are you going to do about it?" An equally impish smile comes to her lips.

"Learn to live with it, I guess."

I shrug then kiss her once more.

JUST THE BEGINNING...